CHASE YOUR OWN STRAWBERRIES

CHASE YOUR OWN STRAWBERRIES

Kenneth J. Hall

PARTRIDGE

A Penguin Random House Company

To order additional copies of this book, contact
Toll Free 800 101 2657 (Singapore)
Toll Free 1 800 81 7340 (Malaysia)
orders.singapore@partridgepublishing.com

www.partridgepublishing.com/singapore

CONTENTS

CHAPTER. 1

Gerald Fatslobe was a successful politician, by anyone's standards. He was in fact The Minister for Agriculture in Antonio Cacophony's New Deal Democratic Party. He was fifty, with that successful fullness that fills the double breasted suits of long standing MPs and gives the electorate confidence. Heavy jowled, and comfortably corpulent, he could pack away endless business lunches, official receptions and Foreign Office banquets with equanimity. Never had he been known to refuse an extra helping of lark's tongue pate or another glass of claret. He was viewed as being a positive asset to both the party and the country. "What's good for the Party, is good for the country." He would often be heard to say, echoing his leader's words, and he would tuck into another helping of lobster provincal, or roly-poly pudding. Dependent if the occasion was being held in Brussels or Westminster.

He had been born with the happy knack of being able to either talk solidly for long periods with both force and reasonableness and not actually say anything. Or bore people into oblivion with his passion in life, pigs. It is a recognised fact of life, that no successful, modern, western, democratic institution can possibly survive without it's Gerald Fatslobes and Spin-Doctors worldwide fully understood his cruciality. Here was a man who could, if necessary move through 180 degree shifts, without batting an eyelid. And get away with it too. His record to date had been four times in one week. The first time had attracted some attention, it was true. The second less so. By the time the third shift had been announced, the populate was tiring and anyway The Chilli Chicks were about to release a new record and their lead singer had run off with a Jamaican Rastafarian. The fourth shift in governmental policy was ignored totally by the electorate.

Gerald had been born into humble surroundings, of which he was ostensible proud and wont to quote. Actually he secretly loathed being the product of a one armed Liverpool oiler off a Greek tramp steamer and a night of passion with an alcoholic and somewhat blousey barmaid from Birkenhead. He felt no regrets when one night, returning to his boat, his father had slipped from the gangplank in Rotterdam and finding that large quantities of Dutch gin, sub zero temperatures, one arm and the waters of the North Sea are not conducive to midnight swimming, slipped beneath their dark winter chill for ever.

If his mother grieved for her husband, her strength of character was such that she never allowed it to show and she continued to raise their issue alone, fortifying her will and determination with the help of one of the cheaper brands of supermarket vodka.

Young Gerald attended a local school and whilst not excelling as a pupil, equally did not attract the attention of the local constabulary. Quite a feat in itself. By a combination of appearing if not virtuous, then not overtly homicidally violent or irrevocably criminal, he stood head and shoulders above his contemporaries. Since the school had never ever managed to place any of its pupils in university since its institution in 1945, though its record for graduates from Broadmoor and Strangeways was legion, Gerald was viewed as their last resort. The whole staff as one, fell in behind Gerald and he was in receipt of their complete and undivided attention. Much to the delight of the other pupils who were then left to freely pursue their criminal activities. Consequently, Gerald scraped a place at one of the minor and new red brick establishments and Gerald's home town experienced a crime wave of epidemic proportions that to this day has remained an unexplained Home Office statistic.

In university however, Gerald was at a loss. Friendless, and out of his depth. Lacking his academic support team. With no grasp what so ever of his chosen subject and with a strong Lancashire accent. He finally resorted to hiding in the college cellars with a tape deck and headphones and a set of elocution tapes he had purchased in Tesco. It was whilst attempting to all but silently master the sibilant tones of a soft ess and a nicely rounded vowel, he witnessed the Dean performing an act of buggery with a fellow student. Gerald had no knowledge of sex, but he was sufficiently astute to realise that this was not the natural manner in which human beings normally procreated. Knowledge that Gerald not only found to be interesting for it's own sake but also instantly realised could be used to his advantage too. The recipient of the Dean's carnal lust being the son of a well-known businessman who had made his fortune in pork sausages. Gerald gave careful thought to what he had witnessed. He considered his own needs and position and decided upon a course of action. He befriended the youth, who, apart from being a homosexual, was also quite brilliant. Through a combination of guile, persuasion and open threats of exposure, he compelled the youth to write all of his papers, work, which he then submitted as being his own. The Dean, being privy to the knowledge that his secret trysts were now the property of a third party, ensured that Gerald obtained a first class honours degree in politics and social economics, smoothing his passage through university in a manner reminiscent of the manner in which he was wont to utilise QY Jelly.

Gerald left university with a good degree, an ability to talk confidently and at length without actually saying anything and having learned very firmly that knowledge is power. He had absolutely no idea of what he would do to sustain in him life, though he realised that had an affinity for both pigs and living well. Politics were then the most obvious choice, but how to begin?

Gerald had been careful not to allow the Dean's lover to wholly escape from his clutches. He positioned himself like a sword of Damocles over his head and he did his homework. One never knew when one would want a bit of extra leverage in life, he reasoned.

St John Pu' Ddings, pronounced Singen Pew' Thins, a double d being a th sound in Welsh and the g being conveniently left silent, was the heir apparent to the family fortune of the Pu' Ddings. This actually was the product of a lot of hard work and good luck in breeding pigs by one Blakemore Pudding, or Black pudding as he was known behind his back to certain envious souls and business competitors. Black pudding had married the daughter of a landed but impoverished Pembrokeshire farmer. His lands bordering on the banks of the Cleddau, pronounced Cleth-eye, river. His wife excelled in cooking and had her own and very personal recipe for sausage and pork pies. She had consistently taken several prizes at the County Show. Black Pudding had the business acumen to realise that this skill could be exploited. He went into the pig business in a serious way and soon the products of his farm and wife's culinary expertise were being eaten nation-wide. A major brewery advertising one of their better brews as being complimented by a one of his pork pies or a packet of scratchings. With his rise in wealth and social station, so too did his family name evolve. Pudding, now seeming too gauche and lacking in refinement. Pu' Ddings somehow possessing more class. Blakemore devoted himself to his business interests, but took time off to sire a son, St John. Their daughter, Mavis, arrived later. Her mother insisting that the child be named after her grandmother.

Mavis grew to be thin, flat chested and spotty. St John beyond the age of twenty-two, never grew at all. Having been caught by the vicar of St. Bartholomew's in flagro delecti and at it with some local boy scouts in the vestry. This caused the clerical gentleman great distress, as he regarded the boy scouts in question as being rather his own personal domain. St John at least, in a fit of remorse had the presence of mind to attempt to hang himself on some pig's entrails. These being left over for sausage making purposes after a particularly ferocious bought of slaughtering in one of the farm's outbuildings. Taking the trouble beforehand however to leave behind a note of a most incriminating nature. As luck would have it, his wildly swinging body and protruding purple tongue was discovered by his father before all signs of life had ceased. Being a practical man first and foremost, he had replaced the stepladder under his son's feet, allowing him to take in great, shuddering gasps of life giving oxygen, before reading the suicide note. Taking note of its contents, he had pocketed it, then quietly left. Kicking away the step ladders once more, and allowing nature to take its course. He had returned later and arranged things so as to look like an unfortunate accident, phoned the Chief Constable, with whom he shared a Masonic Lodge and popped round to the church to threaten the vicar with exposure unless he promptly accepted a posting as a missionary in Central

Africa. Thus having covered all bases so to speak, he was free to continue producing porcine products and only had his gawpy daughter to get rid of. In the mean time she could be sent to a Swiss finishing school whilst a suitable and not too particular husband was sought.

It was whilst Gerald, out from university, out of work and out of his head on Red Dragon Bitter, rolled out of a West Wales pub, fate, so to speak, took a hand.

Gerald had decided upon a short holiday in Tenby, as he had nothing better to do and had developed a partiality for Red Dragon Bitter. Staggering out of his favourite watering hole, he literally fell under the wheels of Mavis's Lotus Elan. She was visiting her parents and had been attempting a bit of shortsighted reversing at the time, having just come out of the cinema. Gerald, more shocked than injured, but recognising the price range of the vehicle that had pinned him between its bumper and gutter, decided to groan a bit. He then insisted that he didn't need an ambulance, but would appreciate transport back to his mobile home. A friend having been sufficiently unwise as to have offered Gerald the free use of his caravan as a stopgap housing solution and hence the reason behind Gerald being in Wales at all. Mavis, naturally being concerned then drove Gerald back to the caravan site. A secluded spot, more so since it was now off-season and very quiet. To their surprise they found that they shared something in common. St John being Mavis's late brother. Naturally recalling St John and his tragic passing was painful to Mavis. Gerald wishing to console the maiden in her grief, promptly relapsed into the more generous form of his nature and insisted on sharing something else with Mavis. Mavis finding the wholly new experience of having some hairy male grouping within her sensible, white cotton panties both exciting and pleasurable, forgot all about St john, who she had secretly regarded as a bit of a wimp, surrendered herself willingly. For his behalf, Gerald through the blur of darkness and alcohol induced lust threw caution to the wind and sowed his wild oats with abandon, thrusting deep inside the squeaking and wriggling female. Awakening in the morning to find that the voluptuous maiden of the previous night had somehow managed to transform herself into a short sighted, stick like creature with bumps for breasts and nipples like pimples.

But who, however, having tasted the delights of the flesh craved more in direct proportion to the size of his hangover. Needless to state that Mavis, after 23 years of virginity, was highly fecund and to put it crudely, was well up the stick.

Blakemore welcomed this development as he saw that Mavis could now be shunted Gerald's way at a high speed of knots. This only left the problem of what Gerald should do for a living. Fortunately, Gerald and pigs were as one, Blakemore welcomed him with open arms. Well, metaphorically speaking anyway. One experience of having a member of his immediate family with leanings towards persons of his own gender having been quite enough. Since Gerald would need to support his daughter in the manner to which she had been accustomed, namely tacky wealth and Gerald liked being close pigs and talking, politics seemed to be the sensible move. So via his Masonic cronies and a few necessary but subtle back handers discreetly slipped into willing pockets of various noteworthy and eminent persons in public office. Gerald stood for the safe seat of Bradford Central and Northwest. Winning the election with bribes and a massive majority. His son being born on the same day and named in honour of the event. From such humble origins did Gerald Fatslobe's success and rise to fame begin.

It was at this time that The New National Democratic Party was formulating its policy. Which was basically no different from the existing hotch potch of a policy of the party in power. That being the ripping off the general public at large, and increasing taxation by stealth, whilst at the same time lining their own pockets and maintaining a vigorous campaign of vitriolic abuse and false statistics. With which they hoped to dupe the electorate and revile the opposition party. In other words the normal crooked mayhem and lies in which most politicians excel whilst in power. Always of course whilst keeping an eye open for either a lucrative directorship or life peerage to occupy their time once Joe Public either catches on to their illicit dealings, sexual philandering, or tire of them. Gerald rapidly became an expert at both illicit dealings and sexual philandering, not finding his wife attractive at all. He secretly held the view that she looked like an anoxic stick insect with spectacles at the best of times, and even worse when pregnant. But being a realist, he knew very well which side his toast was buttered.

The second child, a daughter Tiffany, was the result of a Caribbean cruise. Though, Gerald harboured deep suspicions that the child was the product of a coupling between his wife and one of the younger stewards, as he swore that he never drank sufficient on the voyage to have had sex with the Damn woman. However, he took a philosophical view of the matter, as the girl occupied his wife's time and allowed him to get on with his own life. A compromise situation that suited them both admirably. Bradford being frail and studious, and Tiffany tending towards rebellion.

Gerald was now a rising star in the firmament of Antonio Cacaphonie's New Deal Democratic Party. The party having found itself, rather to it's own surprise, in power by a narrow margin. In incidentally, the lowest polling turn out since nineteen fifty something. A small fact that was conveniently brushed under the carpet.

None of its members having held Ministerial positions before, they could all be safely regarded as being amateurs. But they were not going to allow this total lack of governing knowledge to deter them. They were more than willing to learn the job as they went along, irrespective of whatever collateral damage they might cause, or incur in the process. Under such circumstances good PR men are not just required, they are essential. At all costs the polish on the table must be maintained, even if the legs are falling off. Two such stalwarts were recruited. Both rather grubby and disreputable in reality, but shiny as cheap chrome and with a veneer just as thin. They were given the awesome title of Spin-Doctors and left to proclaim a major electoral landslide and a fresh approach to Westminster.

On the basis that Gerald bred pigs, he was made Minister of Agriculture. All other Ministers having nothing in common and no knowledge what so ever of their post. With the exception of The Minister for Transport. He having been banned from driving due to a judge's ruling regarding the amount of alcohol present in his bloodstream whilst in charge of a motorised vehicle. This was naturally seized upon by the Spin-Doctors as being positively advantageous, as he was now in the unique position of being able to view the statute from the other side of the cell door, so to speak. Gerald, of course basked in the lime light of one all knowledgeable in all things agricultural. Pigs being his speciality.

It wasn't that Gerald in his own heart supported the pig farmers of Britain, though outwardly he was their staunchest ally. Gerald was actually obsessed with his own grandiose and rather megalomaniac schemes. No, what Gerald actually wanted was to monopolise for himself, the British pig industry and better still that of Europe too. To this end did he set his mind.

He realised that for him to acquire every major pig-producing unit in the UK and then to venture into Europe, would not only require vast sums of money. Money the Gerald did not have but also vast amounts of stealth and guile. Obscure off shore companies would have to be set up in The Virgin Islands and The Bahamas and their records concealed. Thus, Pilkingtons Pedigree Porkers, whilst ostensibly being belonging to one John Grundgesmuck of Sunniemead Farm, County Durham, in actual fact would really be the property of Grabmore Holdings, PO Box 23/8B Nassau. Funds being channelled via Liechtenstein. The alcoholic, and nameless resident of the farm in question, in point of fact being perhaps an ageing and homeless ex hippie. Of the kind that can be found at any time living in a cardboard box under the arches of Charing Cross Bridge. Who, if offered a new identity, a place to live, a blank cheque for pizza and beer at the local super market and a double-glazed green house in which to grow cannabis. Would no doubt agree with alacrity to take up residence in Sunniemead Farm, or anywhere else for that matter. Thus could an outward front be maintained, and good pig management be recruited in East Germany. The advantages being that kudos could be gained from employing some poor unfortunate refugee. Preferably one with very limited English, and he wouldn't have to be paid as much as the genuine article. Furthermore he would be more than happy to keep his mouth firmly closed. Work all the hours under the sun with total disregard for any EEC employment directives and all for an extra couple of quid a week.

Gerald liked to be seen as a hands on farmer. Something that the Spin doctors approved of too. Actually, it wasn't the breeding of pigs and the satisfaction that seeing all this new life coming into the world. Little pink porkers eagerly sucking at the sow's teats. Happy pigs grunting at the trough and growing fat. The wonders of nature. The joys and satisfaction that an agricultural lifestyle can bring to a man, that Gerald enjoyed, so much as their slaughter. Gerald liked killing pigs. Gerald would have bred pigs solely for the enjoyment and pleasure he got from slitting their squealing throats and watching their hot blood squirt over his hands. A secret that he was very much at pains to keep to himself. He even kept one special blade with which he dispatched the unfortunate animals. A nasty looking and wickedly curved weapon of Middle Eastern origins that had been presented to him by one, Shuffet Arrod. Himself a somewhat more than dubious character.

Gerald, cleaned, sharpened and oiled the blade with the care and attention a lover will treat the female of his affections. Often, at night he would sit alone in his study, and by the dim and secretive illumination of carefully concealed and expensive lamps, fondle his blade with love and affection. Making the odd jabbing and slashing sweep and obtaining a sexual thrill in the manner in which the light danced and flashed off the damasked steel blade. He had been finding of late that he needed to wear incontinence undergarments when he personally participated in the slaughter of his livestock and that he was apt to experience multiple ejaculations. A situation that left him happy, but exhausted. Even the thought of Mr. Slice, as he had named his blade, would give him an erection. Which was more that could be said for his wife Mavis, with whom he had steadfastly refused to sleep for years.

Shuffet Arrod claimed to be British on his paternal Grandfather's side. An ex corporal in the Pioneer Corps during the days of Palestine being a British Protectorate. A claim, which was to the everlasting chagrin of Shuffet or Al Arrod, as he preferred to be called, dismissed in its entirety by successive British Governments. Al Arrod, had not let this state of affairs either detract him from pursuing his claim, nor from pursuing wealth. He held huge business interests in the UK in both the retail trade and hotel section. He employed thousands, at minimal wage that is, and actually held the Royal Appointment for supplying bath plugs to The Palace of St. James. Consequently, he felt that in all reasonableness that if he did not deserve a title, then the very least that a grateful Empire could do was to make him one of their sons. After all, even pop stars of dubious gender obtained the Nation's recognition and were awarded various Orders. He was often to be seen on television, waving a sheaf of grubby and age worn papers. All written back to front and from right to left in Arabic. That proclaimed to an uninterested world at large, that he, Shuffet Al Arrod was indeed the illegitimate progeny of one Percy, Walter Gobspittle. Late and undistinguished corporal in His Majesties Pioneer Corps and one Fufu La Bonk, belly dancer and part time woman of the streets as circumstances demanded. All of which invariably fell upon the deaf ears of the British Home Office.

In a fit of peak, Al Arrod began backing the PLO, an activity that whilst coming to the attention of MI6, could not actually be proven. Thus was any claim to British citizenship sunk for ever and with the establishment of the Palestinian State, Al Arrod was left at a bit of a loose end. He had no desires to reside within the boundaries of the country that he had so vigorously albeit, clandestinely supported.

Later, fate would throw Al Arrod and Gerald together and it would be to him that Gerald would eventually turn for money. To finance his dreams of a porcine empire that stretched from Ireland in the west to Poland in the east. A realm over which he and Mr. Slice could wield absolute power and dispatch pigs to whatever Valhalla then went to, with equanimity. The very thought made his heavy jowls quiver in excitement. Sweat would break out on his forehead and Gerald Fatslobe would drool. All of which was the last thing that the party Spin-Doctors would wish an admiring public to get wind of. No, right now, Gerald needed an image.

Two very large polecat ferrets provided this. He became known as Two Ferrets Gerald and was wont to sit in The Houses of Parliament on the front bench stroking his pair of slinky pets. Each of which wore an ermine collar emblazoned with the recently acquired "Old Family Crest"

The introduction of wildlife into the Chamber was achieved over all opposition by referring to some ancient statute relating to the business of the House. Whereby animals necessary for the well being of a member could enter legally within the walls of the Houses of Parliament. Though, in days of yorc, this no doubt pertained to a fast steed. Stabled out side no doubt. So as to be close at hand should the general public decide to take a more active part in the running of the county and arrive armed, and in force. Of latter years, perhaps the statute would have encompassed guide dogs. Naturally, Gerald received the full backing of the Green and environmentally persuaded members along with both the Animal rights groups and the pro blood sport lobby too. Quite a fete in itself and a tribute to the skills and expertise of the Spin-doctors involved. Gerald himself, claimed that the polecats were necessary to maintain his wakefulness whilst in the House and having to listen to the constant drivel emanating from the opposition benches. It was a good ploy. As since TV had been allowed in the house, the general public were quite well aware that even on the very rare occasions that the House was full, over 80% of the members seemed to be dozing off. Gerald on several occasions had unleashed his pair of ferrets to savage unwitting and slumbering members of the opposition benches. Worthy persons, who had been bored into oblivion by one of his endless and thoroughly tedious and totally meaningless speeches. The creatures would promptly disappear up the trouser leg of the unfortunate MP bringing him rudely awake by a sharp nip in the genital regions. Much to the delight of both NDDP, or New Deal Democratic Party politicians and the watching public at whole. In fact, Gerald's ferrets were instrumental in making the ratings of any broadcast from the House prime time TV viewing. Gerald was a major success.

The Spin-Doctors responsible for this fait acompli were Noel Gobbleton and Peter Meddlesome respectively. The former being seen to be wholly repectable, if a somewhat boring individual and the latter being a self proclaimed and unrepentant raving homosexual. It was via Noel Gobbleton that Gerald was to come into contact with Al Arrod. Both men, no doubt in some strange and subliminal way immediately recognising the other for what they were, rogues, and seeing the opportunity for profit. Over a short period of time, like lovers, they would grow to know each other, as they probed for each other's strengths and weaknesses. Shuffet Al Arrod wanted to be recognised as a true Englishman. Gerald wanted to become King Pig. Arrod had access to huge sums of money. Gerald had access to the front benches of the party in power. It was a match, that if not exactly made in heaven had at least some spiritual connotations. Wealthyness being next to Godliness, money and personal opulence, being regarded by both parties as being wholly holy. Al Arrod, however, being by both culture and nature, subtle, or down right sneaky, dependant upon one's viewpoint, did not wish to be seen as approaching Gerald direct. In the manner of his ancestors who had invariably sought the assistance of a third party in seeking anything from the purchase of a wife to the poisoning of a neighbour's wells, he looked around for a suitable accomplice. His obvious first choice being that of Noel Gobbleton.

Noel Gobbleton had the ear of Gerald. He also had the ear of the Home Secretary. A particularly unpleasant and xenophobic individual, who secretly harboured dark thoughts with regard to non-Caucasians, but outwardly was all sweetness and light. His father, during the Second World War, had actually been a member of a Lithuanian SS extermination group and his mother a distant cousin of Eva Braun. A reality that had undergone hasty but careful rearrangement at the end of hostilities. The Home secretary's antecedents now having become displaced Polish refugees and resistance fighters, and thus welcomed as such into a grateful post war Britain. Al Arrod knew instinctively that there was no future in a frontal approach to the Home Secretary. No if he were to achieve his goal, then the prize would have to be taken by guile and stealth. He began to investigate Noel Gobbleton and Peter Meddlesome's personal habits and preferences in great detail.

Meddlesome he quickly dismissed as being hopeless to his cause. No way could he exploit him. The man was a raving and open homosexual. The only male MP who wore ear rings. Well known for his preferences for the rough trade lads that frequented certain Chelsea establishments. Especially those that strutted their stuff in tee shirts and black leather jeans. Meddlesome could also frequently be seen openly loitering with intent around public lavatories on Clapham Common. His chauffeur driven Government Plated limousine, parked conspicuously on a double yellow line. In fact, the tabloid press were more likely to comment on a Meddlesome being seen alone, rather than escorted by his oiled and tattooed muscled latest beau. No, attempting to blackmail Meddlesome would be similar to attempting to threaten a rattlesnake that he would let the world know that it was poisonous. The world already knew, and no one cared. He shifted his attentions to Gobbleton.

Gobbleton lived in a large house in Virginia Water. Married, wealthy and with two children, no hint of scandal besmirched him. Al Arrods suspicion's were instantly aroused. No one could be that squeaky clean. He began to sift.

Gobbleton, he found suffered from' "Affluenza." He, exalted wealth. He had thrown himself upon the altar of Mammon and beseeched the Gods for assets, possessions, opulence and richness. The Gods, in the way that Gods are wont to play with mortals, bestowed them upon him, at a price. The price being his wife. A skinny, dried up, vicious creature, whose body had financed and furthered the careers of several well-known European and American plastic surgeons. Pretty well all to no avail, as no one can make silk purses from sow's ears. Frankly, he had married a dog for her money. Money which she was sufficiently astute to grimly hang on to and only dole out in controlled amounts. Much to the frustration of Gobbleton.

Pressure from her family and threats of legal action from his wife's solicitors for non-consummation of their marriage had resulted in them having two children. An act that had required a great deal of courage on Gobbleton's behalf and had necessitated the utilisation of a bottle of whisky to fortify himself and drum up Dutch courage beforehand and his good lady resorting to a mask, leather leggings and a nurse's uniform. The second and last child, as Gobbleton vowed that he would never go through the traumatic experience of coupling with the woman again, followed much along the lines of the first, except that now his wife was a nun and it was Gobbleton who chose to wear a blindfold. She had her children. Her parents had their grandchildren. Children which unfortunately bore an all too unpleasant resemblance to their mother. Gobbleton had his social standing, and ostensible wealth too. Though his wife firmly held on to the purse strings. With what, Al Arrod pondered, could Gobbleton be tempted, an advantage gained and then later be used? Sex, was the obvious answer. If Gobbleton could be persuaded to take a mistress. Preferably an expensive and exotic mistress, one whose upkeep would cause a drain upon the money that his wife doled out to him, Gobbleton would require access to other funds. Funds that Al Arrod held in abundance. Gobbleton had the ear of not only The Home Secretary but the Prime Minister too and the whole of the front bench. He could get questions tabled in The House. In fact there were no limits to the power that could fall upon a man who could manipulate the man who manipulated the general public for the benefit of the party in power. Al Arrod rubbed his podgy hands together, and the heavy ostentatious rings flashed their gemstones and the chunky gold chinked. He had hit pay dirt and he knew it.

Al Arrod decided on a subtle approach. He would not move directly in Gobbleton's direction, no, he would instead infiltrate obliquely. In doing so he could espy out the land. Possible trip wires, snares and quick sands could be identified. Possible allies too. Al Arrod was a great believer in the maxim of my enemy's enemy is my friend. Al Arrod cast around. Two Ferrets Gerald was difficult to overlook. The man had an affinity for pigs and was The Minister for Agriculture. Whilst Al Arrod held no liking for pigs and though wanting desperately to be recognised as an English Gentleman, he drew the line at eating bacon and eggs for breakfast. Anyway, he could quite sensibly opt for kippers or poached haddock, or something, whilst claiming an allergy to pork.

Al Arrod owned a large department store in Kensington High Street. That, along with several up market hotels dotted around the world, comprised his outward and glossy, business empire. He also owned a chain of somewhat lesser supermarkets under a holding company based in The Isle of Man and he held the leases on thousands of corner shops in Bradford, Leeds, Liverpool, Birmingham and the Black Country. All of which were rented out at exorbitant rates to hard working ethnic minorities without the benefit of UK work or resident permits. It was not only a useful source of hard cash, which was collected by a small army of minor thugs, all of whom firmly believed that the monies obtained were going to finance and further the cause on The National Front. A delusion that appealed to them, and the irony of which was not lost upon Al Arrod. Needless to say this operation was also held under the names of numerous off shore holdings and false companies. The transactions, which were on a cash only basis, accrued enormous sums of paper money. Money that each month needed to be moved and stored. This was achieved by transporting it in "Arrod's 'Ampers". To then be locked away in the cellars of his large mock Tudor baronial mansion in Cricklewood. Money that though being very welcome to Al Arrod, required careful laundering and was in fact fast becoming something of a headache to him.

The small corner shops were also a very useful outlet for expired life stock from his supermarkets. Which was re-labelled at a charity printing factory he owned and held under another name in Wedensbury. Being a run down back street charity. Based as it was in a depressed area, and only employing non-English speaking staff, it attracted neither tax nor attention.

Al Arrod was famous for his Arrod's 'Ampers. Stout wicker work affairs, lovingly knocked up for a pittance by the handicapped. Al Arrod being lauded for providing employment for the lesser fortunate in the process. Each 'Amper was brimful with expensive and marvellous foodstuffs of the very highest quality. The cost of which would far exceed the salary of the person who constructed its container. Some 'Ampers specialised in foodstuffs from a particular gastronomic region. Thus were there French 'Ampers, full of exceptional pate, cheese, wine and truffles. Or a traditional English 'Amper with Stilton, Fine hand brewed ale and ham. He had toyed with Irish and Belgian 'Ampers but had to admit defeat as the former seemed to comprise of nothing but Guinness and potatoes and the latter fried potatoes and mayonnaise.

Al Arrod was about to launch his Oriental 'Amper. Here he saw the opportunity to ensnare Gobbleton and in the fullness of time make the acquaintance of Gerald Fatslobe. Thus paving the way to him achieving his goal. Full British citizenship.

Invitations were printed and dispatched to suitable persons of rank and breeding. Al Arrod thought to promote his new Oriental Line by having an Oriental Lady pop out of an 'Amper. Not perhaps particularly original, but still a ploy that would attract attention. His choice of female though would require careful thought. It was with her that he planned to entrap Gobbleton. Al Arrod went about doing his homework. His attentions were eventually drawn to Te' Upp. A twenty-four year old sinuous and sensuous creature. Small, olive skinned and alluring, with long dark hair, firm breasts and almond eyes full of desire and promise, what man could resist her Asiatic charms? Her background was obscure, her passport Taiwanese and her work permit stamped, Exotic Dancer, and due to expire. Al Arrod had her brought in secret disguised as a Philippina housemaid to his suite of offices in the pent house of the Park Lane hotel, which he openly owned.

At first Te´ Upp had been under the impression that it was her body in which Al Arrod had an interest. An arrangement with which she appeared to hold no qualms, providing that she was suitably rewarded for her time and expertise. Al Arrod had more immediate plans. Plans which he outlined to her. She was about to become the secret and exotic mistress of Noel Gobbleton. He, Al Arrod, had chosen her above all others to perform this task. There, what did she think of that? Was she not honoured? She; a nameless working girl, a lowly peasant from Taiwan, was about to become the concubine of no other than Noel Gobbleton. Te´ Upp, said fine, it sounded like a good deal to her, but who was this punter anyway? Why her? And what was in it for Al Arrod?

Al Arrod told her that it was none of her business. She had no need to bother her sweet little oriental head about such matters. All she had to do was to seduce Gobbleton and make sure that he remained totally pussy whipped. In return for this not only would she be able to screw what ever she could get out of an unsuspecting Gobbleton over a period of years, she would also receive a substantial sum of money placed into a Swiss Bank account under her sole name from Al Arrod. This would also be a useful place into which to channel any other funds that she laid her hands upon during the course of her work. All she had to do to earn all of this not inconsiderable wealth was to lead Gobbleton by the nose. Spend as much money of his as possible, the more the better and shag him stupid. All of which seemed to be perfectly acceptable to Te´ Upp and could she have a photo of the punter in question so that she would be able to recognise him when they met as she had no idea who he was? Al Arrod assured her that video footage would be made available and she would be schooled and groomed for the occasion. In the meantime though, just to make sure that he Al Arrod had indeed made the correct choice, would she be so good as to get her kit off so that he could personally check the quality of the merchandise.

Al Arrod found her to be quite acceptable and probably better than Gobbleton deserved. He considered fleetingly the benefits of a menage des trois, but discounted the idea. Gobbleton did not strike him as a man willing to share anything he valued. Anyway, a woman was merely a woman. Placed on earth to pleasure man. One twenty-four year old Oriental charmer, was much the same as another. He dismissed his brief encounter of exchanging bodily fluids with Te´ Upp, as mere diversions of the flesh and gave his attention to the wholly more important and pleasurable work. That of the entrapment of Gobbleton and the acquisition of British Nationality for himself as a result. He decided to lay his plans with care and precision. Te´Upp, would have to learn her script. She would have to make the, "chance" meeting with Gobbleton, memorable, but at the same time, accidental. Al Arrod began to have an idea how all of this might come about. He would have to control seating, and timing exactly. The 'Amper would need to be presented correctly. If Te´ Upp could then spring out at the exact right time, appear to stumble and fall into Gobbleon's lap, in those few brief seconds of confusion, if she acted on cue, spoke her lines correctly, she would command all of Gobbleton's attention. If then she was whisked away leaving Gobbleton with only her perfume and the memory of her warm body close to his, he would be hard pressed to resist the chance of a second meeting. Once that had been inveigled, and Te´ Upp coached, he should be hooked. From there on in Al Arrod knew that he could quite safely leave it up to Te´Upp to maintain his interest and in doing so, drain his pocket. A pocket that Al Arrod would be happy to refill... At a price.

CHAPTER. 2

Del Minki was a huge America food production conglomerate. It's interests spanning from growing and marketing crops, to canning and food production operations world wide. It also owned many subsidiary companies. Their field of activities were as diverse as producing farm equipment under various Company names to animal feed factories in both America and Europe. They even owned huge cattle ranches in South America and fishing fleets and canning stations in Chile. In fact, there was virtually no aspect of food production anywhere on the Globe in which Del Minki did not have an interest.

They liked to portray a benign image to the world, and where ever natural disaster stuck, supplies of food would be rushed to the scene. All in bright blue and white plastic bags. Each prominently bearing the Del Minki logo. All such supplies either having been paid for previously by government subsidies and thus, surplus to requirements, and difficult to unload. Or, approaching their date expiry time. Thus did the grateful people of Bangladesh or some impoverished African state find themselves the recipients of huge quantities of experimental and totally unsaleable guinea pig pate or a sack or two of alfalfa and pine cone seeds. The usual response of the recipients being to immediately dump the contents and then cut arm and head holes in the bags and dress their naked children. Which also made pretty good advertising for Del Minki when picked up by the BBC or CNN.

To use up some of Del Minki's burgeoning global profits and to further their image as a philanthropic organisation, whilst at the same time maximising tax breaks. Del Minki awarded university foundations and promoted research into food lines that they saw as likely to be money-spinners in the future. Thus it was they who furthered and subsidised the study of hydroponics. As a result of which several Middle Eastern countries, with the aid of Del Minki technology and their highly paid team of advisors, could now grow vast amounts of lettuce without the need for soil. Lettuce that was consumed by the rich within the country of origin, or air flown to another and equally rich country. There to be eaten by equally rich and over weight people as part of their Del Minki diet. Lettuce whose nutritional value was highly questionable, but whose profits were enormous.

Of the many subsidiary companies that Del Minki owned, one, Maksufarti was in Japan. Though being small, and virtually unheard of out side of very limited circles, what ever it lacked for in size, it more than adequately compensated for in brainpower. Its speciality was genetically modified crops. And Maksufarti had made a break through.

Kenu Itayaku, was their chief scientist. A small, balding, fussy, myopic and slightly over weight man of forty-two summers, with an ingrown toenail, and a chip on his shoulder, he was obsessed with seaweed. Apart from his natural affinity for eating the stuff himself along with lumps of raw fish. He saw it as being an answer to the world's food shortage problem. After all, was not two thirds of the world covered in seawater? What could be better than growing a high protein, high carbohydrate crop that only required harvesting and not chasing? Suitably genetically modified seaweed was the obvious answer. It was Kenu's dream. It was his obsession.

Kenu had laboured arduously for long years towards this single goal. Kenu had forsaken his wife and children, none of whom he particularly liked, he would secretly admit. Certainly none of whom other than with sharing his name, he shared anything else in common. He also detested living in Tokyo, crowds, rushing, his cramped apartment, banal TV and most of all, his modern and nagging wife, who showed him little respect. So Kenu had found solace in his work and had laboured long hours for a low salary, to achieve this end. Dreaming of feeding the planet and being recognised as such. Finally, at last! His goal seemed to be within his grasp.

His bleak and open pilot plant consisted of ugly concrete tanks, pumps and stainless steel piping. For years he had stood with chapped and raw hands in winter, or sweated in summer, observing, making adjustments to water flow, only to be met with disappointment and failure. Now, finally, it had spawned a bright red and yellow spotted and ugly, wart like growth of a brand new species of marine plant life. Hither to, never seen upon this planet. Kenu's genetically modified seaweed. Its nutriment value was as outstanding as it's highly poisonous and rather off putting appearance. It also tended to glow with a strange orange fluorescence at night. Its growth rate, though phenomenal under the correct conditions, still remained an unsolved problem. It was a fickle and problematic plant, sometimes growing and sometimes not. The reasons for which still remained obscure to Kenu. He sighed in a mixture of wonder and perplexion as he fondled a frond of his prodigy. He would have to do a lot more work upon it, before being able to submit his paper upon its discovery to a welcoming and hungry world. Kenu looked down lovingly at his hybrid and increased the water flow through the tanks. He dreamed that he, Kenu Itayaku would be the saviour of the planet and in one fell swoop wipe out the shame of Pearl Harbour and the losing of the Second World War. It would also put that nagging bitch of a wife of his in her place too. He polished his gold rimmed spectacles, and collecting his clipboard and carefully written notes, he wandered off back in the direction of his computer. Muttering, "Tora, Tora, Tora," and smiling to himself, as he vowed to redouble his efforts.

Meanwhile, on the other side of the planet and oblivious to the knowledge of Kenu and his world saving seaweed, Al Arrod was holding his carefully choreographed Oriental 'Amper launch. The equally carefully chosen guests seated down each side of a table in the function room of Al Arrod's top London hotel. Te´Upp had just popped out of an Al Arrods Oriental 'Amper. Due to careful positioning of both 'Amper and seated guests, a very attractive Te´Upp, clad in a most revealing and slinky cocktail dress and doused in expensive perfume, managed somehow to trip and land right into a surprised but not dismayed, Gobbleton's lap.

Al Arrod held his breath, as flash bulbs popped and Te´Upp quickly regained her composure. For just a split second, she remained seated and immobile. She hung around Gobbleton's neck. Offering him in the process the full benefit of her cleavage and giving her tight little bottom an exciting wriggle. Then, slipping her hand down below the level of the tablecloth, as if by accident, she gently squeezed his genitalia and felt their immediate and comforting reaction. She stoked a little more urgently and harder and was rewarded with knowing that Gobbleton dare not rise for fear of bursting the zip on his Saville Row flies. "Contact me later", she whispered huskily into his ear, whilst smiling in mock embarrassment to the avid journalists, now crowding around.

Al Arrod immediately came forward. Obsequiously, he wrung his hands, all earnest Semitic smiles and apologies. He gave the impression that he was beside himself with embarrassment and shame. A guest had been discomposed. His guest seated at his dinner table. How ever could he, Al Arrod live with the humiliation of such an incident weighing upon his conscience? Such an unfortunate accident, the evening ruined. He would cancel all thoughts of producing Oriental 'Ampers. He could not live with the memory. His most sincere regrets etc.

He helped Te'Upp remove herself from Gobbleton's lap. Admonishing her under his breath as he did so. She would never work again. How could she be so stupid? All the time keeping his fixed smile firmly in tact. The incident was turning into a bit of a front page tabloid press sales figure as the journalists now rushed to make the next day's issue.

Al Arrod took Gobbleton to one side. His manner was fawning. He would have the stupid girl thrown out onto the streets. She would never work again. He would have her thrown out of the country. He was about to suggest hanging, drawing, and quartering, when Gobbleton firmly demurred.

No real harm had been done. If it was handled correctly and he Gobbleton was after all an expert in such areas, it could be advantageous press to both of them. Perhaps he should be formally introduced Te'Upp. Let her apologise in person. Maybe there was some mileage in it for both parties?

Al Arrod positively grovelled. He physically doubled up in servility and obsequiousness. He had too, other wise his obvious mirth would have been evident. No, no, let him dismiss the woman forthwith. Perhaps Gobbleton would accept an Oriental 'Amper by means of redress for the unfortunate incident instead? He wrung his hands in anguish secretly revelling in Gobbleton's need to reassure him that there was no need to go to such extremes. Just a simple apology from the woman in question would suffice. There again he wouldn't say no to one or two hampers and perhaps a free stay in one of Al Arrod's many international hotels? Al Arrod continued to play his fish, enjoying every second.

Gobbleton assured Al Arrod that no harm had been done. An accident, pure and simple and he would be delighted to accept an Al Arrod's Oriental 'Amper, more so if Te'Upp were jump out for a second time, he joked. Al Arrod's eyes just for the briefest second showed his elation. Inwardly he sighed, he knew that he had his fish well on the line.

Te'Upp was brought and introduced. Al Arrod suddenly found that he had some urgent and unspecified business, Gobbleton was left alone with the tiny and delightful Te'Upp. Te'Upp was demure. She twisted a small handkerchief between her fingers in nervousness and looked up at Gobbleton in a mixture of hope and sadness. "I'm sorry." She murmured, "I know that I should not have done that but I have admired you for so long. It was my only chance. I'm foolish." There was a slight huskiness to her small voice, and she ended with a choke. She looked down hopelessly at her feet and sniffed. A tear dropped from her eye, and she made no attempt to wipe it away. A sob racked her small body as she hung her head with its long black hair. "What will happen to me?" She asked, looking up at Gobbleton. "You won't put me in jail will you?" She appeared frightened.

Gobbleton's heart went out to her. He made one quick pace to her side and placed his arm around her, if in a rather heavy and clumsy way. "There, there." He said in a soothing voice. "No need to take on so. No harm was done. Why ever should I want to put you in jail?"

Te'Upp clung to him; her body so small against his, she looked up at him, from her delicate and tear streaked face. "Thank you." She whispered. "I knew that you were a good man."

Gobbleton felt marvellous. He felt protective. He wanted to defend this tiny creature against the thunderbolts of the world. He also very much wanted to strip off her flimsy clothes and ravish her there and then upon the thick pile carpet. It had been a long time since Gobbleton last had sex.

Then, though briefly satisfying, he knew that it was no more than a business transaction with a rather sturdy Dutch woman from the red light district of Amsterdam. She did what he wanted and he paid her for her time and expertise. Basically the woman was a sex technician. He found it all rather unsatisfactory. No, what Gobbleton secretly craved was a loving and tender woman. One who would understand him and his needs. But also one who was vulnerable and whom he could protect. She also needed to excite him and allow him to rise to passionate heights and satisfy his long suppressed and unslaked biological needs. And here, in his arms was a delicate flower, an oriental orchid just awaiting to be plucked. Not only that but she found him attractive too. In short, Gobbleton fell head over heels and hopelessly in love. He held her small body to his, and kissed her head tenderly. "I must go." He said to her urgently. "Don't worry, I will take care of you. Every thing will be all right. Phone me tomorrow on this number." He passed her his private mobile phone number. "Please." He added, in a most uncharacteristic way.

Te'Upp, clung to him and raising her pert face to his, kissed him passionately on his lips. Gobbleton felt an almost electric like surge of energy flood through his body and he responded with passion. He placed his large hairy hand upon Te'Upp's quite ample breasts and Te'Upp, played her part well and moaned obligingly. Gobbleton's hands were in frenzy, like an octopus on ecstasy, he scrabbled at Te'Upp's cocktail dress, frantically attempting to slide his fingers into her briefs.

"No, no! Not now. Please later. I will phone you. I promise, but we must be careful. You are an important man" Te'Upp slipped from his grasp and held his quivering hands. She gave Gobbleton her best imploring and I am only a mere female and putty in your hands look, and naturally Gobbleton fell for it. He was putty in her hands.

There was a discrete knock on the door. It was Al Arrod. He took in the scene instantly, and smiled to himself, but gave no out ward sign of having noticed that anything was amiss. Gobbleton should return to the festivities, his presence would be missed. He would personally deal with the woman. He trusted that she had apologised fully. Te'Upp made suitable contrite and fearful noises. Shooting imploring looks of, "please help me" at Gobbleton as she did so.

Gobbleton made light of the matter. The woman had meant no harm. She was young and inexperienced. In fact, he found her rather appealing. Perhaps it would be worthier if he helped her to better her lot in life, rather than throw her out onto the streets? One should after all be a little charitable towards the less fortunate in life. Gobbleton looked at Te'Upp, she gave him the full benefit of her most desperate and beseeching look. Gobbleton was besotted and made his decision. He nodded firmly. Yes, he informed Al Arrod regally. He wished to assist the young lady. Te'Upp gave him her best thank you mixed with desperation look. Gobbleton was hooked.

Al Arrod agreed dutifully. He dismissed Te'Upp. Once alone, he turned to Gobbleton. Perhaps Gobbleton would wish to meet the woman again? Should Gobbleton wish to meet Te'Upp later, then this could be arranged, discretely, of course. He, Al Arrod, of all people understood the nature of these things. They were both, after all, men of the world. And in the public lime light too. There were interconnecting doorways within the suite. Why didn't Gobbleton stay the night? A suitable reason could be found. Business, a late night, sudden ill health? All things were possible. Meanwhile, Gobbleton really should return to the reception. These things could be arranged later.

Back at the reception Gobbleton could not keep his mind off Te'Upp and the thoughts of delights to come. Al Arrod slipped past him and assured him quietly that all arrangements were in order. For Gobbleton to behave as normal, and not to worry, the maiden was his for the taking. Gobbleton was almost beside himself with anticipation. However, he placed his mind firmly on the immediate job in hand and falling back upon his experience, he continued outwardly as if nothing had transpired. Gobbleton was after all well versed in the black arts of deceit and deception. His very livelihood depended upon foistering a total rogue upon an unsuspecting public as not only a person of unblemished reputation, but worthy of being elected as their chosen representative too. A reception dinner was a mere bagatelle by comparison. So he smiled and joked and made all of the right noises at the right time even laughing uproariously at the aged and not very funny story about three nuns and a cactus. Told for the umpteenth time, badly, by a decrepit High Court Judge, through loose teeth. Thinking to himself that there should be a law regarding being senile and found drunk in charge of a joke.

In number ten Downing Street, at about the same time as Gobbleton was trying not to think too much of Te′Upp and hoping that his semi erection would not blossom forth into full manhood and give the fat and rather sweaty lady from the Belgian Embassy, with whom he was dancing, the wrong signals. Gobbleton disliked fat, perspiring ladies with moles who seemed to be attempting successfully to grow moustaches. The Prime Minister of Great Britain and leader of The New Deal Democratic Party was taking a bath.

Antonio Cacophony liked bathing. The tub in Number ten was large. Not quite large enough for himself and the scale model replica of a nuclear submarine, given to him by his good friend Willie Clayton, the President of America true. There again that model didn't float as well as his little yellow plastic duck that had come free with a bottle of household cleaner. The submarine tended to fill with water and sink. Which was exactly what submarines were supposed to do after all, but then it wouldn't come up again. It just sat on the bottom beneath the soapsuds, sulked and did nothing. One had to lift it out of the bath and empty the water from it. That was boring, and the little bits and pieces came unstuck. You ended up sitting on lots of rather sharp, plastic crew members. No, on the whole, the yellow duck was much more fun. More so when he held a ping-pong ball under water with his feet and then released it suddenly. He could make it pop up under the duck, hitting it. This was altogether far more satisfying and he could also make depth charge noises at the same time. So he had replaced the submarine back into its mahogany and glass display case, now a little worse for wear, and kept it with his other toys in the spare bedroom. Antonio Cacophony, though Prime Minister, was a simple soul at heart. He enjoyed his baths and it was the one time when his wife, the redoubtable Heigar, allowed him to remove his wig. He ran a flannel over his bald plate and it caught on one of the five small platinum projections that decorated his scull.

Heigar was a well rounded, dark haired, if somewhat plain and solid Teutonic young woman. She was deliberate of action, energetic and determined of will. Possessing that rather steam roller approach to life that had characterised her Germanic forebears when they expanded the Hun nation. Her general appearance was not improved by her lack of dress sense. Heigar wore sensible, heavy clothing that was economic to purchase and hard wearing. As a consequence of which, Heigar tended to look like an advert for a line of second hand clothes hanging in back of an OXFAM shop. The disillusioned daughter of an Austrian. Herr Professor, Doktor Frantz Kutzanburnz. Heigar dreamed of wealth, power, and recognition. She also dreamed of sex. None of her dreams to date having materialised. Heigar was frustrated.

Her father had devoted his life to research into the field of electrical stimulation of the neurone transmissions of the brain. Research that involved cutting open the cranium and exposing the living areas of interest to him. Into these twitching, grey cerebral coils of the still conscious mammal, would the good Doktor insert his probes and wires. All in the furthering of science of course. His experiments with chimpanzees and numerous other animals, he regarded as being vital to adding to the overall wealth of man's knowledge. He personally believed that he more than justly deserved a Nobel Prize as recognition for his lifetime's work. Various other bodies, such as Animal rights, and the Anti Vivisection League disagreed. To the extent that over the years, he been the recipient of several death threats, had his laboratory razed to the ground twice and he now found it impossible to obtain staff. Other than ex members of the East German Secret Service, who would willingly work for peanuts, providing they could cut up live animals each day, but tended to be too heavy handed and kill the creatures prematurely. His licence had been revoked by the Town Council of Bad Appanings and he had to resort to bringing in animals on the black market. Times were hard for a dedicated research scientist. For all that, he was now sure that he had successfully mapped all the various parts of the brain that produced reactions. He felt that he had proven beyond all doubt that certain predictable results would occur if when controlled electrical stimulation were given to certain areas. What he needed now was a human volunteer, or even a pressed person, upon whom he could conclusively prove and finalise his work. Then at last he could go public and release his knowledge upon an unsuspecting and amazed world. He, Herr Professor, Doktor, Frantz Kutzanburnz, would at last stand tall, acclaimed by his peers, the scientists of the world. No longer would his work be dismissed as the demented ravings of a sadistic mad scientist and he would no longer be a pariah of the scientific community. Though if he didn't find a suitable human guinea pig, he had to admit, his chances of reaching that particular pinnacle were pretty slim.

He was a scientist first and foremost and devoted to his work. Originally he had spurned wealth or creature comforts but of later years had become disillusioned. Seeing his peers acclaimed and lauded, and rewarded handsomely by NASA, he sometimes wished that he too had studied rocketry.

His daughter Heigar however, was a person from another mould. She placed a very high regard on personal wealth and comfort and objected to the almost Bohemian life style her father led. Not for her old coffee cups and half-eaten sandwiches, Heigar had her sights set very firmly upon a life of luxury and power. She had studied neuro psychology at the University of Vienna, and was in the process of completing her doctorate. She had helped her father over many years but knew in her heart that this was no path to fame and fortune and was dissatisfied with her life. She knew that what she needed was a rich husband. Better still, one with good connections too. Then perhaps could she achieve her dreams. Unfortunately, within the circles that she moved, there were no suitable candidates. Further more, her father's work was scorned. Heigar bided her time, inwardly fuming. One day, her time would come. She knew that her destiny was to rule Europe, all she needed was the tools. Then she would show her despised classmates who really held the aces. Heigar knew that once she grasped and then consolidated her power, she could put into place the founding of an empire that would last for a thousand years. For the moment though, she was rather at a loss as how to begin. She needed a sign. Some signal from the ancient Gods of Middle Europe, that her time was at hand and her hour of destiny had finally arrived.

Gods move in mysterious ways, and her destiny took the form of Antonio Cacophony.

She met Antonio whilst he was on a cycling holiday in the Italian Alps. He had a puncture, and absolutely no idea of what to do. It was Heigar that produced puncture kit and spanners and repaired the deflated tyre. Antonio was suitable impressed by this Ruebinesque, and buxom, dark haired lady. He did what he was good at, and ordered a bottle of cheap local wine.

It was when they were sitting back in the sunshine beneath the vine covered patio of the tavern, enjoying a small bottle of Cianti that the first inklings of an idea came in to her head. Antonio it seemed, was the heir to a fortune. A pleasant, handsome even, bumbling, idiotic English fool, with a totally vacuous space between each ear. He could have walked around with a to let sign above his head, but wouldn't have had the brains to fix it in position. He did however have a British Passport. Heigar saw in Antonio far superior material than the chimpanzees in her father's laboratory. They, after all did possess some degree of intelligence. No, Antoino's background and breeding were perfect for her uses. What she needed was to ensnare him to her will, and quickly. But how?

Antonio Cacophony had been born the grandson of an ex Italian POW who remained in Britain after the Second World War, having dropped the daughter of a small newsagents in the pudding club. Their first child had inherited the newsagency, but had his eyes set on more distant targets. Expanding into a booming ice cream business. He too had married and Antonio their only child had become heir to the family fortunes made upon the nation wide sale of Mr. Whoopee and Whopper-Toffee cornets.

Antonio had been sent to the best schools and on to university. His family knowing the benefits of a good British education. Though a pair of old boots would have displayed a higher intellect. In a word, the lad was thick. Not unpleasantly so. He just mostly appeared to dwell on another planet. This is not seen as being a deficit within the upper and monied ranks of Britain, as there is always the army, politics or the church ready to absorb such dunderheads into their fold. Also on the playing fields of English public schools one meets a better class of person and bonds are made that stand one good throughout one's life. In fact, the public schools of Britain operate a very socialistic policy of each according to his needs and each according to his ability. In later life the better able being, now generally running either countries, armies or merchant banks, able to assist their less capable fellow classmates in scraping a good living.

Antonio, or Toni as he preferred to be called, when he first met Heigar, was at that time in Cambridge studying The Arthurian Legend and Celtic Myths. This area of study having been selected as being one of suitable general disinterest as to afford no competition, and maintain employment for a few senile old tutors who all should have been put out to grass years ago. Whilst at the same time appearing to conjure up a pretence of learnedness. In actual fact it consisted in the main of reading fairy stories. This suited Toni no end and he would no doubt come out with an MA at some point. It only really being a matter of time and a curing process brought about by his body absorbing the second hand pipe smoke of his tutors over a number of years.

Far more important at Cambridge is the ability to punt, play cricket and know which fork to use at high table. The social life is magnificent. Each college in the main in fact, owning vast tracts of highly profitable and leased land. Thus enabling them to maintain an excellent cellar and kitchens. If in the process one manages to collect a rag bag assortment of second hand ideas and opinions and is able at a later date to present them as one's own intellectual deliberations, then so much the better. But Cambridge, whilst certainly having a few excellent brains. Those learned persons generally have no interest what so ever in fields outside of their own highly specialised subject. Furthermore, so esoteric are their subjects, no one would understand them even if these worthies attempted to discus them. No, Cambridge dinner parties tend to consist of self appointed pseudo intellectuals, interested only in impressing others with their brilliance. No one listens. Everyone talks. It follows then if one is unable to remember anything, one only has to be quiet and feign interest to be an instant success. Toni of necessity, kept very quiet.

He was a slim lad. Inheriting certain dark Italian looks from his ancestor's genes that most ladies generally find irresistible. Though Toni had no personal knowledge of women. Shy and clumsy at the best of times, he would become totally incoherent in the presence of a female and tend to knock over tables. However he had one big advantage over all other men. Nature tends to compensate, and whatever Toni lacked in brain cells, he more than adequately made up for in other areas. Toni possessed an enormous phallus. It was huge. Even at slack water it was more than impressive. As a consequence of which he had been named Toni the Pony by those with whom he had shared the showers in public school. This obvious asset was something else that interested Heigar as she took stock of the lean, handsome Toni in his bicycle shorts leaning back in his chair in the sun. Here indeed was something with which she could work. She set about seducing him.

The actual act took place some two or three hours later in a field of tomatoes. To her surprise, Toni seeming to have more of an over view of what was required, rather than detailed knowledge of the specifics. He tended to roll around a lot and move in several directions at the same time, unsure of what went where. It became clear to her that he had no clear idea of what he was supposed to be doing. Eventually Heigar took charge and guided Toni in the right direction. She had been surprised that it had been so difficult for both of them. Not so much the actual penetration, though she did feel as if she had been impaled upon a rolling pin and she thanked the makers of the expanding sized, battery operated vibrators with which she dilated her vagina over several years and enjoyed many a long organism in the process. Toni, she realised, though hung like a donkey, had the brains of one too. Obviously he had no experience of women and had unfortunately only managed to nestle his organ within hers and push experimentally a couple of times before ejaculating enormous quantities of semen in all directions. Still, she reflected, there would be other occasions she knew, and she had a box of tissues on hand. Quietly she set her plans in gear to marry Toni. This she achieved upon his graduation from Cambridge. They set up home in one of the better suburbs of London and Heigar, having now completed phase one of her plan, cast around for leads that could enable her to move to phase two.

Controlling Toni was superbly simple. Heigar, had the voluptuous figure of her Germanic ancestors, well rounded and heavy breasted. All she had to do was to sling one of her more than ample bosoms in Toni's direction and Pony Toni's stallion like urges would dominate. Heigar enjoyed this power to the full and quietly showed Toni that there could be little refinements and it did not all have to be over in eleven seconds flat. But she did not show him all and withheld certain sexual secrets, to be utilised to her advantage later. Whereas Toni before had no ideas what so ever in whatever passed for his brain, he now had sex fixed firmly on the forefront of his mind. Heigar effectively held him in the palm of her hand. She could also afford to dress better and invested secretly in some erotic underwear. She posed in front of the mirror, dressed in something that seemed to be made up of black fishnets, holes, fur and a top hat. She looked like a large, pink German sausage that had been forced into a string bag that was far too small to contain it. Toni, she knew would go crazy.

Noel Gobbleton and Peter Meddlesome were both individually running their own and not too successful PR come IT companies. Both, however firmly believed that they were destined for greater things. The old socialist party was floundering, headless, directionless and useless. Ageing union leaders attempting to behave like robber Barons of old, enforcing their will not by the sword, but with the block vote. The Party in power, under Majory Ironclaw was patently duplicitous and fraudulent. Pursuing as it did the jaded, stale and discredited political policies of its predecessors who had so assiduously lost an Empire through ineptitude and arrogance. Racked with scandal, hypocrisy, perversion and downright theft, it had brought the country to its knees. Time was right for a change. Heigar decided that Toni would enter politics. After all, he had everything that a good politician needs. Good looks, and stupidity. What more could a country expect?

Gobbleton and Meddlesome also could see that it was time for a change and they too wondered how they too might profit from such a shift. They all met by chance a Buckingham Palace Garden Party, in honour of one of the corgies having given birth to a litter of eight. Funding for such functions being allocated on an annual basis by Government in advance and hence had to be spent and thus duly accounted for. Anyway, such occasions allowed one to wear a new hat, meet old friends and make suitable sympathetic noises about the homeless. Also one often picked up a good tip for a bit of insider trading on the stock market too. When Heigar met with Gobbleton and Meddlesome, she knew immediately that these two were to be the viaduct for her schemes and aspirations.

Gobbleton understood wealth and wanted his own. Meddlesome understood computers and wanted power. Both understood public relations and the basic rules of the game. Both had connections. She gently aroused their interests. They met again in secret to decide their plan of campaign, but Heigar kept back the fuller details of her own personal view of a unified Europe under her control. Gobbleton and Meddlesome sat spellbound as Heigar laid before them the outline of her bold designs for a brave new world and their role in such a venture.

Gobbleton and Meddlesome sat transfixed. Heigar, at last having found a captive audience, let full rein to her pent up and suppressed emotions. She spoke not with just persuasion but with positive passion and eloquence. She was careful to lead each of them into a situation whereby they could dream of an unlimited future and envision the advantages to themselves. Whilst at the same time concealing any advantage to herself. They found themselves not just listening to, but believing that her stratagem was plausible. Each could see his role and the personal gains that would be the result. The risks were high, that was true, but should things go wrong in the early stage, then they was still time for them to distance themselves from the project and if necessary, disclaim all knowledge. Should however, the initial difficulties be overcome, as indeed Heigar assured them both, they could. Then the rewards would be bounteous, to say the least. They agreed to go along with the strategy and review the situation once she had completed her initial and vital stage. And so it was that Meddlesome found himself purchasing several black, bouffant style wigs, to which he made minor, but vital modifications as per Heigar's detailed instructions. Meanwhile, Heigar took Toni on a holiday to Austria.

Gerald Fatslobe had borrowed heavily from merchant banks and purchased pig farms. He now owned four units based in England and they were doing well. Not well enough to expand and not well enough to finance his dreams of his empire of pork. Gerald was frustrated. The future lay in pigs. His wife was no problem, all she required to keep her happy was a large bottle of gin. No, the children were being a pain. Tiffany threatening to drop out of university and live in a squat in Camden Town with some of her strange friends. Gerald couldn't quite get his brain around Tiffany's friends. Green and blue Mohawk hairstyles, leather jackets, heavy with studs and safety pins stuck into the oddest of places confused and filled him with disquiet. They scarcely looked human. Certainly not the sort of thing that a successful MP in opposition would wish to be associated. He realised that perhaps it was just as well that the party was in opposition and not in power. The press would have a field day.

Bradford was rather odd too. Locking himself up in the cellars with crates of laboratory equipment and a huge computer layout. No, he really didn't understand his children. Pigs were much more predictable and reliable. He would go and slaughter a few, then perhaps he would feel better.

Meanwhile, in Austria, Toni had agreed willingly to have his head shaved. Heigar had told him that she held a secret fetish for bald men. Having introduced Toni to sex, Heigar had shown him the delights of felitio, and Toni liked it. It had not occurred to him that other bodily orifices could be employed and sacrificing his hair for the promise of continued blowjobs, seemed to his way of thinking, a small price to pay. Though quite why he required a general anaesthetic for a hair cut eluded him. Still, if that what it took to have his Heigar suck away at his member, so be it. It crossed his mind too, that one normally sat in a barber's chair, and not lay on a sort of hospital trolley thing. Herr Professor, Doctor, Frantz Kutzanburnz slid a needle into his arm. Pony Toni, slipped into unconsciousness, unaware of the part he was about to play on the world's stage.

Herr Professor, was excited. At last he had his volunteer. Heigar had explained to him her plans. He knew that they would work. He set up his instruments carefully. There would be no room for mistakes. No margins for error. If he were successful, then in the fullness of time, by stealth, would he and his work be acclaimed. As for those who had scorned him, revenge would be sweet. He prepared his patient, first shaving the scull.

The small platinum implants were placed carefully into the holes that he had drilled into Toni's head. These were then glued into position, sealing the micro holes. A laser being used to effect the final bonding. He had only wanted to put three into position. Their tiny wires penetrating the smarm and charm, earnest and sincere and confidence and aggressive reaction producing areas of the brain. Heigar had insisted on a further two that affected the sexual drive and sleep inducing spheres respectively. The patient would be allowed to recover before any stimulation experimentation exercises were attempted.

Meddlesome arrived in secret two weeks later. Having driven unchallenged, via France. He brought the wigs, laptop and mobile phone. With the EEC open boarders policy in force, no one took any notice of an English man who hired a French registered car and obeying all traffic regulations, legally entered Austria.

Toni, when he came around, if he wondered why he had now acquired five small bumps on his head, paid them no great attention. Maybe they had always been there. He could not remember ever having seen himself bald before. Heigar told him that they were stuck to his scalp and would be used to lock his wig in position. The wig that would arrive any day now, along with the wig maker. In the meantime though, he was enjoying the delights of felitio, and he like it.

Heigar just wished that Meddlesome would arrive with all speed. Her mouth was getting sore and she suffered from cramp of the facial muscles, due to having to keep her mouth wide open but with gums well forward of the tooth line. Still, at least it was giving the thoroughly dilated muscles of her labia majoris time to recover. Toni, she was beginning to realise was OK in small doses, unfortunately there was nothing small about Toni.

CHAPTER. 3

Majory Ironclaw, was the first female Prime Minister of Britain. A lean and severe lady who reminded most people of either a heartily disliked and feared headmistress, or a hated spinster aunt. Indomitable, rigid, thrusting, dynamic and displaying more than a healthy touch of megalomania, she pursued her policies with an unswerving will and determination. Feared by many and hated by all, she was in global terms, a highly successful Prime Minister.

So as not to disturb the calm waters of what she knew instinctively was right and proper for the country, she surrounded herself with sycophantic toadies that would lickspittal to her will. Britain, that had once been a great ship building nation, had in the sixty's slipped into becoming a car manufacturing country. Under Majory Ironclaw's leadership, it became a nation of TV and washing machine repairmen. Or persons, to be politically correct. The opportunity to become a semi skilled, and lowly paid, part time employee, being equally available to both sexes. The washing machines and televisions in question, all having been imported from Japan.

Britain was an island that's geological formation consisted of in the main coal and iron ore, surrounded by seas abundant in fish. Under Majory, both former industries were massacred and the fishing rights to the latter were given away to minor countries of the EEC.

The profits from the recently discovered oil and gas fields were used to pay off the three million unemployed. Jobs, the nation, was assured were there for the taking. Careers, no. Jobs as bar men, launderette persons and a bit of part time cleaning for the newly rich, yes. Under Majory, the paper wealth increased, and some prospered. There again, Krupp did pretty well in Germany from 1940 to 1945. Using slave labour that is. But there are no Nuremberg Trials for ex British Prime Ministers, no matter how badly they behave, just life peerage's in the House of Lords and the odd statue or two.

It's a well-documented fact that nothing boosts flagging a Prime Minister's opinion polls better than a nice little war. Nothing too big, you understand. The last thing one requires on breakfast TV is a long parade of body bags being unloaded. It puts good folks off their Cornflakes. No, what is required is a safe little shindig in a foreign part. Not too far away, and definitely not too close either. Since the army was wholly volunteer, one can expect to incur a few casualties. That's their tough luck. That's what they got paid for anyway wasn't it? One didn't want a lot of nasty looking walking wounded either. Not good press having hideously scarred veterans with bits missing lounging around in wheel chairs and making a lot of unseemly noise. No, either kill them straight out, or have nice valiant wounds. Smiling men with an arm in a sling waving to a grateful country and collecting a gong. That sort of thing.

Majory's press ratings were in a sharp decline. Her plan to offer long-term prisoners the opportunity to purchase their prison cells had not been received well. The homeless were making their presence felt. The streets were becoming untidy. That was bad for the tourist industry and their lobby was getting all together too vociferous. No, something would have to be done to take the general public's mind of things. Providence provided the key. Someone raised the Icelandic flag on Unst, and so the second cod war began.

In retrospect, it was highly doubtful if the Icelandic Government knew anything about the flag, or cared. They were much too preoccupied with the decline in cod fish stocks caused by over fishing by both UK and EEC fleets. After all, Iceland's only natural resources were thermal power, a non-exportable item and white fish. There was the eider down industry but that was seasonal, and totally dependent upon migratory ducks. The advent of polyesters had also driven a large nail into that particular coffin. No longer did hardy Icelandic wives of fishermen prepare tempting places for the ducks to make their nests. Then later, plunder the soft white feathers. Polyester filled pillows were for the buying on supermarket shelves and cheaper too. No, it would have been a brave soul that stockpiled barns full of duck down, in the hope that the bottom would drop out of the oil industry and polyester production dry up. So the ducks, no doubt now suffering from psychological rejection and a feeling of being unwanted, went and built their nests in other and highly inaccessible places, never to return.

Once, on a previous occasion, Iceland had resorted to increasing its sea boundaries from 12 to 200 miles. Britain's objection mainly stemming from realising that if they accepted that then everyone else would wish to do the same too. For a nation that fondly still presumed that it ruled the seas, this rather tended to underpin it's feeling of pride and security. It would be also become debatable as to who owned lumps of France, or the Channel ports come to that. No, the Dukes of Normandy might get restless and the one hundred-year's war start up all over again. Also yew trees and longbow men were both in sharp decline. In any event, France was an independent nuclear power, and had that tetchy, big nosed general in charge. Consequently, on the whole, Iceland seemed to be a much safer adversary and softer target for aggression. There again, one could not be seen in the eyes of the world as being too gung ho. Bully with the big stick etc. No, send a few frigates up there and play tag with their funny little gunboats. Let everyone get used to the idea of a 200 mile fishing limit, then do some deal with regard to fish stocks. That way everyone was kept happy and the Navy could play and their Lordships would be happy having meetings, drinking rum and pushing wooden models around a battle plan. Anyway, 200 miles might just suit us nicely too. There was rumour of there being some oil deposits in the North Sea. And so the first cod war had drawn to a close, but now oil had been discovered and Iceland had raised their flag on Unst.

When she had first been alerted to the situation, both Majory and The Home secretary had been under the opinion that Unst was a railway siding near Shrewsbury. It had crossed her mind that the likelihood of Iceland laying claim to anything so far inland was unlikely. Still, who knew what the Iceland's flag looked like anyway? It could just as easily be The Welsh Nationalists, or Plaid Cwmru, as they called themselves. It took a large map and the aid of The Foreign and Commonwealth Minister to get the actual geographical location correct. Unst, they discovered, was in the Shetland Isles.

Now true Shetland islanders, The Home secretary assured the Prime Minister, have a lot in common with the peoples of the Faeroe Islands. Spelt Færoyar locally. The capital being Torshaven, which roughly translated as Thor's Harbour. Thor is a Norse God. And that both peoples were closer ethnically to Scandinavia than to Anglo Saxons was beyond dispute. The Faeroe Islands belonged to Denmark, as indeed had Iceland previously. The obvious logical conclusion to this train of thought was that Iceland, first having seceded from Denmark and then having got away with imposing a 200 mile territorial water claim, was now putting in a bid for the Shetland Islands and the sub sea oil wealth in their vicinity. This could not be tolerated, and would not be tolerated either. Action was called for. Immediate action at that. Marjory called an emergency Cabinet meeting to discuss the crisis, though she had already made up her mind as to exactly what she intended doing about the situation. Still, in a democracy, she sighed in exasperation, one had to pay lip service and go through these tiresome rigmarole's, prior to getting one's own way. She held no qualms. The opposition party was in magnificent disarray and her own party would do as they were told. Majory could have her safe little war and the nation would forget about the current refuse collection strike and the demise of the National Health Service.

The Cabinet met. It was decided to summon the Ambassador for Iceland and formally demand an apology and for the offending flag to be removed forthwith. Since the flag in question had actually been placed there as prank by a passing lone Yachtsman. Who after several large glasses of whisky, had copulated strenuously with a local lady of somewhat easy virtue upon the cliff top. Having assuaged his natural bodily functions and paid off his accomplice. He had then raised his standard in triumph as his own rather more personal, and less imposing standard drooped. In the morning, suffering heavily from a massive hang over, he had subsequently sailed away leaving the offending standard still raised and forgotten. The Ambassador was sympathetic, but claimed no knowledge of the incident. Through him the demand was passed to Iceland.

Naturally the Icelandic Government too had no knowledge of the incident. Anyway, they were far too preoccupied with maintaining the integrity and sanctity of their Norse language. They were very proud of the fact that should a twelve century Viking suddenly pop up from no where, he would be able to communicate perfectly with any Icelandic citizen. Apparently the likelihood of such an occurrence happening, having slipped past their collective psyche. Committees met each quarter to decide upon new words that would be acceptable. Hence jet plane became, high flying, fast silver eagle of Odin, or some such combination. There was also the problem with the Icelandic telephone directory, as all male names ended in sonn and all females ended in tochter. Hence if Erik had a male child called Fredrick, then his name would be Fredrick Eriksonn. If it were a girl called Martyr, then she would become Martyr Erikstochter. Then if Fredrick Eriksonn had a child that he wished to name after it's grandfather, he would then become Erik Freidricksonn. Which effectively meant that family names changed with each generation. Since all Icelandic citizens were pretty well related to one another somewhere along the line, it didn't much matter, as they all knew each other anyway, but looking up a phone number could get tricky. When informed about some flag stuck on a rock in the Shetlands they didn't take it too seriously. I mean, they didn't put it there, had no idea who had and cared even less. Surely the Brits. were capable of taking down a flag? God alone knows, they had enough practice over the past few years. They seemed to be hauling them down all over the planet. Iceland put it on the back burner and got on with the far more important business of working out a suitable word for a helicopter or microwave. Majory fumed. She had been snubbed.

Majory locked herself in her office with a nice cup of tea and a slice of Madera cake. She would lead the expedition. She pictured herself at the head of her victorious armies, doing Henry V type speeches. Then realised that would also demand that she actually leave the civilised safety of Number Ten and consort with a lot of working class squaddies, who probably smelled unpleasant. Majory shuddered at the thought. No, better she use the Elizabeth 1 technique and address her troops prior to them going off to do battle. It could all be stage managed so much better too and it was far easier for TV coverage. She gave America a passing thought and sighed again. She would have to let that dreadful ex B movie star cowboy that dyed his hair know. What was his name? Pistols? Laser Blaster? No, Raygun, that was it. He would no doubt be far too wrapped up in that stupid idea of his to blanket the world with anti missile missiles. She supposed then that Russia of China would put anti missile, missile, missiles in place. Pretty soon the damn things would be bumping into each other any way. She shook her head in exasperation and impatience at the stupid games boys play. It's all a case of I can piss higher up the wall than you can. Well, she was having none of it. No, they could both keep their noses out of her war. Let them find one of their own. On second thoughts best not. The last thing she needed was to get in the crossfire of a replay on the gunfight at the OK Coral. Done on global terms and at nuclear levels. Better to leave them pissing up walls. She got the maps out again, doodled with a few pencils and then called for the Joint Chiefs of Staff, more tea and cake.

"What I propose gentlemen." She began, "Is a total blockade of Iceland. We will place our warships here, here and here." She indicated with a pointer on the large map spread out on the table in front of them. "We will immediately land a battalion of troops on Unst, here and here. Seaborn amphibious landings here and airborn drops here, here and here. We will protect our beloved homeland once again from the marauding Viking. I shall not go down in history as Majory The Unready. We will starve our pagan foe into submission and then, when he is on his knees begging for our mercy, we will dictate the terms. She sat back, well satisfied.

"What exactly will those terms be Marm?" It was one of her press aids. A young man with no chin, spots and a clip board.

She turned to him in annoyance; "I don't yet. I haven't made up my mind. Don't be picky lad." She had the satisfaction of seeing him go red in embarrassment.

"Uh-humm" It was the army this time she noted with distaste.

"Can't actually do amphibious landings where you indicated Marm...... High cliffs and all that."

"So conduct them somewhere else, for God's sake." He really was being tiresome. "I leave the details to you man. I don't sharpen my own pencils.

Just get your troops there and do it today!" One really had to be very firm with these military types; they had no idea of urgency. The Chiefs Of Staff looked at each other and sipped their tea. "Well, get on with it. Don't keep me waiting." She gave them her best cross look and was pleased to see them all go into huddle. They muttered a lot and pointed at the map, then seemed to come to a collective decision. It was the same army man she noted with distaste, he seemed to have become their spokesman. She sighed, why was it that these people wanted to make things so difficult? It was quite simple. Get the troops in position with a show of force and as that dreadful American President had the habit of saying, Kick Arse. Well, she would just have to listen she supposed. It was just like cabinet meetings. First of all be forced to listen to endless objections of why it couldn't or shouldn't be done, and then tell them to get on and do it. She sat down and adopted her regal pose that she had practised for so long in front a mirror. "Explain." She said in her We are not amused voice.

"Well Marm. First of all we don't have the facilities to mount a seaborn landing. Neither transport ships or landing craft. Secondly, we don't have facilities to mount an airborn operation. All of our transport having been hired out by the MOD on long term commercial leases to OXFAM for that famine thing going on Africa or some where. If you want troops there quickly, then my suggestion is use the railway. But they, as you know are currently on strike due to the number of threatened closures and staff cut backs. You may find that the union refuses to drive the trains.

"So drive them yourself man!" Majory exploded. There was always a famine going on in Africa somewhere and it had been her idea to rent off the planes and their crews quietly to the relief agencies. They in turn obtaining the money for the rental from public donations. It had been a nice little earner. The army chap was shaking his head. Apparently the army couldn't drive trains. Tanks and radar controlled artillery yes. Trains, no. There were some problems with signalling too. In any case if any damage were to be incurred and God alone knows what would be likely to happen if he let a lot of cag-handed soldiers loose on the nations rail system. The subsequent civil actions and legal costs would be unthinkable. Majory had to grudgingly agree to herself that he did have a point. Anyway she had not planned to send off her valiant armies care of British Rail. The food and delays alone would result in most being incapacitated long before they reached their objective.

"Navy." She demanded. One of their Lordships stepped forward.

"Wee bit tricky Marm....... Not enough ships for a blockade."

She waved him away in exasperation, "Royal Air Force? Yes, you. Blue uniform, stick and big moustache. I take it that I still have an air force."

"Lord yes Marm. Still have one of those, my flyboys. dontchaknow?"

"Yes, yes. get on with it. Can you give me air cover?"

"Oh yes Marm." At last! Majory thought, something positive. "Mind you Marm, depends rather upon what you had in mind."

"Air planes man! aeroplanes. You know, those silver metal things that make a lot of noise and have guns and bombs and things and cost a fortune. Fighters for God's sake. What do you think I mean? Balloons and boxkites?" This was all too much.

"Well Marm. I could rustle up a couple of Nimrods to keep an eye on things."

"What's a Nimrod?"

"Converted civilian job, used for surveillance."

"Can it drop bombs?"

"Fraid not Marm. It's actually a converted De Haverland Comet. One of the ones that didn't fall apart in mid air back in the fifties. We got lumbered with them, so stuck a lump on the nose and use them to take photographs. They are quite safe if you drive them around quietly. Bit long in the tooth now though."

"But they don't drop bombs and can't fire guns?"

"Exactly Marm." He looked apologetic.

"What about those jumpy jack jet things that your chaps are so keen to potter around in at air shows, Harriets."

"Harriers Marm. Frightful expensive to operate and they like to have a nice steady deck. Those little through carriers bob about like corks in a heavy chop. Might get them off, bit tricky getting them back. Chaps tend to get a wee bit bothered under those circumstances. Can't blame them I suppose. Anyway no point Marm. The other services can't organise any landings and as far as I know, Iceland has no airforce. So we wouldn't have to protect ourselves from them even if we needed to, which we don't." He seemed quite pleased with his answer.

"So you are no use either?"

"Oh don't know Marm. Might be able to help out with an airborn assault."

Majory sat up and took interest. "Go on. I'm listening."

"Well, there's a couple, maybe three Vulcans." Majory looked blank. "Those big delta wing jobs. Sitting at Duxford Aircraft Museum, I believe. You know Marm. "A" bombers from the early sixties. Quite spacey inside. We could pack in a few brown jobs with parachutes, fly in slow and boot them all out."

Majory sighed. "So let me see, have I got this right? The Navy hasn't enough boats for transporting my army, let alone a blockade." She knew that their Lordships hated their beloved toys to be referred to as boats. Everything was a ship. Even buildings! "My air force consists of some converted passenger liners that didn't manage to self destruct twenty odd years ago and some jump jets that are either too expensive to operate or will be unable to return from their mission if they do? I suppose the army still has enough tents to house the troops in the field?" She turned her icy stare to the towards the Field Marshals. They fidgeted and fiddled with their gloves and sticks. "Well?"

"Actually no Marm. We sold the lot off as a job lot to Indonesia."

Majory picked up at the word Indonesia. It rang a bell in her memory. "What about those Hawk aircraft things?"

"Sold all of those to Indonesia too Marm." It was the spotty aid again. "Next batch aren't built and anyway Indonesia has first claim to them too. Frightfully good business, selling arms, or so Mark tells me. He swears that it's much better than second hand cars. Making a fortune and no MOTs to bother about either."

"SHUT UP!" Majory snapped. The last thing she wanted was that cat let out of the bag at this stage. Anyway, if Mark sold arms to the Arabs or Pinochet, or whoever, it was better than having him running around in the desert in rally cars and getting lost. It made for bad press. She wasn't giving up yet. She wasn't known as the Steel Biddie for nothing. "So gentleman." Her sarcasm hung heavy, "How exactly do you propose to move my army into position? She was sure that the Duke of Wellington had not have had these difficulties. The Joint Chiefs of Staff huddled some more.

A decision was finally reached. Hover Lloyd and Sealink operated large hovercraft. These could be used to not only transport troops, but land them too. Care being taken to select a nice easy going and gently sloping beach. It was only really a case of hiring the craft on a commercial basis and using their existing crews. Caravans could be requisitioned from all over the country and loaded on too. These would then be used to house the troops once the landings had been completed. Just hitch them up behind Land Rovers. The old delta wing Vulcans could be brought out of storage. Apparently these museums looked after them with loving care, far better that the RAF had. No doubt civilian crews would again have to fly them. No museum in it's right mind being willing to let some hamfisted top gun loose at the controls. Anyway the old boys understood navigating with a compass and map. Those old planes didn't have all of the newfangled electronic gear in them. Modern pilots expected to have their destinations programmed in and be directed from the ground at all times. Stick them in an old Vulcan and they would only get lost.

A couple of Nimrods could stooge around and take photographs of each other. If some footage was then dug up of Hawks and Harriers, jumping and flying around, with sufficient good PR and a tame BBC, no doubt Iceland could be intimidated. Anyway, it was the best she could muster for the moment. And so Britain prepared for war.

The tabloid press were happy to latch onto the story. VIKING THREAT ran the headlines. It had been a poor week, nothing to grab attention. The usual type of children starving to death in third world countries. Transvestite vicars dressing up in see through black nylon underwear and frightening old ladies, a couple of drive by shootings in Sunderland and a High Court judge found in compromising circumstances with three underage boys in Sri Lanka. Absolutely nothing. The BBC, when asked to roll some footage of aeroplanes did so in an obliging way. Unfortunately they broadcast some very impressive stuff of carriers and fighter planes blasting off. All very imposing. Snag was Britain had no aircraft carriers and the ones in question belonged to America. This prompted the American President to get on the hot line and ask if the USA had gone to war as no one had told him. Not that anyone told him anything anyway, but he thought it would be best to know about it if they had. Could save a few embarrassing questions. Majory assured him that he hadn't. Then of course he wanted to know why not? I mean they were allies after all. Why should Majory have all of the fun? Couldn't she share her war with him?

Well yes, she conceded. But he had to understand from the outset that it was her war and she was in charge. But, if he wanted to position a carrier some place handy, but not so handy as to grab all of the limelight, then he could play too.

"Great." Said Raygun, "He could get to wear his cowboy hat. His favourite one he wore in the film, "The Wyoming Wanderer" and by the way, who was he fighting. Iceland? Never heard of it. Still, he expected that someone in The Pentagon knew where it was. Leave it all to him. He would send the USS Terminator. The one that had won the Vietnam war. "You didn't win the Vietnam War." Majory reminded him. "Hadn't they?" Well no one had told him that either. Not to worry, they sure would win this one. By the way, who had won. "The Vietnamese? Well, what do-ya-know? still, it hadn't done them much good had it?." He had never seen a Vietnamese built car for sale.

The British ferry companies that owned the hovercraft, were quite obliging. It shouldn't interrupt services for more that two days, so if it could be a mid week landing, it wouldn't disturb things too much, and they would offer a special discount rate. But they insisted that they inspect the landing sites before hand for nasty sharp rocks or sudden swirls of water. Oh, one other small thing, their crews would be driving and they insisted that the bars and duty-free operate on board as usual. Would there be a campaign medal? If so, then they thought that it would be a nice gesture if the crews got one too.

Caravans proved to be far more difficult. For some reason caravan owners strenuously resisted having their mobile homes requisitioned by the army. To the extent that several more bucolic farmers had driven army personnel from their lands at shot gun point. One such operation resulting in a total route of three officers, and pellet damage to a staff car. The officers refusing point blank to return and have anything further to do with the enraged owner. They were not paid to risk their lives against armed civilians who had no conception of either the rules of engagement, or the Geneva Convention. Anything could happen. Eventually the MOD resorted to hiring sufficient for their purpose from Happy Holmes and Sunny View Leisure Parks Limited. Both organisations of which insisted on moving the mobile homes themselves. At a discount rate of course. Majory recollected that her objective of instilling the values of a market economy on Britain, had certainly fell on fertile ground with regard to hovercraft and leisure home companies.

And so it was that on a bright Wednesday morning, a fleet of large mobile homes, officers use only, were loaded onto the backs of Happy Holmes low loaders and they along with a fleet of Volvos pulling other ranks class homes behind them, converged, in secret on Dover. The resulting traffic jam was of stupendous proportions and D notices were served on all newspapers.

The army meanwhile, all in civilian dress, apart from boots and kit bags posed as peaceful tourists. There was a slight hiccup at Customs when a squaddie was asked to open his bag and an SA 80 assault rifle fell out along with several clips of ammunition and the odd grenade. This was quickly covered over by the squaddie reverting to his cover story. Namely that he was with the IRA and popping home on a spot of compassionate leave. The fact that the ferry from Dover went to the Continent and not to Ireland could safely be ignored. I mean, he was supposed to be Irish after all.

The hovercraft nosed gently ashore on Unst. The civilian drivers started up their engines and the battle fleet of caravans disembarked. The army was by now in full battle gear. Unfortunately, the duty free bars having been open for the whole of the trip, and it had been a long one, most of the troops were near paralytic. The drivers all in a similar state. The Beach master had apoplexy, finally breaking down and sobbing. Caravans and tucks got bogged down. Squaddies stood around in groups either singing dirty songs and throwing up, or picking fights with soldiers from other units. The Vulcans came roaring over, far too fast and low and blanket bombing everyone in sight with members of the Third Parachute Brigade. They whistled in with their 'chutes still folded and bounced around like ping pong balls. Eventually some local farmers arrived with tractors and sorted out the mess, towing the caravans and parking them neatly in their fields. Having first of all come to a suitable monetary agreement with the Brigadier in charge, for rent and services supplied. The hovercrafts, having retreated under the fusillade of bodies from the Third Para. and fearing damage to their machines, now returned and picked up the returning trucks and Volvos. The army either collected its dead or went to sleep off the effects of the duty free. More D notices were served and it was decided to do a landing re-run the next day for the benefit press and video footage, when things were a little less chaotic.

Iceland continued on blithely unaware that their country should be on a war footing. Or that an aircraft carrier, the USS Terminator was planning on taking up station 210 miles off their shores, armed with sufficient nuclear weapons to wipe out all life on the planet.

The Irish were being difficult. The Irish were always being difficult. Majory was sick and tired of Orange Men dressing up in bowler hats and sashes and disturbing the peace of Catholic areas with their endless parades. She wished to God that they would stop waving Union Jacks and proclaiming themselves to be British. Why in the name of God couldn't they be quiet. That way the Free Six, as the counties of Ulster had now taken to calling themselves, could be united with the Republic and we could all get on with living within the EEC together. It wasn't as if the Catholic Church held any sway over the masses in the south anyway. Any chemist shop would sell you a packet of condoms and church attendance had been in almost free fall. Most of the bombings of late had been rival Loyalist gangs fighting a turf war and any shootings had more to do with organised crime than religion. On the whole it had been a black day for English history when all those years ago, the Earl or Duke of Pembroke had decided that he had nothing much on one wet Saturday afternoon and grabbing Ireland was a good idea. There had been nothing but trouble ever since. The people there seemed to live in some perpetual time warp, re-fighting battles that took

place over three hundred years ago. It was about the time that the whole
bunch of them was dragged screaming into the twentieth century. The one
good thing about it all was it did allow Britain to rotate every Battalion in
the army through Belfast. Thus subjecting them to battle conditions. If a
few got shot, so be it. They volunteered.

The one big fear in any government's heart is internal insurrection.
All of her officers and troops received invaluable training in this field in
Ulster. In fact, her government actually owed the IRA a debt of gratitude.
Just so long as the bombs and bullets remained over the water, no one on
the mainland took too much notice. Now however someone had noticed
the troop movements and the Republic wanted to know was it about to
be invaded? The north was expressing concern with regard to reduced
numbers of British troops and facilities and Iceland was ignoring her. To
cap it all, that oaf Raygun had got it all wrong and sent his Damn ships
off to Greenland. Well serve him right if he missed his hour of glory. She
certainly was not going to miss hers. Raygun could catch up later.

Iceland first got wind that something was amiss when one of it's
scheduled air busses en route from Helsinki to Reykjavik encountered a near
miss with a Nimrod within Iceland's territorial air space. The conversation
went roughly as follows:

"Captain of air bus to RAF Nimrod. That was too close for comfort.
Are you aware that you are in Icelandic civilian air space?"

"Nimrod to airbus. Yes."

"Oh! Captain of airbus to RAF Nimrod. Why?"

"We're at war old boy."

"Who with?"

"Well, you lot I'm afraid."

"Good God! Are you going to shoot us down? I only have civilians on
board."

"Wouldn't dream old bean, wouldn't dream. Anyway just between you
and me, we aren't carrying any ordinance on this old bus. But the Yanks
have come in on our side and are supposed to have some carrier floating
about below, so keep your eyes skinned for a brace of Tom Cats. Very

trigger-happy are our American cousins. Or, so I'm told. Oh well toodlepip old chap."

Iceland protested to the United Nations.

Majory placed a Polaris submarine in position. Raygun sensible kept his carrier and it's escorts well out of the way. The Brits. were a terribly secretive lot and wouldn't tell him exactly were their secret submarine was. They had told him it wouldn't be a secret otherwise. Just to keep well over to the left of the map and there would be plenty of room. His Tom Cats had lots of fun buzzing Reykjavik and taking photographs of snow and volcanoes. Iceland kept it's fishing fleet in port. They did not want to provoke anyone. They knew nothing of any flag incident and wanted to be left alone to catch cod, rearrange telephone directories and make up new Norse words. In fact Iceland sulked.

Back on Unst, the farmers ran in power lines, complete with their own coin meters, charged rent and sold fresh food. The pubs did a roaring trade and the Chilli Chicks held a concert. In fact everyone was quite happy, no one was actually getting shot and wealth had suddenly appeared on Unst. The worst that could happen would be a few unwanted pregnancies. Majory fumed. Her war was bogged down.

Two events then occurred pretty well simultaneously. With the Icelandic fishing fleet being confined to port, there was a shortage of cod in the UK. Some crazy splinter group of the IRA called the Mc Guinness Brigade, publicly aligned themselves with Iceland. Something about Imperialist British aggression. They took to fire bombing fish and chip shops on mainland Britain in protest. Hit them where it hurts, was their motto. There was a predictable public outcry. Majory threatened to nuke Reykjavik. The fact that a Polaris submarine carried 16 missiles, each with a programmable multi warhead was explained to her. "So program the lot for Reykjavik." Was her answer. It was explained to her that Iceland would be vaporised and the nuclear plume would drift eastwards towards Russia.

"So what?" Was the Steel Biddie's response. "We had to put up with their Chernobyl. There are still sheep on the hills in Wales that glow green in the dark!"

"But Marm, the countries in between might get a little miffed. Denmark, Germany, our EEC neighbours. Things are not quite going to plan Marm. Half the army is paralytic through drinking the home brewed Unst whisky and all of the troops are in debt. The Americans have got bored of photographing volcanoes and snow and have gone home and the British public are now up in arms over the shortage of cod. None is to be had, and that Marm, is very serious."

It was at this juncture that Majory uttered the immortal line that sunk her Government without trace.

"So let them eat hake!"

A general election inevitably followed.

CHAPTER. 4

It wasn't that the British public cared passionately about politics, or even who ran the country. They didn't. For the vast majority, providing there was soap on TV, the price of beer, petrol and cigarettes only went up in small increments, though remained hideously expensive. They could take the odd package tour to Majorca and the football team they supported wasn't relegated, they didn't give damn. Majory Ironclaw was a figure they all loved to hate. A handy peg upon which all the problems of life could be hung. The fact that they lived in the most expensive country in the EEC and paid considerably more for alcohol, tobacco, oil and cars, than their neighbours was ignored. Johnny Foreigner did things differently. Anyway, he didn't have a National Health Service did he? If it was pointed out to the man in the street that France, Germany, Holland all possessed superior systems, it was rather like discussing religion with a Jesuit. The shutters of ignorance were firmly drawn. Objective criticism withered on the vine of preconceived and ingrained believes. No light could penetrate the blindness. Majory was well aware of all of this of course, and was happy to be hated. Just as long as she got her own way. And went about Increasing, albeit legally, the personal wealth of her family whilst holding office, by several hundreds of thousands of pounds. Well, she did represent the party of business and commerce after all.

Under her leadership, and in global terms, the country did appear to move forward and the majority did acquire a higher standard of living. But it was achieved by selling off the family silver, debasing the birth right of the nation and blatant deception. Furthermore, the price that had to be paid by some, was very high indeed. Fortunately for Majory though, they remained in the minority. Naturally voices were raised in protest, but to no avail. The Great British Nation carried on playing Bingo and no one cared. Well, not anyone who could command an audience. No, Majory was left pretty well alone to pursue her own private megalomaniac dreams, sell arms to all and sundry, with no thought that perhaps one day those very arms might be used against Britain. Boost the personal wealth of herself, family and close friends and no one within her orbit objected if a few crumbs fell off her table of largess to be eagerly consumed by her favourite and fawning acolytes. So much the better and all the more reason to fawn. Unemployment could be tolerated and contained. Homelessness amongst the young explained as the actions of ill disciplined youth. An ever rising crime rate could be blamed upon certain factions within ethnic minorities. A collapsing health service upon the mismanaged policies of the previous Government in power. Fingers could be pointed, and tired, worn platitudes paraded. Joe Public showed no interest. Majory was once overheard to remark that populations by and large got the kind of government they deserved, and Britain certainly deserved her. Fish and chips however, were something very different.

That fish and chip shop premises had been destroyed and livelihoods lost were not the prime concern of the public. After all, most of the shops in question had been owned by Turkish Cypriots anyway. It was the non-existence of cod that captured the attention of the nation and fed the headlines of the tabloids. In one fell swoop had the very cornerstone of British culture been removed and one of the traditions that had under pinned and fed the British way of life for generations was destroyed. Majory's classic remark displayed to an anxious and agitated populace the level and true depth to which her esteem for them extended. The mob was riled and her doom sealed. There would be no honorary Doctorate in Economics for her from the University of Milton Keynes. No statue of her would grace the halls or galleries of the House of Commons. Majory had failed to recognise a fundamental facet of the British character. Namely that one can throw flying bombs at them, tax them to the hilt and even threaten them with nuclear destruction and they will take it all with equanimity. Mess with their food, driving on the left or the makings of a cup of tea, and then you have major problems on your hands. In fact Britain went to war with China, became the first country to base an economy on heroin and lost America, all over tea. Fish and chips are equally revered. No, Marjory had shot her bolt and really pissed off Britain. Her days were well and truly numbered.

Not the opposition party was in any better shape. Led by some red haired, freckled and blathering Welshman named Kevin Pillock, they were in total disarray. Racked with internal feuding and internecine warfare, it was in no shape to undertake a snap election. It was onto this political scene that Gobbleton and Meddlesome strode. Well, quietly infiltrated, along with their secret weapon

Toni was first paraded in his smarm and charm mode, moving quickly on to earnest and sincere. Hands were shaken, babies kissed. Poses struck for eager cameramen. The man of the people was among them, making the right noises. The software programmes they had developed to control him they found, needed refining. There was a time delay between question and answer. This could be overcome by giving Toni a note pad and pencil. A quick and meaningless scribble by Toni and Meddlesome was relaying back the correct answer. Other ploys were developed too. The disassociation stratagem was one such clever move. Dreamed up by Gobbleton, it consisted of not giving an accountable answer. A question would be posed. Toni would give his, "I am totally absorbed in what you are saying and you have my whole and undivided attention" look. Then he would nod and look serious. An answer would be formulated by the spin-doctors and relayed back verbatim to Toni electronically. The speech centres would be activated and out would come the answer. Question and answer then being stored on the hard drive back in Austria, to be down loaded immediately, should the computer recognise the same question at a later date. This was the part of the programme that needed refining. It was envisaged that once all of the replies to normal questions had been loaded onto the hard drive, answers would flow automatically. Right now, some care had to be exercised and there was an unavoidable, short delay. No matter, the crowd loved someone who took notes. The small fact that everything was on video tape and hanger ons in their multitudes were ever present, and that there was no reason for Toni to take notes, was either overlooked, or ignored. The disassociation feint came under the heading of non-accountability. Thus

Toni would reply, "Personally I." Or "Well the Party believes." And finally, "If I was prime Minister." Thus on each count he could claim to be giving an hypothetical and perfect answer but unfortunately it was an imperfect world and the facts of life were......."

No one, least of all the struggling opposition party had any idea from whence this gift from the Gods had arrived. They just adopted him with all rapidity to their bosom, gave him a back dated party membership card and amended the records to reflect this. The Party then took on a new image, new logo and became over night The New Deal Democratic Party, with Toni at it's head. Kevin and his pushy wife Edna, were both given highly lucrative jobs in the EEC with offices in Brussels. Work that required them to spend long periods away from Britain. They were quickly forgotten by an ever increasing and adoring Toni fan club in the UK.

The best that Majory's party come up with for a leader was either some funny little grey man that looked like a door to door insurance salesman from the Pru, or some strange, gravelly voiced Yorkshire skin head that wore roll necked sweaters beneath tweed jackets and looked as if he had spent the greater part of his working life as a bouncer out side of some Bradford night club. There was no contest. That hardly anyone bothered to vote, was glossed over, and a landslide victory declared for Toni. The New Deal Democratic Party was swept to power, and Gobbleton, Meddlesome, and Heigar, each with their own agenda saw the way to achieve their dreams.

The only one who had no idea of what was going on was of course Toni. He was amazed at the ease with which he swayed crowds. And he didn't have to think about anything, the words just flowed from his mouth and they loved it. He loved their adoration, revelled in their accolade and basked in his own popularity. Toni had discovered the pop stars fame and recognition and he was hooked on their idolisation. He ate well, slept perfectly, waved to the crowds and Heigar obligingly opened her legs and also gave him blowjobs. Life for Toni was perfect

So it was, the Party got its leader and won the election. Toni got sex and veneration. Gerald got his ferrets and to sit on the front bench. As a consequence of which he acquired access to draw upon more funds with which to finance his dreams. Gobbleton got Te'Upp. Britain got around to having its turn at heading the EEC. Heigar saw the way to uniting Europe under her rule via Toni. She also got to be able to afford Viennese coffee, chocolate eclairs and black cherry cake. None of which helped to improve her already sturdy figure. Herr Professor, Doktor etc. got proof positive that his theories were correct and no one gave a thought to what Meddlesome was getting. Other than a lot of work fine tuning and honing the programme and database that ran Toni. Al Arrod of course still did not have his much-desired British passport, but he could see it in the distance. The stage was now set, all the players in their places but not unfortunately all reading from the same script.

Throughout Europe, suddenly cattle started to behave in an extraordinary manner. Actually, it had first been noticed in sheep.

If sheep are allowed to graze upon fresh clover, the nitrogen nodules in the roots of the plant find their way into the sheep's stomach. The resultant nitrogen gas, bloats the animal. It will stagger and fall and the resultant continuing build up of gas pressure will eventually be sufficient to stop the creature's heart. Death occurs. Unless the offending gas can vented. This can be sometimes be achieved by piercing the creature's abdomen and inserting a small hollow tube. The gas can be released, at the risk of course of deadly pathogens entering the peritoneum.

For some time now, unbeknown to the general public at large, bits of dead sheep had been included in the high protein pellets fed to all livestock daily, as a matter of course. Some faceless person somewhere no doubt working along the lines that animals need protein. Dead sheep need disposal. Why not kill two birds with one stone, so to speak?

The small fact that cattle are herbivores and not designed to assimilate nor digest flesh, not appearing to have entered the heads of those responsible for implementing the plan. Not only was it energy conscious, not having to incinerate dead sheep. It was economically viable as the feed pellets produced could be packed out with a cheap source of protein. Thus saving on the costs of importing soybean and the down stream products of the overseas cooking oil industry. Therefore, de facto, it had to be right.

Cattle throughout Europe suddenly and slowly at first, began to suffer from what was originally described as Bovine St. Vitus Dance Syndrome, or

BDS for short. They would roll their eyes, then start to swell up and dance about, emitting vast quantities of evil smelling gas from their rectums as they did so. They would prance and fart about, completely uncontrollable, until finally collapsing in a heap exhausted, and still farting gently. This process would then be repeated at irregular intervals and the number of beasts exhibiting the symptoms was growing at an alarming rate.

Milk yields dropped dramatically. The downstream industries of butter and cheese making were adversely affected. The weight of beef on the hoof fell. Stockmen and vets alike were at a loss to explain BDS.

Next it was the turn of the pigs. The stench was terrifying. Any pig farm with BDS made it's presence felt and could be scented 2 Km. down wind by a person with a heavy cold. Europe quite simply, stank.

Some wag suggested that the situation could be turned to advantage, and the enormous quantities of methane gas being released into the atmosphere could be collected and utilised commercially. This promptly inspired the workforce on the off shore gas platforms in Morcome Bay to go on strike. They saw their jobs being threatened. How exactly one was supposed to collect the gas from half a dozen excited and prancing animals, the person who made the suggestion, failed to explain. The attacks came spasmodically, without warning and were very violent in their nature. They were normally also accompanied by prestigious quantities of faeces being expelled at high velocity. How then one was to go about controlling a beast under these circumstances, so as to be able to jam a flexible pipe up it's rectum and harness the expelled gas, was beyond the wit of man. There was also the engineering problem of slugs of faeces within the pipe system too. No, it was generally considered better to keep well away from the beast, let the spasm pass and clean up the damage and mess afterwards.

Immediate research was called for and government funds made available. It was discovered that something called a prion was the cause of the symptoms. No one had ever heard of a prion before and that the Damn things were virtually indestructible came as a bit of shock. That human beings suddenly began to dance around wildly, throwing off their clothes as they did so and farting in a most unpleasant manner was all the more shocking.

Supermarkets began to experience a spate of middle aged and wrinkled, cellulite-ridden females, discarding their clothing and with eyes rolling wildly in their sockets, would charge around the isles behind their trolleys shouting WHOOPEEEEE! and farting like a brickie after a heavy night of stout, and egg sandwiches. Men were also prone to behave in a similar manner, though what some men chose to wear as undergarments was, if anything came as even more of a shock. The old adage of putting on a clean pair of underpants in case one got knocked over became all too true. The only major difference between the animal version of BDS and human was that animals didn't try to get out of their skins and humans just danced and farted, without squirting crap every which way. Small conciliation.

Official Royal Functions were cancelled for fear of either party succumbing. Business ground to a standstill as directors cavorted and farted. All flights with European crews in charge were banned throughout the world. A ten-mile an hour restriction was placed on all EEC roads, including motorways. Output fell, factories limped along. Europe was in turmoil, the prion had insidiously moved up the food chain

The first really positive step that was taken was that a total ban was imposed throughout the EEC on the movement, or sale of sheep, cattle and pigs. Sale of all meat and meat products was also banned. This was an open ended and panic measure. It would be in force until such times as rectifying action could be implemented. No one had any idea of what form that action would take. Each day Europe sank deeper into chaos as animals and humans alike succumbed to the sickness.

The New Deal Democratic Party had already formulated a system whereby they got a subtle plug each day on TV. Now a concerned Toni could be seen making suitable calming noises. Generally at length, but not actually offering anything positive. But the population were close to panic. Super market shelves no longer stocked meat. Beefburgers had to be imported from America. School dinners now consisted of chips, peas and semolina pudding, and not a sausage in sight. Riots had already broken out in Chipping Sodbury and Bury St Edmonds. Both big pig breeding centres and not normally the kind of place associated with violent, civil dissent. Germany no longer ate blockwurst and Italy ceased production of

Parmesan Ham. Only America and Australia were immune. The former quite happy to supply as much meat as Europe required. At a price. The latter, still smarting under Britain joining the EEC and demanding an entry visa, said Stuff you cobber and went about their plans to become a republic with renewed vigour. Meanwhile, Gerald was facing ruin. He had borrowed heavily to finance his pig farms and purchase product processing production lines. He was a worried man.

International scientists grew concerned. Not just at the risks of BDS infecting their countries, but from it's long term effects too. They warned that the sudden high rise in the percentage of methane gas in the stratosphere was having a highly adverse affect upon the ozone layer. A hole was developing over Europe, and the greenhouse effect was beginning to melt the polar ice caps. If a cure was not found within the foreseeable future, then several Pacific nations would disappear beneath the waves of an ever-increasing rise in sea levels. The higher levels of radiation over the planet due to the destruction of the ozone layer would threaten the growth of crops. Europe could starve. Warnings, that apart from the small Pacific Island Nations, who had all by now taken to boats, were studiously ignored by Europe. When it did finally dawn that the globe was in trouble, the finger of blame was firmly pointed towards Britain. Which is fine if you want a scapegoat, but doesn't actually do anything to going towards solving the problem in hand. The British Government promptly placed the blame firmly upon the shoulders of the previous administration, stuck it's collective head in the sand It's thumbs up it's bums and sat back as if the problem had then been solved.

None of which seemed to bother Gerald's son Bradford, one whit. A loner by nature, and heavily into computers, he had left university with a good degree and no idea of what to do for a living. Starved of funds, as his father assured him that he had his own problems, and was also Minister For Agriculture, and far too busy. He had surfed the Internet for ideas. He chanced upon a web site happyhobies.com/amsterdam. Out of curiosity he logged on. The result being that he then proceeded to down own load a step by step instruction manual for making designer drugs in your basement. Bradford, being a geek and having an interest only in computers and hacking, promptly set about funding his chosen way of life. He found that manufacturing illegal drugs was not only simple, but also highly lucrative and very boring too. He limited himself to only producing sufficient quantities so as to enable him to pursue his real interest in life. Hacking.

The Scots, not a slow race when it comes to catching on to making an easy profit, cornered the illegal black market haggis industry. Meat and meat products now being banned, there was a growing and lucrative, black economy in sausages and Spam. Bradford found that his now nation wide drug distribution system expertise was in demand by certain shady characters north of the boarder. His business interests prospered. He called in his sister Tiffany to assist.

Tiffany had endless contacts at street level, Tiffany ran the business, allowing Bradford to play with his computers. Meanwhile their father was facing financial ruin and unbeknown to him, in the cellars of his very home lay large, wicker laundry baskets full of unused cash. The proceeds from Bradford's and Tiffany's activities. Gobbleton was also having cash flow problems. His beautiful and secret oriental mistress, Te'Upp was proving to be far more expensive than he had envisaged, planned, or could afford, upon the meagre allowance his miserable wife gave him. Al Arrod had assisted him in setting her up with a secluded mews flat in Bloomsbury. It had been lavishly furnished with no expense spared. The bill for which was causing Gobbleton some concern.

Though he spent as much time as he possibly could with her and had attempted every move in the Karma Sutra and few more besides. Te'Upp, was not a girl to sit at home watching TV when Gobbleton was not around. She got bored. What does a bored girl do? Either take a lover, or go shopping. Te'Upp was getting quite enough sex thank you. In fact she was beginning to tire of Gobbleton's hairy, pawing hands. His insistence on her cooking, was also trying. Te'Upp hated cooking and was not too good at it either. She solved this problem with a little help from Al Arrod, and one of his better chefs. Exotic meals were prepared by the chef, in advance of Gobbleton's arrival, to be produced with a sweet and submissive smile by a submissive Te'Upp, as being all her own work. Gobbleton was entranced. Other times if he felt like a snack he had to knock himself up a bit of cheese on toast. "You do it darling, I cooked all that for you yesterday etc." being Te´Upp's method of solving that problem. Then she would lean over towards him and bat her long lashed, almond eyes. All though of food would leave Gobbleton's mind, as he stripped of his underpants and made a grab for Te´Upp's slinky little olive coloured body. So, Te´Upp shopped and Gobbleton got the bills and wonderful sex. Al Arrod was well pleased with his protege and paid some more money into her off shore account. He began to set his plan in motion for obtaining his much desired British Passport. Fatslobe, he knew was in difficulty. Due to the total ban on all meat and meat products, Gerald had only outgoings and no incomings from his pigs. Not only that, but he dared not reveal just how large was his failing empire. Via Gobbleton, Al Arrod went about effecting an introduction.

Kenu Itayaku was also not a happy man. Also, he was not a stupid one either. He could see the immediate potential for his genetically modified seaweed as a foodstuff. Europe had become a continent of vegetarian's overnight. Forced vegetarians at that. Not for them the joys of a personal conviction in the advantages of a lettuce and mung bean salad. They longed to satisfy their cravings for red meat. Unfortunately, there was a total ban on the sale of all meat and meat products. There was even talk of destroying all livestock throughout Europe as a means of stamping out BDS.

Increasing pressure was being made itself felt from the world scientific community too, with regard to the methane being produced and Global warming. All governments feared to take this draconian decision, knowing that the resultant backlash from the agricultural community could easily slip into anarchy and civil unrest of gigantic proportions. As it was, every European capital was periodically brought to a standstill by irate farmers and their tractors on an almost a daily basis. Insurrection simmered just below the surface, not assisted by the population being reminded three times a day that no meat was on the table. A couple of life long vegans, in Germany, who had been foolish enough to lecture to the world at large and some frustrated local carnivores in particular, on the benefits to be gained from an animal free diet, had met with a very unpleasant, cannibalistic end. Other vegetarians, took note and sensibly kept their views to themselves.

Kenu knew that since his seaweed grew under water, and ultra violet rays are absorbed by water. His crop was immune from the effects of an ever-depleting ozone layer. No, what concerned Kenu was not that he had as yet failed to solve the difficulties of persuading his fickle marine vegetation to grow. Some times it would, and sometimes it refused. That he felt he could answer. Given time and study. It was the lack of respect and status with which America held Japan and more to the point, the way in which his own family behaved. His wife, a product of post war Japan was not the submissive wilting flower, dominated by her husband and a tradition of subservience, that he felt was his due. In fact on the contrary, she was a successful commercial translator, working herself for Del Minki. Their two children did nothing else than chew gum and watch endless American films on TV.

Kenu harboured a deep hatred for America and all things American. Was he not after all a Samurai? The truthful answer was in fact was that he was not, but he liked to see himself as one. He imagined himself as a lean, dark featured warrior wielding a Samurai sword and slicing off the heads of the hated American foreigners with an ease and will. Actually, he was short, over weight and wore spectacles. Had he have been given a sword he would have in all probability only have sliced off his own fingers. Which psychologically only went to reinforce his views and feed his feelings of discontent. Matsufarti would never get recognition for the seaweed. His seaweed. No, all acclaim would go to Del Minki, an American company. He might get a few crumbs, but he would never get to control or even have a say in the use of his discovery.

Kenu could see that the time was right for him to make his move. He set about looking for an ally that would assist him in first stealing and then marketing his crop. Then he Kenu, would spring it upon the world. Then too, he, Kenu would have the control and the true respect that was he felt due to himself and Japan. His dream of fame and recognition would be realised. He too began to surf the net and send out tentative feelers. Feelers that were picked up by the CIA, and relayed back to the President.

The President of America was in trouble. Willie Clayton had taken over office from Reel Raygun. Willie didn't know much about Presidenting, as he tended to name his calling. He believed that all one had to do was leave it all to one's aids and advisors, smile a lot, kiss a few babies, publicly deplore the number of shootings that took place each day, but do nothing to repeal the gun laws. That, and swan around the world in Air Force One and allow American states to maintain the death penalty, seemed to be about it.

Willie liked big women. He loved to fondle large breasts and well rounded buttocks. He had been having a long ongoing affair with one Lulu Lewhisky, an ex Ukrainian Olympic shot putter of more than generous proportions. Lulu had skipped her Nation's team and sought political asylum in America. That fabulous land of huge cars and enormous helpings of ice cream. That she ended up in the President's bed was the fairy tale come true.

She had come to the President's attention when he happened to be watching the Olympic games on TV. They were being held in America at the time. The sight of a muscular Lulu was more that Willie could take and he recorded Lulu's sweaty work up, on his video. Later he would secretly view the footage and fall into a paroxysm of self-abuse. He had long ago given up poking anything in the direction of the hatchet-faced hag to whom he was married. Once Lulu had defected, he personally made a point of making her acquaintance. From that point on their affair had begun. Lulu would strip off her kit slowly. Her heavy peasant face perspiring a little below her severely trimmed blond hair. She would raise a muscular arm to reveal an armpit of more thick, curly hair and then removing her double reinforced bra, of East German manufacture, display her pendulous breasts. Willie would sit on the end of a White House settee in his red and white striped boxer shorts and tee shirt, chewing on his hands and rocking back and forth in ecstatic excitement. By the time Lulu had got down to having removed her black, military style, heavy skirt and stood before him in her knee length black woolly socks and regulation Russian cotton knickers, Willie had a fearsome erection and was pawing at the object of his desire. Willie was enthralled by her hairy armpits, rolls of fat, legs like tree trunks and buttocks like two balloons. When she sat on his face, enfolding his cheeks within hers and pushing a further mass of blond curly curls into his face, Willie was beside himself in a frenzy of sexual pleasure. He could not have been dragged away even if World War III had broken out. Willie was happy with his Lulu. Even more so when she wore a ballet skirt and bridle and he could don a fox hunting jacket and approach things from the rear. Just as long as the American Nation never got wind of his cavorting with her, let alone the manner and substance, or World War III never actually broke out, all would be fine.

Lulu was quite happy with the arrangement. She was a simple and homely soul at heart. She had no strong feelings with regard to wearing a ballet skirt or anything else for that matter. Willie was nice to her and if that made him happy, so be it. She had a nice apartment, secret service cars to drive her around and a big TV set. She also unlimited accesses to money. Not that she spent any, other than on food. Lulu loved to cook. The peasant dishes of her homeland. Pig's entrails and bean soup. Red wine, black bread and chicken's feet. She actually never had any intention to defect, and the whole thing was a mistake. She had been stopped for Jay walking by a policeman. Having limited English, and only knowledge of the police systems within the Eastern Block, she had been so terrified as to sign anything that was placed in front of her. When the police realised that they had a member of a foreign Olympic team on their hands, they called the FBI.

The CIA, who spend a lot of time keeping tabs on the FBI intercepted the message. From that point on matters became totally confused. The CIA, mindful of their need to flex their muscles over the FBI, demanded that Lulu be handed over to them. The FBI demurred. This was after all a police matter. The original charge of jaywalking now long consigned to the mists of time. The CIA then got a highly nervous Lulu to sign a document that stated that she wanted political asylum. Thus in one move taking the ball firmly out of the hands of the civil authorities.

When Willie Clayton found out that the big Ukrainian shot putter was in a safe house, he demanded that she be brought to his presence immediately. His personal aids, knowing full well what was on their President's mind. Namely the furthering of very personal relations between East and West, they sighed and sat down to plan the trysts. From Lulu's point of view, she was just happy that it was only the boss man that wanted sex with her and not the whole of the 49ᵗʰ precinct. It took a little while for it to register with her, that the President of the United States of America fancied her something rotten. But she was quite astute enough now not to do anything that would jeopardise her new-found lifestyle. She was genuinely fond of Willie. He was funny and like a small boy. She really wanted to cook and mother him and would much prefer to have gone to bed with a big feather quilt and have sex sensibly with her darling Willie, rather than all this strange fancy dress stuff. She dreamed in her heart that once his term of office was over that Willie would ditch, "The Bitch" as he so lovingly called his spouse. Marry her, and together they could spend their time, eating pig's entrails and bean soup, watching TV. She especially liked the adverts, and they could make lots of children. And if that involved in wearing funny clothes and doing strange things with chocolate eclairs and cigars. Well, after all this was a rich foreign country and people could afford to indulge themselves in such luxuries.

Willie Clayton was due to visit Britain. He had no desire to visit Britain. They didn't have air conditioning, nor even hamburgers any longer. The Brits had a new Prime Minister with a name like an Italian. It was all very confusing since the Europeans had become one bunch. You never quite knew who the Hell was whom or what country they represented. They also took it in turns to be boss of Europe. A Europe that seemed to get bigger with each passing year. They all had funny accents and none of them knew anything about baseball. Europeans were, as far as he was concerned, a bunch of weirdo's. He had no wish to go there, but had been told that he had to. Consequently, if he had to go, then he would go on his terms.

He had two missions, one personal and the other foisted upon him by his advisors. It seemed like the Europeans were still starving, so he would offer them some beef in exchange for a major but secret share holding in some of their Blue Chip companies. What ever they were. No, Willie was much more concerned with fixing Lulu up with an American passport and having her accompany him on the trip. No way did he intend taking that smart bitch of a wife of his and everyone knew that the British women only had sex with the lights out and even then is was strictly functional and missionary position. No, he would take Lulu along. Hell, what's the use of being President if you couldn't do what you liked? Now his aids were adding to the confusion by telling him something was going on in Japan. Something was always going on in Japan. Pearl Harbour had demonstrated that. Those slant eyed, buck toothed little toads were forever coming up with something new. There was a rumour that maybe someone had discovered some new foodstuff made from seaweed and if the Brits got wind of this, then it could scupper any plans for swapping beefburgers for Blue Circle Cement. Who in their right mind, other than the Japanese ate seaweed anyway? He wished that just for once there would be a clear-cut path, and goals that he understood and someone would tell him exactly what was going on. He had asked for this before, but the explanations that had been forthcoming only served to make him more confused and wonder if in fact his aids knew what the Hell was going on anyway. On the whole, tonking Lulu was much more fun and a Damn sight simpler too.

Kenu Itayaku thought that he had found his safe haven. His guarded enquiries had at first gone unnoticed or had been ignored. Then one night, in a bar down on the Ginza he had met a man of his own heart. A big red haired foreigner, who claimed to be descended from Viking warriors. A man who understood honour, tradition and the warrior code. He too had no love of America. In fact he went so far as to claim that his people had actually discovered the place and the story of Christopher Columbus was nothing more than deliberate fabrication to discredit his people and steal their birthright. Which, after eight Scotch whiskies, seemed wholly reasonable to Kenu. If Kenu were to consider defecting to Iceland, then his genetically modified seaweed could be produced there. There was ample seawater available and Iceland's climate was not too far removed from that of Northern Japan. Also, it too was a geothermal active region. His nation would ensure that all of the credit for the seaweed went solely to Kenu, thus granting him great face. In return, Iceland would become a world power overnight, with the ability to feed the world. Thus in the process, humbling the despised Americans and at the same time their fawning little lap dogs, the British. Kenu leapt at the idea, and began to make his plans.

On the other side of the world, Antonio Cacophony and the New Deal Democratic Party were in ascension. Farmers throughout Europe were facing ruin and taking to the streets. Livestock was prancing about, venting huge amounts of methane gas. Civilised, middle aged women were stripping themselves naked in supermarkets and farting. Gerald Fatslobe was being threatened with foreclosure and bankruptcy. Noel Gobbleton was besotted with Te´Upp. Heigar, now a few pounds heavier, was watching with satisfaction as her husband, under her and Meddlesome's control swept all before him, and more small Pacific Island nations took to the boats as sea levels continued to rise world wide.

Bradford was absorbed with his hacking and had partially penetrated the American defence system. He was down loading some very strange information.

CHAPTER. 5

Kenu Itayaku was impressed with his new found friend, even if he did have trouble with his name. The sound of the letter R and L tend to give Japanese problems. So Erik Bludax moved from Ellik Wudax to Ellik San, which was near enough for the big red haired Icelandic. Erik's real name was actually Sven Svensonn and he was head of the Icelandic Intelligence gathering service, Far East Section. As large, occidentals with red hair and huge busy beards are somewhat difficult to disguise in Japan, his cover was that of Captain of a whaling ship. The indiscriminate slaughtering of intelligent sea mammals, being one of the few things that the Japanese and certain Nordic peoples, share in common.

Sven or rather Ellik San, claimed that he was in Japan to take delivery of a brand new hunter vessel, Wjhale KillÆr IV. Japan being the only country in the world that would manufacture a ship to the stringent Icelandic specifications. Sven plied Kenu with whisky. The real, 12-year-old malt stuff. Not the Japanese home produced barbecue starting liquid. Which no self respecting Scotsman would touch. With the advent of devolution, and a Scottish Parliament that would probably constitute a traitorous act and be regarded as such by the latter day high land Chiefs that now ran the country. No, the genuine article. Which in Japan normally requires a second mortgage. Sven regaled Kenu with the prospects of fame and fortune. Honorary Icelandic citizenship and fair skinned, big busted, red haired female company. He produced photographs and centre fold girlie magazines to illustrate his point. Kenu was sold. Japanese women, and Kenu's wife in particular, tend towards being small and having a bra size to match. Their pubic hair is often sparse and straight. Little inverted volcanoes of dark

67

fluff. As they get older, they, and Kenu's wife again in particular, incline towards being bow legged.

These Nordic Goddesses were heavy-breasted females, with forests of curly, red pubic hairs, and large voluptuous bodies. Kenu drooled over the glossy photographs and his spectacles steamed up. He rubbed them vigorously with a tissue and flashed his gold teeth. Yes, he would leave his disrespectful wife and his two ungrateful children. He would leave Japan, with it's millions of ant like and milling people. Not for him a life in a crowded apartment, doing the same each day as everybody else. No, he Kenu Itayaku would be free. Free from the limitations of his American owned company. Free from the constrictions of Japanese life and constantly touching elbows with his neighbour. Free from his foolish wife. He would have his very own detached house, with space to move and breath. There, with his new found wealth and fame, could he indulge himself. He would own a Volvo, drink real whiskey and have an endless stream of large, smooth, white skinned, heavy breasted women with masses of curly red pubic hair. He began to plan ahead in earnest.

Sven sent a message in code to Reykjavik and his controller. That message spelt out that a method had been evolved in Japan for genetically modifying seaweed. The result only needed sea water in which to grow and had the potential to feed the World. Kenu, no doubt in his enthusiasm for the more obvious and illustrated benefits of his emigrating to Iceland had obviously neglected to mention the fickleness and problematic nature of its growth, for Sven never mentioned it. He stressed the point that if Iceland held all patents and more to the point all stocks and the technology for making the product, Iceland would overnight become a major player in the world league. Britain and the EEC couldn't push it around any more and it would take over America's place as the world's major food producer. The Viking at last could take his rightful place on the World's stage. The hat with horns on would become renown and respected and all without having to wave a battle-axe. Operation Longboat, the transfer of the seaweed to Iceland had begun.

All of which the CIA found to be most interesting. One of their agents, who had managed to seduce some secretary from the Danish Embassy in

New York had passed the code on to them years ago. The Danes themselves having broken it some time before then and dismissed it as being information not worthy of retaining. They had used it as a bargaining chip with some American CIA agent who they had managed to get one of their secretaries from their New York Embassy to seduce. The outcome being a useless bit of information that had cost both the Danish and American taxpayer dearly. The two agents in question having then run off together and married in secret. They had managed to set themselves up with a bar in Fiji on the profits, had two children and were doing very nicely thank you. It was the sudden burst of strange code emanating from Tokyo that alerted the agents in the first place. Russian, Chinese, Korean and British being more the norm. Langley was informed.

Langley immediately understood the magnitude of the problem. The interests of the United States of America were at stake. What should be done? The first reaction was as usual to go in shooting from the hip. Smash the lab, burn the crop, kill all of the personnel. And serve them right for flooding the USA markets with cheap electronic goods, fuel efficient cars, split system air conditioners and for buying up half of Las Vegas and the film industry, oh yeah, and let's not forget Pearl Harbour too. Someone had the nonce to point out that the actual owners of the GM sea weed were actually an American company and vaporising Maksufarti, was in fact a bit like shooting yourself in the foot. Anyway, think of the fuss and legal actions that would ensue, should the truth ever come out. The truth had a nasty habit of late of popping up in the most unexpected of places. No, that would be unthinkable. The last thing that the CIA wanted was the truth to be known. It undermined the whole foundation upon which they were built, namely, deception. They would have to think again.

Obviously, the ship would have to be taken over on the high seas, in International waters. The same person who had pointed out the flaws in the original plan, now pointed out that such an act constituted piracy. For which hanging was generally still enforced. The next question was; should the President be informed? This got more difficult and opinions were divided. One faction believing that he should not. Reason being given that either he wouldn't understand what the Hell was being explained and wouldn't care as he was far too busy shoving his face between the legs of that fat Ukrainian cow. Another faction pointed out that having the President know meant that he took the blame, should things go wrong. Always a useful ploy.

This was considered too. A compromise solution was opted for. They would tell the President what he needed to know. Sufficient for him to approve the plan and secret funding, but not enough to scare him off. Meanwhile, someone had better get down to planning Operation Watercress.

A take over on the high seas was ruled out. One had to find the ship. A ship is pretty small, the Pacific Ocean in comparison, is rather large. Anyway, they didn't know as yet, its planned route. No, their best bet would be to substitute the crew before the ship sailed. Naturally no one considered contacting Del Minki. They were after all a civilian company and as such had no concepts of security. No, it would be far better if the ship just disappeared for a while. Then its mysterious cargo could be removed and subject to Agency scrutiny first and foremost. What should be done about the Icelandic agent and the Nip, was not as yet finalised, but if they wanted to play hard ball, well, it was a big ocean and very deep.

The story for Willie Clayton was kept as brief and as simple as possible. No one wanted him to get confused. The Japanese had stolen some American trade secrets, through their industrial espionage net work. These secrets, were the sole property of America. The Japanese planned to sell them to Iceland, who no doubt was acting as middleman for those sneaky Brits or possibly one of those other EEC outfits. America wanted back what was after all, rightfully hers. Willie was sold on the idea. But he was off to Europe now. Had to meet that plastic looking new Prime Minister of theirs. He didn't want any fuss. Anyway he had his own problems in trying to prise a US passport out of the State department for Lulu, and slipping her in to his entourage as Sports Attaché. They were being most difficult. No, he would give the CIA his blessing if they in turn could put some pressure on those passport jerks in the Immigration Service. He was sure that the CIA must have something on some of them. Oh yeah, another thing. Best not to use known CIA agents by the way. Couldn't they use someone expendable to do the actual dirty work? Then perhaps any of their men that needed to be involved could wear ski masks and act in more of a managerial capacity. That way there was less risk all round. Willie, if nothing else had a very strong sense of survival when it came to his own skin.

The CIA took this one on board, and promptly blackmailed some Immigration Department officials with exposure. All of them were keeping mistresses or queer boyfriends anyway. Then they looked around for a third party fall guy, should things go wrong. Solly Capacino fitted the bill perfectly.

Solly Capacino represented the Jewish American wing of the Mafia. A rather minor player in the Costa Nostra and organised crime in The United States.

Solly itched to get into the big time and mainstream crime. He was fed up with shaking down pickled herring and bagel sellers. He longed to be recognised in his own right and be able to hold his head up high in front of Rabbi Shekellkounter in the Synagogue on a Saturday. He also felt the need to impress Father De Betta, of The Christian Brothers. An organisation that Solly secretly admired as representing the East Coast para military wing of the Roman Catholic Church.

Solly was a peculiar hybrid. His grandfather having been a very minor Sicilian Don. An immigrant that slipped into both the country and the bootlegging business at the time of prohibition. He had met and married some Polish Jewess, also from a recently arrived family. Rumour had it that the music for the wedding service consisted of Oivai Maria. From such humble origins had the Jewish wing of the Mafia been born. It had not been an easy struggle to keep control over its small patch of turf. But both Jews and Italians know all about oppression. Consequently, the victims of their criminal activities had taken a strange pride in having been done over by their own kind. They promptly closed ranks on the mainly Irish police. Now a days however, with a more liberal attitude in force and positive steps being taken by the Government to protect minority ethnic groups and their cultural backgrounds, things were less complicated. Now, as a gesture of racial integration, none other than the CIA was offering them a job. Solly knew that his hour had arrived. He had finally hit the big time. He would not fail his country, or his ancestry.

Solly was a simple man. He saw things in simple terms. The CIA wanted him to take over a ship. A very small ship. Simple, bump off the crew. The CIA however preferred a more subtle and plausible approach. They decided that Solly and his gang would substitute for the real crew. This called for a carefully planned operation, to be known as Puffer Fish.

The puffer fish is strange creature. When left alone to get on with whatever puffer fish do, it minds its own business and does just that. However, if disturbed, or frightened, it starts to swallow seawater. This distends its body and sharp spines stick out. It looks a bit like a cross-eyed pincushion and can end up the size of a small football. If then removed from its natural element, it spits out the water and gulps air. It will continue to do so until it is incapable of retaining any more. Then it sits there. A spiky, rotund, cross eyed football. Gulping air at one end and farting it out at the other. If one slings it back into the ocean, as would seem sensible, it will float upside down on the surface, then suddenly vent all of its contained air and shoot off like a released balloon making the same sort of noise. All in all, a strange and peculiar creature and not one that would in the more usual circles be deemed haute cuisine. Naturally, it's regarded as a delicacy in Japan.

It is eaten raw and costs an arm and a leg. As if all of the above were not enough to warn off the average person, unfortunately, it is also highly toxic. It has to be prepared by only licensed and highly specialised chefs. If not, then the person who partakes of its gourmet flesh gets to loose more than just an arm and a leg. More like his life. Since all of the chefs in Japan who were allowed to prepare puffer fish for the table were not only licensed but also highly paid and few and far between. It would be highly unlikely that a chef could be bribed to knock off a whole crew, but there were ways around that problem.

The CIA loved gadgets. Ever since they had seen the James Bond Movies with Q handing out exploding cabbages and oxyacetylene fountain pens, they had been hooked. The Bulgarians too were lovers of technology and also quite inventive. Sometime ago they had shot some dissident in the leg with a poisoned pellet from an air gun disguised as an umbrella. In broad day light, and on Waterloo Bridge, in the heart of Olde London Towne no less. Something that had always impressed the CIA.

A 3mm. ball made from a metal that promoted little allergic reaction, had tiny holes drilled through it. These had been filled with a natural poison produced by the castor oil plant. The ball had then been covered in sugar and fired into the leg of the unfortunate victim. The British National Health Service, unused to dealing with such cases, had been powerless to prevent the death of their patient. The CIA had been dying to try out the technique themselves. Now a suitable opportunity had arisen. Operation Puffer Fish, far from being part and parcel of a much larger operation, began to assume proportions of its very own. The main objective became side lined and clouded. Still, if you are up to your arse in alligators, one can tend to forget that the original objective, had been to drain the swamp.

The manufacture of the pellets proved to be the least of the problems. Building the mini guns into the backs of chairs and then organising it so that all the chairs were at the same table, and that all of the crew attended the Last Supper, was something else. Somebody once said that that if something can go wrong, it will go wrong and it did. Some of the chairs failed to fire their lethal darts. Some of the chairs got moved and a couple of innocent guests got shot. This the CIA placed under the heading of collateral damage, and ignored. No, more to the point, some crew were never even fired upon. Solly stepped in at this point, and placed the unaffected crew members in a taxi of his own. He then shot them. Having apologised to them before hand and explaining that it was nothing personal, just business. Those bodies were never recovered. Meanwhile, the recipients of the poisoned pellets suffered and died. Operation Puffer Fish, apart from a few slight hiccups was declared a success. The Japanese press got hold of the story.

How could it be that not only had all of these unfortunate persons eaten ill prepared puffer fish, but a couple of others in the restaurant who had been eating whale meat also died. Then there was also the question of the missing crew members too. Kenu and Sven were also suspicious. They had not been present at the meal. A meal that had been ordered in their name, without their knowledge. What was going on? Suspicion fell upon

The Green Brigade. A global organisation that used public sympathy and subscriptions to fund their political aims world-wide. The fact that they had overlooked that an Iceland Whaler had been built in Japan and was about to sail caused them to smart a little. They decided that their best policy would be one of active denial. Thus confirming in the eyes of the World that they had indeed been behind it. Any way, if the French could blow up one of their ships in a neutral harbour. Killing a crew member in the process. They were well within their moral rights to bump off a few Icelandic and Japanese whale killers, even if they had not done so. So the emphasis turned towards environmental issues and whale hunting in particular.

Meanwhile, special tanks had been welded into the hold of Wjhale KillÆr IV and the seaweed was on board along with its associated pumping system. All was ready, apart from the small but rather necessary detail that Kenu and Sven were now without a crew. Solly and his boys, at this point presented themselves and stepped into the vacant slot. Langley received the message that operation Watercress was under way.

In the general euphoria of operation Puffer Fish being completed and Watercress getting up a full head of steam, no one had though to ask Solly if in fact any of his happy gang of hoods could actually get a ship under way, let alone navigate it over several thousands of miles of open ocean to the East coast of America. Sven was quite capable of doing so, and took the helm once the pilot had cleared them into the roads. It was then that Solly showed his hand. It was a Mexican stand off. Sven wanted to sail to Iceland. Solly had the firepower, but was incapable of navigating the boat. The answer was obvious. For the moment, Solly needed Sven, just as much as Sven needed Solly. Sven could play for time.

He had the choice of two routes to Iceland. West and via either the Suez Canal or a longer passage around The Cape of Good Hope and the Southern tip of Africa. Alternatively, he could sail east across the Pacific and through the Panama Canal into the Atlantic and then turn left. He opted for the Western course. There were too many American controlled territories involved if he sailed east along that particular route. No, best they head for Singapore, then Sri Lanka and up the Gulf. Slip through the Suez Canal and into the Med. Once out and into The Bay of Biscay, he was almost on home territory. All he had to do was take a West and Northerly course around Ireland and Iceland was within his sights. Plenty of time to plan. No need to rush things. Meanwhile he would whip this bunch of landlubbers into a crew. Yes, he would look forward to that. Right now they needed him. Sven sighed in satisfaction as he programmed the GPS navigational computer for Singapore.

Meanwhile both Langley and The Green Brigade started to log the course of Wjhale KillÆr IV.

Tiffany's latest boyfriend, who she rather fancied and with whom she shared a bed in a squat in Camden Town, was a member of The Green Brigade. Fate in the form of sex and young people took a hand.

Tiffany was quite a pretty girl. Once one gave her a bath, washed off the make up, removed the safety pins from her ears and did something about the green and purple coloured, electric shock hair. She had been a bit of a rebel, wanting to carve her own path. She had some inverted snob complex about being the daughter of a Cabinet Minister. A dark secret that she held close to her soul. She had become sexually active at the age of 18, losing her virginity in a rather clumsy way to some spotty youth in the back of his father's rather battered Ford van. His father doing some part time, cash in hand building work around their housing estate. She hadn't felt any particular desire for the lad. In fact, the whole thing had been over rather too quickly for her to all together grasp the significance of the occasion. From there on in, it had all become rather a case of, well it's what boys and then men do. Drink a bit, slobber in your ears, poke their tongues in your mouth, feel your tits, push sharp and dirty fingernails into your vagina, and then slip you a length. Finally to make a fast and welcomed thrust and gasp and wiggle a bit. That, or extract themselves quickly and masturbate all over your stomach." All in all of which, Tiffany found to be pretty boring but the price one had to pay for having a boyfriend. Not that she really wanted a boyfriend, but it seemed the sort of thing one did.

Peter was somehow different. He was quiet and protective in some odd way. She felt comfortable with Peter. He talked to her, rather than at her. He listened too and took notice. She decided that she liked Peter.

He too came from a moneyed background but had not, like most of her acquaintances dropped out of college. Peter had a good degree in economics. An academic path chosen for him by his parents. He actually wanted to become an environmentalist but was unsure how one went about this. In the meantime he was working as a part time mini cab driver and wondering how to achieve his goals and at the same time deriving some degree of satisfaction in driving his parents into mental agitation and anti depressants in the process. Tiffany found him to be a gentle and all together much more satisfying lover. He was also particular about personal hygiene. Another eye opener for her. Peter not only didn't smell. He smelled good. She found that she was not only happy to make love to him, but she enjoyed the process. Tiffany's concept of sex underwent a fundamental change. Tiffany's concept of sex underwent a fundamental change. Peter held her in his arms at night, having made love to her. That in itself was a revelation. All her other partners had turned their back on her, broke wind and gone to sleep. Tiffany's hormones began to make their presence felt. She found herself thinking of babies and the future. One day Tiffany decided to broach the subject of their future together.

"Pete. Do you like living here and driving a mini cab?" She looked in the mirror with its large crack that she had rescued from a rubbish skip.

"Not really Tiff. I do it for you."

"But I don't like it either Pete, so why are we doing it?"

"I don't know Tiff. I mean, I could get a job in the City, but I wouldn't be happy. But I'll do it, if that's what you really want. The old man would give a sigh of relief and Mother would stop drinking so much gin. What do you want? Where do you want to live?"

"I don't mind really Pete. I'm happy if you are happy. But I was sort of thinking more long term. I mean I can't go on for ever wearing pins in my nose and a leather jacket can I? I'm getting bored with it too. But I will if that is how you like me to look."

"I don't like you looking like that Tiff. I hate all of those stud things, and they catch when I kiss you. You have nice hair, once all that multi coloured dye is washed out. I much prefer you normal."

"So why didn't you say so before?"

"I didn't want to upset you. So shall I give Dad a bell and ask to borrow enough for a suit and bowler hat?"

"No silly. I have money. Lots of it actually. No, come and sit down by me and let's decide upon a plan that would make us both happy."

So they did. The outcome being that Tiffany would wash out the dye, it was only vegetable based anyway, from her hair, and have it straightened, oh, and take out most of the pins. Peter would give up the mini cab business and together they would settle in Carmathernshire in West Wales. There they would purchase a smallholding and be self-sufficient. Peter could put in his wind generators and solar panels. Oh yes, and they would get married and have a baby. To fund all of this, Tiffany would use the money that was still building up alongside Bradford and his computers. There was far too much for him to spend and he had no interest in the stuff other than as a means of buying more and more, ever more powerful electronic equipment. Bradford was a 24 carat, 100% solid gold Geek! So a now fresh faced, and rather pert Tiffany, dressed in shirt and jeans, drove with her equally sensible looking husband in their second hand diesel Land Rover along the M4 Westwards to meet her brother.

Al Arrod was a satisfied man. The New Deal Democratic Party had appointed "Experts and Advisors" These unelected, and non answerable persons were instrumental in moulding Government policy whilst at the same not being held responsible for the results. Nor were they in any way representative of the electorate. In fact, as jobs go, it was the best. Lots of money for not actually producing anything, and responsible to no one either. Only a government could dream up, instigate and actually get away with a scam like that. They were given the title of Sultans and seemed to spend a lot of their time producing speeches they would appeal to the, "Heartlands" and "All sensible thinking People" Since most people would like to regard themselves as being sensible and the exact geographical location of the Heartlands was never disclosed, it was rather difficult to pin anything down. So Government rolled along with Toni being all things to all people at all times and the Sultans spun their webs of words. In fact, so successful were they, that a small group of singularly gifted musicians produced a clever pop song called The Sultan's of Spin, which made the charts. In point of fact, the Government was neither much better, or much worse and very little different from that of Majory's, other than it spent a lot time and public money telling people that it wasn't. It was quite obvious that since they had come to power subtle extra taxes had been introduced, the Health Service was terminally ill, education was a joke with everyone getting a qualification, irrespective of how worthless it was, and the farming industry had ground to a halt. "What's good for the Party, is good for the country." Was the watchword. Again, no one cared to be too definitive, but generally it appeared to mean, let's reduce to the lowest common denominator and one will never have a problem if one's standards are low enough. Under this regime, Al Arrod felt his long awaited British passport was a certainty. Gobbleton was now getting nicely into his debt. Te'Upp shagging him stupid and claiming day trips to New York on Concord for a spot of shopping in return. He had also had Gerald Fatslobe under careful examination too. The time was ripe for Al Arrod to make his move.

Gerald was a worried man. He held huge interests in pigs and due to the BDS scare and Government regulations, he was unable to sell so much as a sausage. His outgoings were enormous and the incomings were zero. He would have considered bankruptcy, but then the full extent of his illicit dealings would have become public. Al Arrod had offered a solution. He knew all about Al Arrod, in fact it would have been difficult to have had such a flamboyant character escape one's attention. Gobbleton however, had effected a personal introduction and hinted that friendship with Al Arrod could be advantageous. Now, having met, he was due to meet with him again, in secret. Gerald went to Al Arrod's department store and using a concealed and private lift, was whisked up the penthouse suit of offices to meet the owner. Once there, Al Arrod offered Gerald a deal.

Gerald bred pigs. Pigs were a liability. Rabbits were not. People were desperate to eat meat. Therefore what Gerald needed to do was to get out of pigs and into rabbits. Gerald pointed out that he agreed. It was a lovely idea. The snag was however how to dispose of his pigs in exchange for the folding cash required to move over into the rabbit breeding industry? There was no market for pigs and even if there was, it was illegal to move them anyway.

Al Arrod pointed out that the manner in which Gerald had acquired his holdings didn't bear scrutiny and if he didn't do something soon, he would be forced out into the glare of the spotlight of the public domain. Whether he liked it or not. That was something Gerald did not want to contemplate. Not only bankruptcy, but shame and disgrace too. Gerald knew when he was over a barrel. He was also quite astute enough to realise that Al Arrod had some solution up his sleeve. The only question what was it? and how much was it going to cost Gerald? He nodded his head, yes, he agreed that he had a serious problem on his hands, what did Al Arrod suggest by way of a solution?

Al Arrod smiled. Perhaps, he Al Arrod could help in the transition from pigs to rabbits. Obviously Gerald could not slaughter all of his stock. The disposal of so many bodies would in itself cause a problem. Equally, their disposal would cost money and money was at a premium at the moment. No, what Gerald need to do was to sell his infected animals, and then, use the cash generated to restock with rabbits. Gerald could see the economic sense in this suggestion, though he personally held deep misgivings that killing rabbits would give him the same degree of satisfaction that slitting the throats of pigs did. Still, when needs must, the Devil drives. How, though, he wondered could this transformation take place in secret and safely?

Al Arrod supplied the answer. All he wanted was a British passport. A legal one, he already had half a dozen fake ones. Half the asylum seekers in the World had fake British passports. He personally felt that they were available on super market shelves in certain countries.

Gerald pointed out that that passports came under the responsibility of the Home Secretary and it was almost a matter for record that he loathed all foreigners. No offence of course. Al Arrod knew all that. No, Gerald had the ear of the Prime Minister. Personally Gerald thought that the Prime Minister was a buffoon who was incapable of organising a round of drinks in a bonded warehouse, but he kept his opinions to himself. Still, he reasoned, if he couldn't fix a genuine British passport for this grubby little foreigner, then no one could. He tentatively agreed and indicated that Al

Arrod should outline his schemes. When he had done so, Gerald had to give him some measure of grudging respect. His plan had merit.

What Al Arrod proposed to do was drug the pigs. Then they would be secretly loaded into sealed trucks, labelled Bananas and placed aboard ships as empty containers ostensibly being returned to the West Indies, or some place. These ships in turn would then meet up with a mother factory ships that had canning facilities. These ships operating under the guise of fish canning operations and positioned in International waters. The pigs would be processed into pork and luncheon meat. The cans being labelled as originating in South America and then sold on to China and Korea. If it spread the BDS sickness to those countries, well, there were too many Chinese anyway and who gave a Damn about a few Koreans? Al Arrod would fund the operation, and take the lion's share of the resulting profits too. Though there would be something in it for Gerald too. He would however bail Gerald out of his present financial constraints and that money could be viewed as an interest free loan. To be repaid later, once the rabbit business took off. Gerald knew that really he had no choice.

Meanwhile Bradford and Peter were getting along splendidly together. Peter understood computers too. Bradford had told them to take as much money as they wanted. It was stacked in cardboard boxes in the far cellar. In fact there was so much that even he Bradford had begun to get a little concerned. So he had moved the wine racks around a bit and now the money was in another room at the end and he had disguised the door. Bradford was much more interested in showing Tiffany and Peter the signals that he had been receiving from Langley. There was something odd going on with that whaling ship. It seemed that it originally had intended to sail for Iceland and had some unspecified cargo on board. Now the Americans had somehow gained control of the vessel and were intent taking it to America. Some plan was being hatched at Langley whereby once the Ship had cleared The Med. and was into the Bay of Biscay, they were to drop the sextant over the side. Then Solly could sit back and leave the rest to Langley. Meanwhile the ship was transmitting some coded message of its own too. Perhaps Peter would like to try running a decode programme and finding out what those messages said. Peter did and pretty soon came up with something that was obviously written in a foreign language. Icelandic would be the most likely language. Bradford just down loaded the text and hacked into Langley's Super Cray, which obligingly translated it for him. At that point the three of them became spectators and could view the cards held by both sides.

Whatever was on board that vessel was obviously wanted by both Iceland and America and both seemed to have a similar plan to obtain it. That being that both sides wanted their operative to allow some unfortunate accident to occur to the ship's sextant. By doing that, then there would be no way for anyone on board to check the vessel's longitude. The ship would depend solely upon satellite navigation and its GPS system. Langley would then control the navigational message that the ship received and send it secretly on a course for Virginia. Iceland had a similar plan, but would route the ship to Reykjavik. Having had their appetites whetted, the three plotters wondered if once the sextant was destroyed, if they could reprogram the programmes and sail the boat into Milford Haven on the West Coast of Wales? They too now wanted to find out the contents of its mysterious cargo.

Sven smiled to himself. Solly hadn't realised that he Sven had actually caused Solly to fumble and drop the ship's sextant over the side. Sven had feigned almost explosive anger and berated Solly as a clumsy, landlubber fool. Solly would never know how he had played into Sven's hands.

Solly laughed to himself too. That fool of Captain. All red hair. and beard. Now he had no way of knowing that the good ship Wjhale KillÆr IV was bound for Virginia along with its precious cargo.

Bradford just waited until both Langley and Reykjavik confirmed to their own parties that the program had been sent and loaded into the ship's GPS and that false co ordinates would be shown but actually the ship was on course. Then he sent his own set of data, which superseded that of both Langley and Reykjavik. He also included a programme that would send back to each of the parties a suitable false position for Wjhale KillÆr IV.

Kenu was worried. His seaweed was loosing its ability to glow in the dark. This he knew from experience meant that his precious plant was unhappy. He had a sinking feeling in the pit of his stomach that his crop was about to expire on him. What would happen then? Here he was in the middle of nowhere on the high seas with a bunch of armed cut throats intent on sailing to America. Ellik San would say nothing and now they had lost the sextant. If his seaweed died, then the whole purpose of the exercise was in doubt and along with it, no doubt his life too. He had to keep the plant alive somehow. Even if he ended up in the USA he could claim that he had been kidnapped. No doubt the Americans would see the advantage of keeping him alive. There again, why would the Americans have wanted to kidnap him and the crop in the first place, when Del Minki was an American company? America would have had the seaweed in any case. It suddenly occurred to Kenu that perhaps America did want the secrets of his seaweed, but for far more sinister reasons than feeding the world. May be the reverse was true. Dreams of a new life in Iceland with heavy-breasted white women began to fade. Even his skinny, and shrew like wife began to seem more attractive by comparison with what might be in store. Kenu decided on one last strategy. His very life now depended upon him keeping the seaweed alive. It very much looked like the seaweed was not going to oblige. What he needed to do obviously was to some how fool both Sven and Solly that the seaweed was healthy and thriving. He would chill the tanks down and claim that he was placing the seaweed into a state of suspended animation. Then, once they reached America, which would seem to be the most likely of the destinations, he would negotiate with the persons in charge. He would claim that he had been forced to take drastic measures during the voyage due to prevailing circumstances. Incorrect water supply, temperature problems. Anything, he could think about that later. His life now depended upon him being able to convince all persons on board that all was well with his weed.

CHAPTER. 6

Brenda Crabpenny was lonely. Brenda Crabpenny was always lonely. In fact, Brenda Crabpenny could not recall any time in whole life when she had not been lonely. Life for her was only a question of degrees of loneliness.

She had been an only child of elderly parents. Her mother had not planned on getting pregnant and was quite surprised when she found that she was with child. She and her husband having given up hope of having their union blessed. So Brenda had been cosseted. Her father was a clerk in a small, rural branch of a large national bank, and her mother had worked in a building society. Giving up her job when Brenda came along. Both of her parents had been non-smoking and tea total. Staunch members of the local Methodist Chapel. They had a nice bungalow that overlooked the Cleddau Estuary in Pembrokeshire, on the Milford Haven side of the river. Her father had been a bit of a local historian in his time. He had written, though never had published, a history of the area. So Brenda grew up in an atmosphere that was steeped in information regarding the second largest natural harbour in the world. Though one that had last seen any degree of activity in Nelson's time. The good Admiral even then basing his ships there more as a convenience for himself, than for tactical reasons. He was at the time having it away something rotten with Lady Hamilton who happened to be living in Milford Haven. To give some degree of credibility to his warnings that Napoleon was likely to sail all the way from France and land on the west coast of Wales, just about as far as one can get from London, he had a whole bunch of fortifications built around the entrance to Milford Haven harbour. This would then require him to inspect them closely from time to time and Lady Hamilton likewise. Information, in which Brenda found, few people showed an interest. Brenda had no friends at school, nor later at Trinity College, Carmarthen where she did her Teacher's training. Finally to find herself back on the banks of the Cleddau, having inherited her parent's cottage, and teaching history at a local school. The pupils of which also showed no enthusiasm for history or anything else either. Other than each other and sex.

Brenda's parents had died tragically. They owned a caravan, which they kept locally. On top of the cliffs at Castle Martin. They used to spend a lot of time there, including their annual holidays, bird watching. Also taking long healthy, invigorating walks along the beach and collecting snippets of local history for later inclusion in her father's already bulky manuscript.

The Ministry of Defence also had a vested interest in the cliffs at Castle Martin. They rented it out each year to the German Armed Forces. Panzer Brigades would arrive each summer and play in their tanks. All of which frightened the birds and annoyed her parents no end.

One day, her father, having spotted the nest of some migratory specie. A small, dull brownish and uninteresting looking bird called a Godwits lesser spotted pluvit, had rushed out with his wife to remonstrate with the young, blond haired commander of a leopard tank. Unfortunately, the young blond commander had his mind on other things at the time and was busy visualising himself over running Poland. The result being that both Mr. and Mrs. Crabpenny ended up longer and wider, but considerably thinner, having been run over by the leviathan. This gave the undertaker a difficult task, as he had to sort of fold them into their respective coffins. Brenda was left the family home, and alone.

Brenda was thirty-seven and longed for a husband. A man with whom she could share her inner most thoughts, her very soul and better still her body. Brenda was a virgin. Well, technically so anyway. Her hymen having long ago been ruptured by a cucumber, with which she had been experimenting. Later she had graduated to vibrators and other self-stimulating devices. All of which she kept under careful lock and key. Brenda, to put it simply was gawky. Small, skinny, with short and nondescript hair tending towards ginger. Her features were not improved by her being myopic too. Brenda wore thick spectacles. Her over all appearance was that of a ginger ferret with specs. So Brenda was lonely. She lived with her two cats and a cocker spaniel in the same bungalow in which she had always lived. She taught history to a bunch of moronic kids that had no interest. Every day she walked her dog along the estuary edge and dreamed longingly of a man and sex. Brenda's luck was about to change.

President Willie Clayton had brought his beloved Lulu to Olde London Towne. She had been slipped in as Commercial Attaché's assistant. Willie now had her all to himself in the hotel suite and Willie was enjoying himself slipping in to her. He was busy running his favourite pornographic video on the TV. He had taken the trouble to bring them with him, and was faithfully following every action of the main star Stud Shafter. Lulu was stretched out naked on the bed, a huge expanse of white flesh and Willie was busy coating her with great dollops of ice cream and chocolate chips. Later he would roll all over her and lick it off. Lulu quite liked this game as the cold ice cream made her giggle. She dipped her finger into and licked it experimentally. Willie promptly offered her something else to lick. She tried it with a mouthful of ice cream. She decided that it was better that way and Willie seemed to be enjoying it too.

Heigar was feeling frisky too and had switched Toni into sex mode. She was lying on her back, with her legs wrapped over Toni's shoulders enjoying the feeling of Toni's massive, throbbing phallus being thrust inside her. Later, when she had enough, she would switch him off. The inclusion of those two extra electrodes had been inspirational. She lay back to enjoy her moment of pleasure to its full.

Gobbleton was also moving into a paroxysm of sexual frenzy. He had bought a nifty little French Maid outfit for 'le' Upp. It came complete with black suspender belt, stockings and tiny wee skirt. The skirt was now up around her waist and Gobbleton, with one leg still inside his trousers, was frenetically trying to take her partially standing and backed over a dressing table. Gobbleton, she felt was getting boring, but the money was good.

Everyone was getting his or her oats, except Brenda.

On a dark, wet night at around the same time, but over on the West Coast of Britain, Wjhale KillÆr IV had just entered the mouth of the Cleddau River, and was on course for Milford Haven. Sven had long given up trying to mount watches. Solly's gang, whilst making admirable thugs and gunmen were not cut out for a life afloat. Most had been sea sick for most of the voyage, and Sven had been hard pressed to all but sail single-handed. The first inkling that he had that all was not as he imagined, was when the Wjhale KillÆr IV ran aground on the rocks of St. Annes Island at eco-speed. The ship virtually stopped dead. Loose bits and pieces, like crew and cups; due to the effects of laws of momentum, did not. When Sven picked himself up off the floor and had looked out of his cabin window into the rain of the dark night, he found himself looking up at a Martello Tower that according to his calculations should not have been there. Sven was confused.

If Sven was confused, then Kenu Itayaku was totally dismayed. The ship had been badly holed and though in no immediate danger of sinking was well stuck on the sharp rocks of pre Cambrian limestone that are as hard as granite. What really caused him concern though was that the tanks had broken loose and overturned. The dark waters of Milford Haven were flooding into the hold. Worse still, his precious seaweed was now, before his very eyes slipping into the sea from the upturned tanks. What little was left alive was disappearing into the rising tide through the holes in the vessel with an eerie orange glow. This was a disaster.

Kenu threw himself into the cold waters, in an attempt to rescue his precious weed. His actions were futile. His spectacles were covered in seawater, he could not see clearly, but he could see sufficiently well to watch helplessly as the last strands slid away. Kenu knew immediately that there was only one thing that he could do. Being a sensible, calm, rational and logical thinking male Japanese he made his decision. There was only one solution. He would commit ritual suicide. He scrambled aboard and headed for his cabin.

All the lights on the vessel had gone out. Kenu had managed to reach his quarters in the gloom, ignoring the noise and confusion going on all around him. He removed his clothes and sitting naked, it occurred to him that he had no knife. He cast around and took the first sharp thing to hand. A small tin opener. Kenu found that no only did he have enormous difficulty in committing suicide with a tin opener, it was painful too. It was all too shameful, he couldn't even commit suicide properly. He decided to leap back into the cold waters and drown himself. Upon impact one of the life boats had broken free and was now floating gently under the side of the ship. Kenu leaped into the darkness, committing his immortal soul to the shrine of his forefathers, secure in the knowledge that he had behaved honourably and landed headfirst into the empty craft. Knocking himself unconscious as he did so. Quietly, silently and unnoticed, the lifeboat drifted up stream before the strong onshore wind and making tide.

On shore, Brenda, with nothing better to do, had been staring out over the expanse of water that made up the Havens waters, from her dining room window. She had watched in amazement as the Wjhale KillÆr IV's distress rockets lit up the dark night sky. Brenda knew from experience that some vessel had driven straight on to St. Annes Island. She decided that it was worth a closer look. So, in a very leisurely manner she had collected her boots, jacket, the dog and her late father's bird watcher's binoculars, and headed for the beach. It was much further along the foreshore that she came across the naked and unconscious Kenu lying in the lifeboat. A boat that had grounded onto the shelving shingle. She thought at first that he was dead and, oh what a waste of an able bodied male, crossed her mind. She rolled him over and Kenu groaned. Brenda's heart leapt in her spinster's 32A-cup bosom. She quickly wrapped Kenu up in her jacket and tying the boat off to a handy rock, she rushed back to the bungalow to get a wheelbarrow. Very aware that the tide was coming in and time was of the essence. This was one man that she was not going to either throw back, or allow to get away either!

Kenu came around, all wrapped up in a big bed, with some strange lady looking at him. His first thought was that he had died and ended up in the wrong queue in Heaven. Obviously, there was a mistake and he should be in the dead Japanese section. But no, now this skinny little woman of about 35 years was looking at him kindly through thick lens spectacles and spooning hot soup down his throat. He was still alive, had a fearful headache and chilled to the marrow. The shame of it stung. He, Kenu Itayaku had even failed to drown himself. The strange female was talking to him.

"There, there. Don't take on so. Brenda will look after you. Here, drink your soup lovely boy. That's a nasty cut you have on your tummy. But Nursey Brenda has put a nice big plaster on it. Your Dinky Doo was all shrivelled up too. Must be all that cold water, but we will soon have it fit and well." Her eyes glinted a little when she said that, but she continued to spoon hot soup down his gullet in a most conciliatory manner.

The Cleddau River Conservancy Board vessel took charge of the shipwreck. They were not at all sure what they were supposed to do, but sure as Hell they were not going to allow the police or the Coast Guard to get a slice of the action. No way. They were after all a QANGO or quasi-autonomous national governmental organisation. Which basically means a non elected non-representative body with a lot power, a big budget and answerable to no one. It found that if it made local people register their moorings, later they could charge them for the privilege. Out siders could be really fleeced. They even claimed ownership of the swans on Pembroke Castle pool. That was until some one pointed out that all swans in Britain are owned by the Crown. They didn't want to upset Her Majesty as they were hoping that she would put in an appearance for the Tall Ships Race. So they sensibly settled for the ducks instead.

Before they arrived though, Solly got off one last coded message to Langley. Bradford intercepted and decoded the transmission. "Watercress aground in British waters. Send the Marines." Meanwhile, Brenda having obviously having read somewhere that hypothermia kills, and not wanting to loose her patient, had slipped quietly beneath the sheets with him. Her objective to keep him warm with her own naked body heat.

Customs and Excise were confused. Their first thought with regard to Wjhale KillÆr IV was drugs. More so when the captain could not be found and those persons claiming to be the crew and obviously knew nothing about seamanship. However, a through search revealed nothing. There was no cargo and there were no drugs but one lifeboat was missing. A lifeboat that some enterprising local lad, knowing the laws governing salvage and items found between high and low water line, was even now busy repainting and renaming.

That effectively left Customs and Excise with the story that the ship was in fact an Icelandic-whaling vessel that had run aground. Though why it should be in Milford Haven was a mystery. There was also the crew problem to be explained. It was obvious. This entire motley bunch spoke English with heavy American accents. They all looked like Arabs; they were all heavily armed. Quite obviously they were PLO members, trained to masquerade as Americans and had come to assist the IRA. This bunch of ruffians must, have disposed of the original crew. They, poor souls, having been done to death most foully once the gang had realised that they intended to beach the ship. The cargo must have been arms and explosives and these had been consigned to the deep too. They informed the police authorities accordingly. It was a neat story. It caught the press headlines. It made the Authorities look good and was plausible enough to be believed. All in all a satisfactory outcome and the whole issue could be filed under case closed. The IRA disclaimed all knowledge, but who was going to believe them?

Iceland asked for their ship to be returned. Naturally they were not going to let anyone know of their original intentions and the CIA also breathed a sigh of relief that there was no hint of any mud sticking to them. There was still the question of what had happened to Sven, Kenu and the cargo. The CIA, being suspicious by nature jumped to the obvious conclusion. Kenu had thrown in his lot with Sven. The CIA issued a directive to its entire operator's worldwide. They were to be terminated with extreme prejudice. The fate of the cargo however was an unanswered question. Still, at least Solly and his gang of inept hijackers were safely taken care of by the Brits. No leaks there. They sent a message to Willie Clayton in London, "Watercress lost." Bradford read that too.

The Green Brigade was also confused. From their headquarters in London, they too had been trying to track the progress of Wjhale KillÆr IV. Without success. They lacked access to sophisticated satellites and didn't have either Bradford's equipment or expertise for hacking into the American secret service network. Peter had conveniently neglected to inform them he knew exactly where the ship was at all times, as it was he and Bradford that had decided upon it's course. Once however, they knew that the ship had actually run aground in West Wales, The Green Brigade had thought to claim some degree of responsibility for wrecking the ship. Another killer vessel sunk etc. But once the connection with the IRA had been established they thought it better to stay silent. Those sort of wild actions were the sort of thing that Animal rights groups got up to. They, The Green Brigade, were after all an almost respectable World movement. Best not to tarnish their name. The Green Brigade slipped silently away.

Peter, Tiffany and Bradford were suspicious and confused. What was Watercress? Where had it been lost? Why were both Iceland and America involved? Why did the British seem unaware of either Watercress or Longboat? Where was the captain of the vessel? Who were the so-called Arabs and what the Hell did the IRA have to do with it all? No, there were far were all too many unanswered questions.

Peter and Tiffany went to an auction. They bought themselves a very nice, secluded but rather run down farm. It's owner having shot himself in protest against the decline and collapse of the British farming industry. A protest that went completely unnoticed.

Bradford moved in with his now extensive electronic equipment. He had decided to stop making designer drugs, and being involved in the illicit meat trade. Both activities impinged upon his time too much. There was more than enough money for all of them and he much preferred to spend his time hacking. He was still getting frequent bursts of an odd signal for which he had no explanation. Peter looked in from time to time. He was busy with a solar heating project. Tiffany seemed to be perfectly happy. She went around in old jeans, an old shirt of Peter's tied at the waist and with her now rather nice looking hair tied up in a scarf. She spent her days stripping old pine chairs, painting and cooking meals.

Bradford gave the signals some more thought. He enjoyed a challenge. He didn't hack for the pleasure of obtaining secret information. He hacked for the pleasure that he received in beating the defences. Perhaps if he hooked up an oscilloscope into the circuit. Perhaps he could work out some way to record the signal; he could then reproduce it. If he superimposed it over the signal on the 'scope, he would be sure that he had an identical match. What he would do then, he wasn't sure. He decided to give it some more thought.

Willie Clayton was worried. Somehow the Damned CIA had not only managed to sink that blasted boat, but had done so in a British harbour. Whilst he was on an official visit too. If that wasn't bad enough, the cargo of GM seaweed had disappeared along with that slant eyed Jap and crazy Viking. It was quite obvious that he could place no trust what so ever in his intelligent service to deliver the goods. He decided to trust to his own judgement in future.

Then there was this very odd new Prime minister of the Brits. God alone knew that the Brits as a race were odd at the best of times, but this guy was right off the wall. Willie was almost sure that the guy was wearing a hairpiece. Never trust a man that wears a wig his daddy had always told him. The fact that the expression derived it's origins with Apace Indians rather than his father, was lost on him. No, this Toni Cacophony was a weirdo. He decided that he didn't really like him. Another point against him was that he was too damn popular, and Lulu seemed to find him attractive too. No, all in all, he would be glad once this visit was over and he could go back to the White house and humping Lulu on the carpet in the Oval Room. He was pissed off with this stupid little country, it's God-awful weather and all these Limey jerks that walked around like tailor's dummies with plumbs in their mouths and a handful of brambles stuck up their backsides. What Lulu saw in that smarmy jerk Toni was beyond him? Jesus! Anyone could see that the guy was pure political plastic and brainless to boot. And what to do about the sea weed? Where was the seaweed?

Sven Svensonn, was not at all happy either. He had seen the glowing cargo slide into the waters of the Haven and knew that it was lost. Well, for the moment certainly. There again, the sea, in his experience tended to give up its dead. The question was more one of would the seaweed survive and if so, how would it be recognised? Mind you, the orange glow was a bit of a dead give away. He reasoned though, that if it did survive, even in small quantities, a careful search would reveal its location. Then as he knew of its value, he could grab some and be on the next plane to Reykjavik. and to Hell with that crazy Jap and his fetish for big tits and red haired pussy.

He decided to phone his controller. He would say that he had no idea of how the Wjhale KillÆr IV ended up in West Wales. That must have been Reykjavik's fault. He had been overpowered, but having fought valiantly in the manner of their glorious Viking forefathers, escaped over the side. He was now in hiding and waiting his opportunity to grab a few samples of Watercress and return with them to Iceland. He had no idea of what had become of Kenu Itayaku, but assumed that he had been killed by Solly and his henchmen and the body not as yet discovered. Either way it was highly unlikely that the Americans had any sea weed either. Naturally the Brits had no idea of what was really going on and were happy to put the whole affair down to the IRA. He went along to Woolworth's and purchased a pay as you go mobile phone and rang Reykjavik.

Kenu Itayaku was also confused. Here he was in some strange house, overlooking the river and estuary and being looked after by some strange but very kind young lady with a sing song voice. She waited on him hand, foot and finger, and was most respectful too. She also had some thing about sex. She seemed unable to get enough of it. Kenu quite liked that. It was a pity that she had such small breasts though. There again, her pudenda were very exciting. Having as it did, masses of ginger coloured hairs, curly hairs too. When he told her that he liked eating seaweed, she had been delighted. She promptly took him down onto the foreshore to gather basketfuls. She called it lava bread and cooked it with mushrooms. It tasted rather nice. When he had been down on the foreshore with her, he had looked carefully for traces of his life's work, but could find none. Not too surprising really, it had been most difficult to grow.

He thought about his life to date. All that time and energy wasted and for what? A pokey little apartment in a tower block in Tokyo. Confined to rush to and from work on over crowded underground trains. Hustle, bustle, stress, noise, people and a family that showed no respect. No relaxation, no peace of mind, a difficult wife and a stressful existence. Yes, he decided, it had only been an existence. Here by comparison, it was green and peaceful. There was room, enormous amounts of room in fact. A garden, flowers, a nice view and two cats and a dog. Then there was Brenda. She showed him great respect. She had told him that he was a teacher. She cooked for him, and tended to his every need. She even allowed him to start building a Japanese Garden. In fact she was happy for him to do so. No, he was happy here and obviously Brenda wanted him to stay. No, he would complete the garden, and build a teahouse. Then he could teach Brenda the intricacies of the tea ceremony. Maybe buy her a kimono. His wife had never bothered to learn. Kenu was at peace at last. He would live with this woman and be at peace with the world. He would forget all about seaweed. He would build his garden and practice his Zen.

Al Arrod was quite happy too. He had presented Gerald with a ceremonial dagger, to seal their bargain. Gerald was moving drugged pigs in secret, from all points of the compass by road to Pembrokeshire. There they were being shipped out in containers that were labelled bananas, to be turned into neat little cans of ham on the larger factory ships that lurked off shore.

Gerald felt confident too. No one was taking any notice of the numerous empty containers, full of his drugged pigs, that were finding their way into the docks. The numbers of pigs was being reduced, he was showing a profit and quietly he was planning the move into rabbit breeding. Things were going quite smoothly. Al Arrod, he was aware, was desperate for a British passport. He could play him along for quite a while and really establish his rabbit business before he delivered a passport. He wondered if he could deliver one page at a time? but dismissed the idea as being unlikely. Meanwhile the Chinese could eat the infected meat.

Bradford worked at recording and copying his strange signal. He knew that it was of a digital nature and being transmitted on the microwave frequencies used by mobile phone bands. He also knew that this was no normal chit-chat conversation. He was intrigued. Peter occupied his time with erecting his solar power system and Tiffany stripped old pine chairs. She could not recall being happier in her life. They had a huge AGA cooker and Tiffany was learning to cook. She was also considering throwing away her contraceptive pills.

Willie Clayton was in two minds. Should he tell that dick head of a British Prime Minister about the seaweed or not. He decided that discretion was by far the best course. On the other hand, if he did nothing, then he would lose control of the situation. Not that he had much control at the moment. No, a ploy was called for. He sat and thought, picking up a tourist blurb as he did so. Then he saw the way forward. Ashdale Field Centre, he read idly. A centre open all the year round and available for use by the public as well as schools, colleges and universities. Ashdale provided bed and board and provided an understanding centre for those persons or educational groups involved in coastal research and natural activities. They even ran their own field trips. They provided a base for normal marine study activities and for private and more esoteric studies. Perfect, He would get the CIA to infiltrate, under the guise of marine biologists or some thing. That way he would have his people on the scene and he need not tell that donk of a Prime Minister a Damn thing. He drafted his signal, which was intercepted by both Bradford and MI6. MI6 advised the Minister that the Yanks were up to no good, something about using Ashdale Field Centre as a front for finding a missing cargo of genetically modified seaweed. The light began to slowly dawn in Whitehall and in the new and very expensive MI6 building on the South Bank. So that was what the Wjhale KillÆr IV had been carrying. The Prime Minister was informed, he in turn told Gobbleton. Who in turn, wishing to impress Te′Upp with his importance and by association his male virility, told her across a silken and scented pillow. In the darkness, Te′Upp's eyes gleamed. She would report to her masters in Hanoi. For far from being a penniless Taiwanese gogo dancer, Te Upp was actually Vietnamese, and held the rank of colonel in their intelligence service.

In the cold dark waters, deep in a crevice a foraging crab thought that he had chanced upon a morsel of food. He tasted it, and decided that he didn't like it. It glowed in a strange way too. He scuttled off in search of more appetising things to eat.

CHAPTER. 7

Meddlesome did not trust Gobbleton any longer. In fact, Meddlesome decided, he had never really trusted him in the first place. To start with, Gobbleton was heterosexual. To Meddlesome's way of thinking, no one could ever trust a man who went with women. Women were unreliable, fickle creatures. No, with a man one knew where one stood. Which way round things were and how to approach matters. He stroked the black masses of curly hair of his latest lover, who lay asleep beside him. A delicate, Turkish Cypriot lad he had met out side a kebab bar when he had been cruising around Waterloo Station, late the previous evening.

Meddlesome also loathed Te´Upp. He distrusted her on principle. She was after all female. Apart from which she had far too much control over Gobbleton. He was well aware that Gobbleton was in over his head in debt to Al Arrod. Al Arrod had introduced Gobbleton to Te´Upp. Obviously for his own ends. Al Arrod, he knew full well, was not in the habit of doing anybody a favour for nothing. Now Gobbleton and Te´Upp had been spotted by chance, by a tabloid reporter. They had been spending a weekend together in one of Al Arrod's Abu Dhabi hotels. Gobbleton had publicly denied it and at the time in question, was claiming to have been in London. The press, scenting a scandal, were sniffing around. On top of that Gobbleton had now told her about some missing cargo of genetically modified seaweed that the strange Icelandic ship had been carrying. Meddlesome, congratulated himself on having had the fore thought to have organised the bugging of Te´Upp's bedroom. All those boring hours he had spent listening to tapes of Gobbleton grunting and puffing his way up to an orgasm had finally paid a dividend. He decided to run his own programme on Toni. He would get him into best smarm and charm mode and use the hot line to Willie Clayton. This GM seaweed needed further investigation. Maybe he could use it to his advantage. He would however have to speak to Heigar. He didn't trust Heigar either, nor her crazy father. He wondered what they were plotting? Well, neither of them understood computers and Gobbleton was far too busy with that minx of mistress. All the workload was falling upon his shoulders, he thought. Meddlesome began to feel a sense of injustice. He was the important cog in the machine. He ran Toni. All Heigar did was feed and water him. As for her father, all he had to do was make sure he paid the electricity bills on time at that stupid castle of his. His mood grew blacker as felt sure that somehow, though he was doing all of the work, the others were plotting against him. He would be careful and let them know as much as they needed to know.

Meddlesome contacted Heigar, but took care not to tell her too much. This would take a little organising, he realised. He wanted to make sure that the main frame computer still hidden in the depths of her father's cellars in Austria was all booted up and ready and all of the microwave link lines were in order. He couldn't trust the mad professor. They had been caught flat-footed at Question Time in The House the other day. He didn't want to be caught out again. Taxation under Toni's government had risen by 12%, but all in carefully hidden taxes. The opposition had been doing it's sums and had a wonderful time quoting the Prime Minister's own words, from the early days of electioneering, back to him. The electoral pledges that he himself had made that taxation would not increase, and had then quite obviously been broken. Meddlesome cursed the early programmes and the holes in them that had allowed such a gaff to slip through. The very idea of a politician saying anything that could later be quantified was abhorrent to him. The damage however had been done. And now this gravel voiced, slap head, of an opposition leader had well and truly got his teeth into something. Getting Toni to stand up and claim that what he had actually meant was that the basic rate of taxation would not be increased, and that anything else was fair game. And any way, he was only cleaning up the mess of the previous Government. Even to Meddlesome this sounded a little hollow.

Meddlesome ran his programme. Toni rang the President of the United States of America.

"Willie, it's Toni. How are you? Err, just a wanted a word, you know, nothing that's important. It's about that ship that ran aground when you were over here. I, I err, have a snippet of information, thought that you might be interested. Get to see the big picture and all that, but if you are busy........."

Willie Clayton was quite occupied, though not with matters vital to the State. He had been practising in front of a mirror whilst sitting behind his enormous Presidential desk in The Oval Room. He wore a jacket and a shirt and tie. That was all he was wearing. He leaned forward in his chair, giving his best, you can trust me, I would not lie, face. Lulu however, was crouched between his knees busy giving him a blowjob. It all worked quite well. If only he could keep that silly grin off his face that had a habit of creeping in. He would have to work on it some more, he decided. For all that, he had better listen to what this stupid Limey had to say, and find out how much he knew.

"No Toni, nothing that won't keep. Only planning the nuclear destruction of Iran, for next Thursday. Those Ayatollah boys just keep pissing off my Generals. So what's new on the boat scene?"

"Well, the big picture is that apparently there was some genetically modified sea weed on board. That was, in the broadest sense, that is, something to do with your boys. Seems like they were hitching a lift from Japan. Then they got hi jacked, and it ended up over here. That's about all really. Snag is the old environmental people are likely to make a dreadful fuss over here, if they get wind of it. No reason that they should, but they have their aspirations too. And in the fair and democratic society that New Deal is implementing, appealing to the heartland's and all reasonable people, they have to be allowed to speak. We don't have to take any notice. Not in the big picture. Just wondered if you could shed a spark of light on the seaweed. What it did, you know, anything interesting? Don't want a lot of three headed prawns or ten legged crabs or anything. We have enough trouble keeping the lid on the odd things that keep popping up in the water around Dungeonfield Nuclear Reprocessing Plant out fall. Had some child swallowed by a giant mackerel the other day. Frightful fuss the parents made. Can't think why, disgusting looking child from the photographs and the parents can always have another. Two if they like. We pay excellent family allowances. So, nothing like that then? No little surprises?

Willie did a quick bit of thinking on his feet. "No, no, Toni. Apparently our boys had some idea to use the stuff as a base for marine paint. You know, sea weed. Sea water. Nothing to worry about. Has the weed turned up then?"

"No idea Willie. I mean, taking a global view, one bit of seaweed looks much like another bit to my boys. Any distinguishing marks? Lib-Dem stickers, or anything? Then we will know what to look out for."

"Don't think so Toni. Not that I know of. I'll ask my boys and let you know."

"Right you are then. Have a nice war." And Toni put down the phone.

Meddlesome, who had been listening in mulled over the information. So they haven't found it and we haven't found it and we don't know what we are looking for, other than it's sea weed. Nor do we know it's true purpose. Meddlesome dismissed the idea of it being a base for marine paint as a smoke screen and therefore, worthless. The Americans wouldn't have taken all the trouble to ship the stuff in secret it had no value. Where did Iceland come into the picture? He decided to discreetly ask MI6 to keep their eyes peeled for American agents operating in the Milford Haven area.

It was Te´Upp that finally cleared up the matter for all parties. Vietnam informed her that via their source and agents in Japan it had been confirmed that the seaweed was a new and valuable food source. She was ordered to obtain live samples at all costs. If Vietnam could grow the stuff in the Mekong Delta, over night they would become a World power. Their food production out stripping that of their old adversary the USA. Vietnam and its glorious socialist policies would be seen as a shining beacon to the starving and oppressed masses of third world humanity.

Te´Upp decided upon subterfuge. That night, once Gobbleton had finished taking her doggie style, she blew in his ear and tickled his neck, and other places, with her delicate fingers. "Why don't you leave your wife

Gobbies? You could live with little old me and I could cook and look after you." She turned her big, dark cat shaped eyes to him. "Little Te'Upp is tired of sharing her big Gobbie baby with that nasty old wife of his." She ran her long finger down his cheek.

"Where would we live Te' Te'?"

"Oh, in my home."

"You mean in Taiwan?"

"Mmmm... We could have a nice little house by the sea, and I could cook your favourite food and we could be happy. Just me and you. And I could wear my black fish net bikini. The one you bought me in Amsterdam.." She knew that Gobbleton had a thing about her fish net bikini. He used to love taking her out of it and getting himself into her afterwards.

"But it's money Te' Te'. My wife has all the money. You know that."

"Al Arrod has plenty."

At the name of Al Arrod, Gobbleton flinched. He even stopped rubbing his hand between Te'Upp's thighs." I owe that man thousands as it is!"

"But if little Te' Te' knew of some way of finding enough money and tricking that nasty Al Arrod, then would Gobbie be interested?"

Gobbleton certainly was. If he could get away with dumping his wife and Al Arrod at the same time and get to keep Te'Upp and have wealth too, Gobbleton was very definitely interested. He sat up and took notice. "How do you mean Pussycat?"

Te'Upp sat up in bed. Her breasts, shrouded in her long black hair, poking their dark nipples towards Gobbleton. She sat with her legs crossed, her pubic hair hidden from view. Gobbleton almost took his mind off money. He reached for her.

"No, in a minute Gobbie darling, this is important." She pushed his exploring hand away gently. "You remember that ship you told me about. The one that crashed on the rocks and no one knows why?" Gobbleton nodded. "Well a little bird told Te'Upp something."

"What little bird?"

"Te'Upp can't say. A bird from Taiwan maybe. Anyway Te'Upp knows what the secret is!" She leaned forward and pushed her small nose into Gobbleton's face. "It's sea weed."

"Sea weed?"

"Mmm." She nodded her head and shook back her long hair. "Special sea weed. Very special sea weed. You know that we can't eat meat, because of this nasty BDS disease. Well this sea weed was developed by the Japanese for America. The Americans want to sell us all of their expensive meat, and feed the rest of the World on the sea weed. That way they control the World's food supplies. They were taking the sea weed in secret to America on that Icelandic ship. Perhaps they promised Iceland something, or maybe they just wanted to steal it. Anyway, something happened and it ended up here. Now the Americans want it back, but it's all fallen into the water."

Gobbleton sat listening to her. He was unconvinced. "So how does that help you and me, even if it's true?"

"Oh my Gobbie is clever enough to check if it's true. If the Americans want it back, then they will be looking. And looking for seaweed too. Now, my Government wants the seaweed. If Taiwan could grow it before the Americans get hold of it, we can claim that we invented it. You know how we are good at copying things. Then we could offer it to Mainland China. They have dreadful problems in feeding all of those people. We would have some control over them. America could not make too much fuss as they protect us from Beijing, and they couldn't very well complain without everyone knowing what their plan had been in the first place. My Government would be very grateful and we could live there in luxury. All we have to do is find a little bit of old seaweed and not tell anybody. Then we will send it off to Taipei by DHL, they guarantee to deliver anything. It can be our secret." Little did they realise that they had just let Meddlesome into their secret too!

Someone once said that a secret is only a secret, if only you know about it. The moment that you share the knowledge with someone else, then it is by definition, no longer a secret. Meddlesome knew that the secret was out. Not yet common knowledge, but too far loose to be contained. He would have to act fast. His first move would be to check on any strangers in the Milford Haven area who were acting oddly. That took about twenty minutes. Ashdale Field Centre had all but been taken over by a party of American marine biologists, who were the oddest bunch of marine biologists that

Ashdale had ever come across. For a start, they had wanted exclusive rights to the place for an unspecified time. They were also prepared to pay very handsomely for the privilege. They had some sophisticated communication systems, but little else. They all were clean shaven, tanned, and always wore dark mirror sunglasses. They all wore black belted trench coats, smart dark suits and were very polite. They never wore gumboots. Preferring instead Italian loafers and all carried suspicious bulges under their left armpits. Furthermore, they avoided any conversations about marine biological matters like the plague. They seemed to spend most of their time in groups of three, with the last man in line constantly casting about as if expecting a surprise attack. They were also constantly followed by some huge red haired man with a large red beard. Something of which they seemed to be totally unaware. Obviously they were CIA. Once that mystery had been cleared up to the satisfaction of the locals, it became common knowledge and they were ignored and left to get on with what ever they were doing. The price of calf's laxative in the local farmer's co-op and the ban on meat products being much more important.

Meddlesome knew that he had to find the sea weed first. Well, not him, but Britain. If Britain had it, then effectively he had it, as he controlled Toni. Gobbleton was working for the Taiwanese. Obviously the blasted Te´Upp woman was some agent or other and Al Arrod was involved. He felt that the suspicions that he had harboured for them were well founded. Well that could be sorted out later. Equally obviously, the Yanks were here in force. He guessed that the red haired giant, would be the Icelandic connection. He could get rid of him first. Have him kidnapped and smuggled aboard freighter bound for The Falklands. So, the Prime Minister would have to be informed, and duly programmed. This of course would involve Heigar too. He really needed to find some way of eliminating both her and her father. Perhaps a skiing accident. He would also have to dispose of Gobbleton and Te´Upp too. Then he alone would control Toni. Toni would be head of the EEC soon. It was Britain's turn to sit in the high chair. Then he, Meddlesome, would effectively control Europe. If he had the sea weed secret, then Europe, still in the grip of BSD, would no longer be held hostage to America for food. Also, Britain could feed the world. Starvation is a very powerful and strong economic weapon. Population's tend not to want to stand by and watch their children die from hunger, whilst their well fed political leaders tell them that it is all for the greater good of the country. He sent an E mail to Heigar who was in Austria with her father. An E-mail that due to the systems that Bradford had put in place, promptly appeared on his screen too.

Kenu Itayaku was happy. Never had he know such inner peace and tranquillity. He had started on making his Japanese Garden and had been critically examining various stones that would have to be placed in mind pleasing and calming positions. He rather liked the hard blue coloured stone that could be found locally. Brenda had told him that it was Pembrokeshire Blue Stone and the only place in the world that it could be found. She had produced some information that she said had belonged to her father. Kenu learned that the strange stone had a long history. Apparently prehistoric man had valued it so highly that Stone Henge had been built from it. He marvelled at how with only wooden tools, those peoples had laboured all of those thousands of years ago to cut and transport such large pieces of stone over such a distance. He did a little more research and found that the stone was claimed to have odd magnetic powers too. He knew little of geology, but thought that perhaps the stones had some odd isotope and emitted a weak radioactive signal. Or maybe some strange trace element even. Anyway, he found their shape and colour pleasing and tranquil, and ideal for his planned garden.

He liked Brenda too, although she did have small breasts. He wished that she had larger breasts. He was very fond of her strange, curly red pubic hairs. They fascinated him. Brenda had said that she was going away for a week, and when she came back she would have a nice surprise for him. It was some school holiday or something. He was quite happy to play in the garden. The weather was warm. The flowers were blooming and there were birds, butterflies and squirrels. Kenu found his life to have meaning at last. He decided to remain with this kind and gentle woman. He would overlook the smallness of her breasts. A Samurai Warrior would grant his woman one small failing.

So Brenda placed lots of cold Lava bread in the freezer for him, along with his now favourite fish, kippers and showed where the Uncle Ben's long grain rice was. So much nicer than the sticky Japanese type that his wife had so grudgingly cooked, and off she went. Unbeknown to him to keep an appointment with a top plastic surgeon that did breast implants. Brenda too longed to fill a 34C rather than leaving space in a 32A. For years she had saved her money for this operation, but had been loath to spend the cash without good reason. Kenu Itayaku, her gentle Japanese lover, who she had rescued from certain death, provided that reason. He had told her that he was at peace with his soul at last and would remain with her. Brenda was far too astute to question him about his past life. Why remind him? No, far better to allow him to concentrate on the present and future with her, than dwell on the past. Brenda had also found life to be meaningful.

Bradford, Peter and Tiffany were sitting around the AGA cooker. Tiffany had made cheese scones and also brewed some beer; they were discussing the Meddlesome's E-mail to Heigar.

"So it's genetically modified Sea weed and has the potential to feed the world." Peter was in the chair. "That's pretty mind boggling stuff. Any one, who controls the world's food supply, ultimately ends up controlling the world. No wonder everyone is trying to locate that missing cargo."

"Would it have survived Pete? These scones are pretty good Tiff and your beers not bad either. I never knew that you could cook."

"It's easy Brad. Bucket chemistry. You just dole out the ingredients in the correct ratios and add heat. Simple really. What do you think Pete? Would it survive? I know that Milford Haven waters are part of the Gulf Stream, but it's still pretty cold."

"Hard to say Tiff. Japan's sea is not exactly in the tropics. Maybe it likes cold water. Either way, I can't see that there is much we can do about it, other than blow the whistle if it's found and marketed. I don't see that we could affect the outcome of that either. Eat GM seaweed of starve? No choice is there? Why did Meddlesome send the E-mail to Toni's wife? That's a much more interesting question."

"I'll tell the pair of you something even more interesting." Said Bradford secretively. I did a little bit of signal chasing on all of those odd signals." He looked at them both through his huge horn rimmed spectacles and nodded, smiling as he did so. The other two listened Bradford rarely spoke and when he did it was usually worth paying attention.

"Well. Some signals originate from here in the UK. They are directed to, would you believe Austria. Then the odd ones start up from Austria and are received, where ever, and by who ever. I ran a survey. Every single time the start signal is sent from Britain, the odd ones follow immediately from Austria. Therefore it follows that someone is sending an initiation code from here. Those codes are received in Austria. Then they generate some other signal and that is the one we are getting. Now, what is really interesting is that those transmissions from Austria are all originating from the same place. And guess who lives there? Herr Professor, Doktor Frantz Kutzanburns."

"Heigar's mad father!" Exclaimed the other two simultaneously

"Exactly! And... I can reproduce the signal"

"Can you modify it?"

"No point Pete. There are only five set signals. Obviously these are the key signals that set some programme running. Variables have been built in, but basically they all remain within the parameters of the original signal. It's a programme. It's a clever programme, but not that clever. My guess is that there is some large database in Austria. In the mad professor's castle, or what ever. It's a self-learning programme. Which is really only a fast comparison act. I am confronted with this problem. I have this set of options. What happened before? It's bit like teaching a robot to move through a maze. Same principle. It chooses the best option from what it has and runs it. Then it looks at the feed back it's getting and adjusts accordingly. Then it saves the results. Consequently, it learns, and gets a bit faster and bit smarter each time. The big question is what the Hell is the programme running? It's obviously big, whatever it is. No. I won't attempt to change the signal. What I want to do is transmit the whole five programmes one after another and then sit back and keep my eyes and ears open for clues."

"Hang on Brad. If you could trace them, then surely they can trace us?"

"True, but I know a way around that. I will transmit a virus programme into their mainframe using their own wavelength. This will be a descrambler and storage programme. Then I will encode and speed up my signal to them. This I will send as a micro second burst transmission. My programme, now bedded down nicely in their brain will recognise it, and store it. Then, at any time in the future I can send my own signal, on a different wavelength. This will be recognised by our Trojan Horse and that will active their hard drive to transmit. Not only won't they be unable to stop it from happening; other than by shutting down, cleaning their hard drive and then starting again and programming from scratch. When their machine begins transmitting, we will no longer be on the air. It will look like a glitch in their programme. It's fool proof." Bradford sat back with a satisfied smile.

MI6 were busy following Sven, who was equally busy following the CIA operatives who were busy looking for the seaweed. There was plenty of seaweed about. They would skip along the fore shore, prodding with sticks into piles of the stuff that the sea had cast up. Or, like children, peer into rock pools. Then, having found some item of interest, they would photograph it with a digital camera and load it into laptop. Transmitting it by a portable satellite link, presumably back to Langley for immediate identification on real time. MI6 thought that all they would have to do, was plot each point on a large scale map from which the CIA men took samples and when they stopped searching, that would be the seaweed in question. Meanwhile they were organising the trip to the Falklands for Sven.

Sven was getting tired. He was posing as a bird watcher and had rented some damp and not very convenient cottage. He wasn't eating too well, living in the main on beans and cheese sandwiches. He had failed to find any sign of Kenu. The cottage had no hot water. He wanted a bath and his only clothes stank and had shrunk from their immersion in the sea when he had escaped from Wjhale KillÆr IV. He wished that the whole nightmare were over as he was heartily sick and tired of the whole business.

When the British Intelligence Service did finally get around to capturing him, he went without a murmur. He was more than happy to tell them the whole story in exchange for a hot bath, a change of clothes and a pickled herring on rye bread along with some lumpfish roe. When he was told that he was bound for the Falklands he fell to his knees and grasping the legs of his interrogator, thanked him for his kindness and had to be prised loose and dissuaded from kissing everyone. The Falklands had a lovely cold wet climate. Was suitably barren as to remind him of home and had big, buxom, women who ate half a sheep each morning for breakfast. And there was plenty of whales around and the odd penguin if he felt peckish. Iceland had been removed from the equation and presumably Japan too. For if Sven had failed to locate the missing scientist, then he could safely be assumed as having drowned. MI6 went back to watching the Americans. They were still getting their feet wet, ruining their expensive shoes and playing in rock pools. The message went back to the Prime Minister. Bradford received it too, but as he had now accessed the American defence system Super Cray, he already knew that so far, no one had discovered a trace of the missing sea weed.

Brenda returned a new woman. Her hair had been restyled into a pageboy cut and she had invested in a Kimono. Kenu was putting the finishing touches to the teahouse. He was entranced and set about teaching her all the intricacies of the traditional Japanese tea ritual. Brenda was a willing pupil. She had even invested in a Japanese language course, published by BBC Radio 4. They had settled down comfortably together. Brenda with her new bust, and mousy hair, now straightened and dyed black. Kenu was fascinated by her new figure, and hairstyle. The fact that her collars and cuffs didn't match only served to increase her sexual allure for him. It was whilst they were sitting quietly in the tea house, in the warm gathering gloom of a late summer's evening that he caught his first glimpse of the orange glow. Perhaps it was a trick of the light. No, with a sinking feeling Kenu realised, his seaweed was alive and well.

Kenu sat quietly alone in his teahouse, in the gathering warm darkness of the summer's dusk. The garden overlooked the river. Brenda's bungalow was called, "See Waters" The reason being that the two arms of the Cleddau river, East and West joined together at this point to form the tidal confluence that then opened out into the expanse of water known as The Haven. He wondered why his weed had chosen to establish itself so far up stream. Here the waters temperature and salt content varied with the state of the tide. Perhaps that was the factor that had been missing in his attempts to grow the weed successfully in Japan. His mind ran around the problems and in doing so he was reminded once again of his former life style and he shuddered. He realised that the very thought of leaving this peaceful and serene setting was anathema to him. He had grown used to the strange female with the new and exciting body who cared for his every need so tirelessly. Kenu grunted to himself. He had no desire to return to his previous life, nor his irksome wife. He also realised that if he had spotted the glow in the water, then pretty soon others would too. Once that happened, then the secret would be out. The whole area would be flooded with activity and his pleasant new life style would very much be under threat. Perhaps if he could destroy the weed before anyone else got to it? Certainly he would have to inspect it closely.

Kenu knew that along the foreshore of the creek, local people left their rowing boats and small dinghies. These they used to access the few yachts and pleasure craft that were moored in the mouth of the small tidal creek. If tomorrow he borrowed one of these dinghies, he could row across to the other side of the river at slack water, and inspect the weed. He made a careful note of the position of the diffused orange glow and joined Brenda in bed. Brenda had invested in a new double bed and also some exciting night attire. Kenu busied himself in exploring the topographical details of Brenda's new mammary glands and soon all thoughts of seaweed were placed aside as he concentrated on the matter in hand. Brenda was in Seventh Heaven. Life was complete. She had a nice little house, a not too demanding job and a wonderful oriental lover. Not only that, she now filled a bra to her total satisfaction. She was determined that nothing would be allowed to disturb he newfound way of life.

The next day Kenu mentioned that perhaps he might go fishing. Well not exactly fishing. Just look at a spot that he considered would be conducive to quiet contemplation and at the same time stood a chance of catching a meal too. Brenda was most helpful. There was an outboard motor in the shed, and the blue and white dingy, "Puffin" belonged to her, though she never used it. Just as long as he wore a life jacket, she had no objections. Anyway it was Saturday, so she could keep an eye on him from the kitchen window, and don't forget to take an anchor, and oars and a bailing bucket too. She would even pack him some sandwiches. So Kenu set out to inspect his seaweed and take some samples.

He motored across the river to the spot where the night before he had spotted the glow, and dropped anchor. He found himself in a backwater eddy. The river and sea water constantly mixing together, and sweeping around in a lazy circle. There was some flotsam quietly floating there, and the whole spot was a secluded, South-facing suntrap. A large outcrop of the strange blue stone fell, almost sheer into the river and large trees over hung the water. There was no obvious route down to water's edge from above. The backwater was shielded from each side by the rocky outcrops. In fact, the only approach was by water and Kenu realised that the glow could only be seen from an observer, standing above and directly opposite on the opposite bank. He breathed a sigh of relief. It could only be seen from exactly the spot upon which he had sat the previous evening. For the moment at least, his secret was still safe.

The growth was however, prolific. Kenu had never seen his seaweed so happy. The fronds with their bright yellow and red blisters waved up to him in greeting from their deep, dark and new watery home. Kenu looked a little more closely and fished out a strand. No, if anything, the colours were less striking than they had been in Japan. His mutant had mutated to adapt to its new environment. It didn't feel quite the same either. It was slimy, and rather unpleasant to the touch. Kenu was intrigued; the enquiring mind and years of background training taking over. He smelt it. It had an offensive smell. Experimentally he tasted it and immediately spat it out. Kenu Itayaku knew immediately that his weed had become inedible. He breathed a sigh of pent up relief. His life's project had failed. All those years of unremitting work had been for nought. The outcome of all of toil was worthless. This growth would no more feed the World than grass cuttings and Kenu was glad.

Kenu sat back in the small boat and relaxed. He pondered, now rather academically, on what had attracted the seaweed and offered it the perfect growing conditions. Obviously, the mixing of the fresh and salt waters. The constant stirring and temperature too, but no, there had to be some other factor. He looked more closely and suddenly it dawned on him. The weed was only attached to the Pembrokeshire Blue Stone. It grew on nothing else. Kenu looked up at the small cliff side above him. This was an isolated outcrop of Blue Stone that ran down into the river. Blue Stone, he knew from Brenda was rare and had always been regarded as being rather special. So that was the answer. Not just water, temperature and saline content, it needed the rare Blue stone too. Kenu knew in his heart that his secret was safe. His weed had mutated so that its glow was far more subdued that it had been previously. It was of no use as a food stuff and grew only in this one spot. Furthermore, its glow could only be seen from his teahouse.

It was with a feeling of total contentment with the world, and knowing that he was a scientific failure that Kenu chugged happily back over the sunlit waters of the river. Back to his teahouse and his Brenda. He would never leave this strange, kind and caring woman who had saved his life. Kenu Itayaku had found his place in the order of the World at last.

The seaweed was equally happy in its newfound environment and also flourished.

All would have been well if in fact the seaweed had not have found its new location as being quite so conducive to growth. Though, it looked a little less poisonous, and glowed less brightly it grew prolifically, though still confined to anchoring itself firmly to the Blue stone and like a loyal lover, forsook all others. However, the rich deep-water kelp beds of California had nothing on Kenu's mutated marine plant. Its roots massed themselves deeper and ever deeper into the riverbed. Its thick, kelp like arms, some the thickness of a man's thigh, spread ever wider. Eventually overflowing from their nice secluded backwater. The long arms of weed now sweeping first up stream and then down, with each movement of the tide. Twice a day.

Autumn was approaching. Gerald had secretly moved vast numbers of pigs through his Pembrokeshire farm. It had now become his clearing station and virtual railhead for moving them on to meet their end safely beyond British territorial waters, on Al Arrod's factory ship. He knew that soon the autumn gales would whip through the Irish Sea and call a halt to his illegal activities. Relations with Al Arrod however, were strained. Gerald delaying the passport until he was safely out of pigs and taking what small profits were grudgingly slid his way by Al Arrod. Al Arrod in turn holding back on any money that would allow Gerald to expand legally into rabbits. Meanwhile pigs passed through Pembrokeshire and Gerald's farm, with the efficiency of a Nazi Death Camp.

Al Arrod was also now trying to divest himself of Gobbleton. He had after all served his purpose. Gobbleton however was still pushing him for money to fund his love nest with Te'Upp. It was difficult for Al Arrod, he could not as yet afford to dump either Gobbleton or Gerald. Still, soon the factory ship would have to sail away until the better weather arrived in four or maybe five months time. Then Gerald would be left once again with out goings and no incomings. If he squeezed Gobbleton a little too, then both of them would realise who actually held the cards.

So Gerald built up his numbers of live pigs at his farm in Pembrokeshire, and viewed with dismay the amount it would cost to feed them over the winter.

Gobbleton looked in dismay at the amount he owed Al Arrod.

Te'Upp kept asking him about the seaweed. Information Gobbleton didn't have, and consequently without it, no chance for him to fund a runner with his beloved Te'Te'. The CIA, having drawn a blank was about to pack up and go home.

MI6 were beginning to realise that the pleasant summer of lounging around the bays and inlets of Pembrokeshire, disguised as tourists and drinking beer and pulling chicks, and taking photographs of topless bathers, was drawing to an end.

Willie Clayton breathed a sigh of relief that the seaweed thing had not drawn him into some scandal. More so as there was a rumour that some newspaper was sniffing around his relationship with Lulu. Still, that could be taken care of. The CIA was organising the break out of Solly and his bunch of henchmen from The Maze prison in Northern Ireland. In return, they would break into the offices of the paper concerned, steal what they could in the way of incriminating evidence and bug the place at the same time.

Meddlesome was sitting quietly waiting and watching and had Toni in smarm and charm mode most of the time. Heigar overrode his programs now and again and switched Toni into sex drive and then sleep. Meddlesome fumed.

Toni was swanning around making speeches and generally trying to look good, but without actually committing himself to anything. The public loved it and at night he pounded an ever increasingly corpulent Heigar.

Heigar ate more chocolate cake and got fatter and at night waved her now respectfully chubby legs in the air.

Bradford set about duplicating his strange signals perfectly and putting his Trojan horse deep in place within the main computer in the cellars of Herr Professor Doktor Frantz Kutzanburnz.

Kenu showed Brenda how to drink Sakae and play Go and Peter and Tiffany began to think about a family.

The seaweed however began to cause problems for small boats. The shear pins on the propellers of small out board motors tended to break each time a small craft encountered the now thick, heavy, colourful kelp. The Cleddau River Conservancy Board was duly notified. After all, they claimed responsibility over the river, the foreshore and just about anything else that they could lay their hands on and charge someone for. Therefore it must be their problem.

The Cleddau Conservancy Board noted the complaint. They did not normally have cause to sail quite so far up river, so it got placed on the back burner. Pembrokeshire attitude to life being rather laid back. Locals tend to go with flow and when they say they will do something, well it does get done, but not necessarily in that year, or even century. So they waited until they had a suitable niche and a nice warm day and nothing much else to do.

The Conservancy vessel Boggle 1 sailed serenely up the area of confluence of the two Cleddau Rivers. This being just about the limit of their territory, though in actual fact the exact parameters of their jurisdiction had never been wholly confirmed. QUANGOs being rather like that. They spotted the weed with no problem and sailed in. Promptly entangling their prop as they did so and becoming marooned in a mini Sargasso Sea. Just as effectively as The Ancient Mariner. They dropped anchor, made a cup of tea and had a little think.

Their plight had not gone unnoticed. On the far side of the river was a lone WARFI, as locals like to refer to folks from away who own large floating gin palaces and have far too much money. The WAFI's, or wind assisted flaming idiots, in turn, whilst not having any axes to grind with regard to locals, do find both the imposition of endless rules and ever increasing mooring fees a pain. Generally, then they hold little love within their hearts for Cleddau River Conservancy employees. The WARFI had been pulling his rather splendid yacht out of the river, presumably to lay it up for the winter months. He would no doubt load it up onto its enormous road trailer and drag it around to the nearby Jolly Matelot pub, where it could be stored. The Jolly Matelot being a well known watering hole that had nice gardens that fronted onto the water's edge. To effect this, he had some huge American Jeep thing, equipped with a winch. The WARFI now unhitched the wire winch rope and chugged across the river with it in a small dingy. He stopped well clear of the weed and threw out a small anchor, still with power on he manoeuvred into line throwing range with Boggle 1.

"Ahoy Boggle 1. In a spot of bother are we?"

"Er, yes. Got the prop fouled."

"So, we're rather stuck then are we old boy?" The WARFI wore a jolly yachting cap and a very self-satisfied smile.

"Well, um, yes. I suppose we are."

"So will you be needing a bit of tow then will we?" The WARFI looked expectantly at the crew of Boggle 1 that were now lining the deck and looking rather sheepish.

"How's you going to that then Boy?" Boggle 1 was intrigued.

"No trubs old bean. You just take this line and I'll wind up the eight cylinders of the old tank over there." He pointed in the direction of the huge red and chrome monster of a 4 trak, squatting on the beach for all the world like a large fat crab. "Have you out of there in no time. I take it that you will accept the terms of a Lloyds open charter?"

This statement caused grave concern on the Boggle 1. Lloyds open charter being the laws of salvage. If they accepted a line, Boggle 1 would become the salvage rights of the WARFI. Boggle 1 decided to radio base.

Base dispatched Boggle 2 to assist. Meanwhile the WARFI and the captain of Boggle 1 were discussing the finer points of marine law.

"You's putting a line on me from the shore boy. You's got put a line on me from a boat for Lloyds Boy."

"I am doing just that. I'm only pulling you from the shore."

"Well, then. That's the same thing boy."

"No it's not! You will have accepted a salvage line."

"Well, we's not at sea."

"So what! Jetsam along the shore line between high and low water belongs to who ever claims it."

"Here! Don't you go calling my boat jetsam. This er's a registered Conservancy vessel this is. I dare say that I would be within my rights to order you to pass us a line."

"You won't order me to do any such Damn thing! I'm just about sick of your endless letters. Moorings have to be this and moorings have to be that. Charge me for access to the foreshore. Who the Hell do you lot think you are any way?" The arguments swung back and fore, until eventually the WARFI tired of it all, and told the crew of Boggle 1 to all rot in Hell. He went back to his vehicle to watch and wait.

Pretty soon Boggle2 appeared around the bend and promptly ran full speed into the weed, entangling their prop too. The WARFI fell about laughing, took some photographs with an expensive looking camera equipped with a long lens and drove off. No doubt to sell them, along with his story to the Milford Haven Weekly Gazette.

That night the full force of the first and sudden gales, which always heralds the start of the bad weather to follow, swept in from the Atlantic. The good news being that it freed both Boggles 1 and 2 from their all entrapping weed. Weed whose eerie orange glow had caused grave consternation to both crews, who had speculated wildly upon its nature. All of whom, being ardent followers of The X Files, a popular TV series, decided that it had been dropped from UFOs. That, or it was caused by the pollution from Pembroke Power Station. Either way, "T'wernt natural Boy." The bad news being that they and a considerable amount of seaweed ended up being swept ashore and beached in front of Gerald Fatslobe's pig farm. A pig farm now stuck with a considerable number of pigs to feed. The factory ship, at the first sniff of a storm having now long disappeared over the horizon and was on its way to sell on its infected cargo to the unsuspecting Chinese and Koreans.

CHAPTER. 8

Myreg Cwmyurr was a Welshman. Not only was he a Welshman, he was a Welsh nationalist. A Welsh speaking nationalist too. Welsh speaking, Welsh nationalists are generally regarded in Whitehall as being either an anachronism and dismissed as such, or, if any one is taking any notice of them, a thorough, and on going, pain in the butt. Myreg Cwmyurr fell into both categories.

He had actually been born as one Rodney Bogg of Diamond Terrace, Splot, Cardiff. The son of a welder and part time car mechanic. Rodney graduated to become Myreg Cwmyurr through a series of life's little quirks, and a brief flash of inspiration, rather than design.

Rodney had been born with a speech impediment. That in itself made him difficult enough to understand, but coupled with a strong Cardiff accent and having all his teeth extracted due a gum infection at an early age, and all subsequent sets of false teeth sitting loosely in his mouth, had now rendered him as being totally incomprehensible. Consequently, not wishing to be dismissed as a gibbering buffoon for the rest of his life, Rodney decided to maximise upon his affliction.

Rodney was not stupid, nor inarticulate, just unintelligible. He could see that Wales, being a Principality, was effectively one of the few remaining Colonies that England still possessed. The English, rather like the French, for some obscure reason, made a virtue out not speaking any language other than their own. The course open to him for success was obvious, change his name, purchase a set of language tapes, and claim to be a monolingual Welshman. As such he fell within the band of an ECC designated ethnic minority and able to claim all benefits therein. That no one understood him was immaterial. No one ever had. A further blessing was that due to the very nature of his chosen tongue, and his loose fitting false teeth, was that he tended to shower any persons with whom he attempted to hold a conversation with vast quantities of spittle. This in its turn then being seen as proof positive beyond all doubt, that he was indeed speaking some archaically pure and esoteric form of Welsh. Myreg was immediately adopted by the budding Welsh Nationalist Party, and soon became their head, if not their spokesman.

The fact that no one understood him was not viewed as being a drawback. As it is, North Walians don't understand South Walians, and no one understands the language that is used by the BBC. It's not so much of what one says in Welsh that counts, as being able to say it, you understand. So it follows then that two learned Welsh speakers are able to hold a long, deep, but meaningless conversation with each other, in which neither actually understands a word the other is saying. But of course would never admit as much. What is all-important is that they said it, and in Welsh. It's very much a case of never mind the quality feel the width.

Once Myreg was adopted, so to speak, the matter of his antecedents was quickly brought under control by a spot of arson at the Welsh Records Office. Myreg had become official. All that was required now was for him to wear a daffodil or a leak, be seen at rugby matches waving his arms, talk unintelligibly, but with emotion and spit a lot when he did so. That as far as anyone was concerned, was Welsh.

The Scots had their own parliament. This was a clever move by Whitehall as it meant that the Scots now had to pay their own bills, but were still subject to being taxed from Whitehall by stealth. Whitehall also still called all the major shots, leaving Scotland free to make such monumental decisions as what colours to paint their road signs and how long the pubs could stay open.

Naturally, Whitehall recognising a good thing when it saw it, assumed that the same deal could be foisted upon the Welsh. This they did by first claiming that there would be no devolution for Wales. Which, as planned, incited the nationalists to react like a pantomime script and reply, "Oh yes there will!" The whole situation having been originally engendered by

Whitehall by the suspension of the Government of Northern Ireland at Stormont, and sending the army to annoy the populace. This being due to the inhabitants of Ulster preferring in the main to shoot each other rather than talk. Something that the rest of Britain ignored completely. Not that this bothered Whitehall particularly, it was after all rather expected of the Irish, as they had been carrying on that way for the past three hundred years or so. By suspending parliament and sending in the troops, Whitehall had saved on heating bills, given the troops some battle experience and generally had Carte blanch to bump off any one they didn't like the look of. Not necessarily confining their actions to the landmass of Ulster in the process.

So Wales, in the fullness of time, had a referendum with regard to devolution. The results of which upset Whitehall no end. Wales didn't want a government thank you. The one in Whitehall generally being regarded as more than enough.

Whitehall sat around for a while and then concluded that Wales had democratically voted the idea down, but the result was incorrect, could Wales go back and have another go and this time, please get it right. So Wales did, and still said no thank you. This didn't suit the mandarins of Whitehall one bit, so it was decided that what Wales really needed was a devolved Assemble. Sitting in the recently renovated and we don't know quite what to do with it, but it looks nice, Cardiff Docklands.

The Welsh were on the whole getting a little bored with the whole game by now. They knew very well that most of the Welsh either lived abroad, or in the Cardiff, Newport areas. Newport actually being in Gwent and only having been recently assimilated into Wales. Before it had been in England, but with the opening of the Severn Bridge, the English found it easier to regard Wales as starting on the other side of the bridge. Anyway, if Whitehall did that, then they could charge people for entering Wales. A toll was placed on the bridge, one way only. In to Wales! The majority of the Welsh, were therefore non-Welsh speaking.

Previously, Whitehall had merged the boundaries of several counties together. Disregarding that some, with just a sprinkling of population actually spoke Welsh. The other and more densely populated counties only spoke English. The obvious result was then ensured. The minority claiming lingual persecution and threats of ethnic cleansing in Cardigan. A council chamber was set up in Carmarthen with instantaneous translation services and everything was conducted in Welsh! A blind eye being turned to the fact that all persons concerned could speak English perfectly well and for most it was their mother tongue. All road signs were bilingual, all official forms and documents written in both languages. Hence everything from a driving licence to a Danger Men At Work, sign became twice as large and twice the cost. The Welsh had learned a lesson and knew very well that any Welsh Parliament would end up the same way. An expensive talking shop for "Goggoes". Knee deep in bilingual paper work! No matter, the Assembly was thrust upon them. In some ways though the Welsh did get the last laugh. They democratically voted out Whitehall's man and refused point blank to purchase an Assembly building at GBP 26 million and thus denying lucrative opportunities for English construction companies. They were however stuck with Myreg Cwmyurr and the nationalists.

Back in Pembrokeshire, the storm had blown itself out, and Boggle 1 and Boggle 2 were high and dry on the beach, and on the other side of the river. A somewhat ignominious fate for both of the Conservancy's vessels. An irony that was not lost on the editor of The Milford Haven Weekly Gazette, as he now had both before and after photographs. They ran the story, and with it wrote about the peculiar seaweed that had been the original cause of the incident. It was an excited CIA man, on the following Saturday morning that broke the news to his colleagues over their Ashdale Field Centre breakfast of boiled eggs. This at last was the break they had been seeking! The CIA went to Code Red.

Fifteen shot, 9mm. automatic pistols were produced and stripped down on the tablecloth, and chambers of Smith and Wesson magnums spun. One of the younger men produced a couple of Armourlite rifles and a rocket grenade launcher. All of which was observed with growing horror by the short, fat foreign waitress with the vestigial moustache. She was an economic migrant from Eastern Europe. Of late, hordes of such people had descended upon Britain seeking the good life. Unfortunately, the concept of a good life to some had been one of begging, along with their children on the London Underground. Begging being regarded in their own country as being a perfectly worthwhile and honourable occupation, more so in a rich country. That obviously being the best place in which to ply one's trade and thus be able to send money back to Aunty Retski and Uncle Bezovik in the old country. However, the sight of endless, shapeless, beady, black eyed women in head scarves, baggy boots and shawls, poking their unwashed and scruffy children into the faces of passengers, whilst holding out a dirty, claw like hand, did not sit too well with either commuters or Government alike. Britain, in spite of the incompetence of its leaders, was after all, still the forth-richest country in the world. When all was said and done, some tourist might mistake one of these vagrants for the home produced article and that would never do. Consequently, they were collected up and forcible dispatched and dispersed around the country in an attempt to keep them as far away from London as possible.

Pilka Drobranowic was one such person. She had been interred, behind barbed wire at the local refugee camp at Trcwn. An ex Ministry of Defence establishment sited in Pembrokeshire that the Government had upon investigation found that they owned, maintained and hadn't used in donkey's years. It had taken Pilka and her colleagues about fifteen minutes to find a way out and five days for her to find illegal employment at Ashdale Field Centre. The wages from which along with UK Government handouts, she found more than satisfactory. However, she still did a bit of begging outside Woolworth's in Haverfordwest on the odd Saturday afternoon in the summer, just to keep her hand in. For all that, Pilka knew all about guns and the damage that they can inflict. She assumed that these dark suited individuals were in fact secret police come to drag her away from her soft job and perks of nice tins of dog food she had been stealing and sending back to Aunty Retski. Her aunt specially favouring the ones with the extra jelly. She promptly, threw her hands in the air with a shriek. Hands that seconds earlier had been holding a tray, upon which were extra Cornflakes and milk. Pilka dropped into a fainted heap of large pleated black skirt, billowy blouse and red headscarf.

The warden appeared. To see what all the fuss was about. That his guests were CIA, he knew and accepted. After all, their business was their business. They paid the bill on time, were no trouble and were nice to his dog. Playing in the sea was one thing, tooling up with high-powered weaponry and upsetting his staff was another.

"Here now. What you boys think you're all up to then?" He stood there in the doorway in his shirtsleeves. He wished now he had put on his official warden's hat. The one with the nice shiny chrome badge. It made no difference. He was ignored as the CIA team pushed him aside and headed for the beach and their powerboat.

The warden scratched his head and poked Pilka with his toe, hoping that they hadn't shot her and thus make life even more complicated for him. Thankfully she stirred. "Clean up this mess gal, then push off home back to the camp. I'll have to phone Pritchard the police about all this lot. Don't want you around complicating matters." He helped her to mop up the spilt milk and broken crockery, then slipped her a couple of quid to keep quiet and sent her back to the government refugee internment camp with instructions to keep her mouth shut. Pilka nodded gratefully and took the proffered cash. The warden phoned the local constable as he heard the motor on the powerboat finally start. He had hired it to the CIA and he knew full well how temperamental it could be.

"Pritchard Boyo, its Williams the warden from the field centre here. Yes, Williams. Yes I knows its early boy, but this might be important. You knows all of those CIA boys that have been staying with me. Yes, good as gold theys been boy. No trouble, Well........ Not until this morning like. Nows theys all got big guns and shot off in the boat somewhere. How the Hell do I know wheres theys gone? I'm standing here on the phone to you! Well I don't care if your bunions is giving you gip. Don't wear your boots Boy if they hurts you. Best get yourself around here. What you mean your cousin Alf up at High Beck Farm has borrowed the Police Range Rover? Well, when will he be finished moving the caravan? That's too late. Best you come on the push bike then. I knows it's all uphill coming here from the village, but you won't have to peddle on the way back then will you?"

And so it was that Police Constable Pritchard, carefully put on his trainers, lacing them lightly over his bunions, and peddled off to take charge of investigations at the field centre.

The MI6 team was holding an important meeting. They could see from the activities of their CIA counterparts that the Americans were getting ready to give up, pack up and go home. This placed the MI6 team in rather a dilemma. Syd Gammage threw a mean dart, whilst Gordon Sprew was a dab hand at dominoes. The darts league, in which they stood a fair chance of taking the championship, would not wind up for another four weeks. Whereas Gordon Sprew was through to the semi finals in the domino team. Though up against stiff competition from the boys at The Dog and Ferrets. They had it on good authority too the The Dog and Ferrets were about to bring in a substitute player. The twin brother of one of their team from Tenby or some place. They had all the facilities of their offices on the South Bank checking this out, and if it were true they intended to have him kidnapped on the night in question and placed aboard a fast train for Greenock. The agenda for the meeting being one of deciding should they remain in their present lodgings at The Ferryman and go with the darts, hoping to string the job out for another four weeks. Or move to The Jolly Matelot and concentrate on the domino championship. Also on the agenda was whether or not to send a nice letter to Sven in the Falklands in reply to his postcards.

Syd Gammage was in the chair and fending off a motion for moving to The Jolly Matelot, on the grounds that he was having it away with the barmaid and they were all benefiting from free beer from time to time. It was into this hot bed of top secret discussions that Syd's barmaid, the over proportioned Rita, yelled across to them from over the pumps, that it was MI6 on the phone. Something about sea weed and did they want to take it in the office, as it sounded private like? It was whilst Syd was on the phone that the CIA team was spotted zipping upstream and past the The Ferryman's panoramic window that overlooked the Haven. MI6 swung its well-oiled machine into action.

Constable Pritchard meanwhile, mincing along on his bunions and sweating profusely, was pushing the bike up hill and regretting that he had hired out the Police Range Rover to his cousin Alf, in exchange for some sacks of potatoes and onions, for the purpose of moving a caravan. It was a warm day, and an Indian summer had been forecast.

The CIA team was doing about 30 miles per hour. The boat was capable of more, but tended to take on a lot of spray, and they didn't see the need to get wet. It wasn't until they were actually on the water that they realised that no one was quite sure of where they were supposed to be heading. So, they just headed up the river, cutting a neat creamy wake across the estuary in the early morning sun light.

The MI6 team, all piled into their white van, and knowing that they would be faster by road headed for where the Cleddau River began to form into The Haven and the toll bridge that connected Neyland to Pembroke Dock. Two places that time had long since forgotten. Neyland, they knew had a yacht club. Yacht clubs contained boats. Their cunning plan was to requisition a suitable boat, two in fact. One they could use to effectively blockade the river mouth in the area of the bridge, and with the other, pursue the CIA. They would then have only one route, ever up stream.

The Haven is a very large expanse of water, running roughly east west. The second largest natural harbour in the World. Sydney Harbour, in Australia holding the prime position. At roughly the point where The Cleddau River begins to open out a large and expensive bridge had been constructed linking each side of the river. During its construction, it had actually collapsed, thus adding to its cost. An argument then took place between Welsh and English authorities as to who would foot the bill for the burgeoning construction costs. A compromise situation finally being agreed whereby a heavy toll was placed upon the bridge and the costs then being passed onto the motorist. For all that, the bridge was quite a splendid affair, tall, slim and elegant. Anyone, who didn't know, could actually be fooled into thinking that they were crossing some important, major, geographical gateway. An illusion that would be quickly dispelled by the row of Victorian houses and launderette that comprised Neyland on the one side. Or a sign that informed one that Flying boats used to take off from Pembroke Dock, 50 years ago, on the other. From the bridge, up stream, The Cleddau continues as one river, then splitting into its two arms. It was close to this confluence of those two arms, Boggle 1 and 2 lay beached, and on the foreshore that fronted Gerald Fatslobe's property.

The MI6 team, out ran the CIA to Neyland with ease. Confidently they swung their white van into the entrance of Neyland Yacht Club. NYC, as displayed upon its jolly little triangular pennants, had been established for many years. It had a nice snug little bar, a darts board and a friendly atmosphere. It also owned a large compound, full of sailing dinghy's. This being the original purpose of the club. Of latter years it had grown and now also involved itself in water skiing and jet skis too. Though the power boats types had fought many a long battle with the purists of sail. Neyland Yacht Club served a useful social function in as much it provided a harbour of peace, pipe smoke, ale and tranquillity, for those souls wishing to escape from the rigours of domesticity and their wives. Or, alternatively, provided a venue for other and more extroverted souls who otherwise would have been the subject of cruel jest, should they have minced along the High Street dressed in funny little caps with gold braid on them and striped jerseys. For all of its cosmopolitan attitude though, NYC was not exactly geared up to having an MI6 team suddenly descend upon it and demand, "We want a power boat. Two."

The ageing custodian of the bar, being fully aware, as he was, of the laws governing the sale of alcohol and tobacco to underage customer and non club members demurred. "Are you members?"

"No. We're MI6" The agent waved a wallet with his identity card, at the custodian.

"Not members then?" The custodian was very calm and deliberate. He had after all attended a course entitled, "How to deal with situations of confrontation, within the hotel and catering industry." Held at a local college. Not that at the age of 59, he had wanted to, but it had all come as part and parcel of taking the part time job, under the Governments, Back To work Scheme, and he hadn't had a choice if he wished to continue drawing benefits. He quietly took the proffered wallet and patted his pockets for his spectacles, as he did so. Finally locating them next to him on the bar counter. He placed them carefully upon his nose, whilst the MI6 man hopped up and down with impatience. "M.16"

"No. M.I.6."

"Says M.16 down here boy. What's you doing then? Building some motorway are we?" He looked over his glasses expectantly at the agent.

"No you fool! We're Secret Service."

"Ere! Who you calling a fool then? Anyways, if yous Secret Service, what you doing telling me for? Wouldn't be a secret then would it? Stands to reason boy. That's called logic that is." He nodded his head in self-confirmation. The custodian had once attempted an Open University course in Philosophy, but given up after a week as he found that most of the words were too long. The cleaning lady, the only other occupant, stopped mopping and looked on in interest.

"We want two boats."

"Well, you'll just have to fill out a membership form and you will be considered at the next meeting. That's the rules." He looked belligerently at the MI6 man from over the bar top. Then mollified a little, and said almost grudgingly, "You can have associate membership straight away, if you want a drink. But the bar's not open until ten o'clock." Further discussions being interrupted at this point by one of his team sticking his head around the door and shouting, "They're coming around the headland boss." Which galvanised the team leader into decision taking mode.

"Commandeer suitable craft." He declared, importantly, and turning to the somewhat bemused barman said in his best authoritative voice, "This is Government business!"

"You 'ain't commandeering nothing boy, and you can move that van too."

The head of the MI6 team was in no mood to bother with troublesome barmen, he produced his Walther PK9 and waved it in the general direction of the bar.

"And you can put that bloody silly thing away too!" Declared the now annoyed and rather red-faced custodian, who added firmly, "I'm phoning the Secretary. We don't want no hooligans in here. And the police." He added as an after thought. "Pritchard the Police will soon sort you lot out. Skin Heads is what you lot are!" He picked up the phone as the MI6 man disappeared through the door, shouting after him, "And move that van!"

Down at the water's edge, Phillis and her sister Dorris, had just completed putting the finishing touches to their recently purchased and very over priced, multi coloured wet suits, and were about to go water skiing. They were both in their early thirty's and lived in Birmingham. Their respective husbands both being in the second-hand car business. All four of them had never quite completed secondary education, and possessed impressive Midlands Accents. However, wealth whilst not changing them had caused them all to aspire to a higher social level. They regarded water skiing as being the sort of thing that a certain class of people did. People that occupied the niche to which they aspired. Therefore, it followed that they too should learn to water ski. Further more, they had all paid a deposit on a forth-coming package holiday in The Bahamas and wanted to at least acquire some degree of proficiency, and thus be able to impress their friends upon arrival. Friends, all of whom without exception, were of a similar background to themselves and also all frantically trying to acquire skills that they too regarded as being essential social attributes and thus elevating their station within their own peer group. A peer group that invariably was at a loss as to know which fork to use, thought Plato was a washing up liquid and wanted tomato ketchup with everything. No, wealth had not altered them one jot. Whilst their respective husbands sailed close to the law, Phillis and Dorris remained basically the same pair of big breasted, painted, cheerful slappers they had always been. Consequently they could afford to drive down from Birmingham at weekends and don fancy ski suits. Naturally, their powerboats were also state of the art machines. Impressive fibre glass beasts, with sharks jaws painted on their prows and engines large enough to be the envy of a formula one racing car driver. It was these two boats that MI6 commandeered.

The husbands of the two women were standing by their craft. Enjoying a last minute cigarette, and discussing the demise of the British Motor Industry, when their attention was drawn to the fact that a bunch of armed men had jumped aboard their two boats. Then they cast off, fully opening the throttles of the already running engines. The boats had literally blasted off and were now shooting away from the astonished men. With their two unfortunate women still tethered behind. They stood bemused, and unsure, Benson and Hedges, drooping from their lips, watching silently as the kidnapping took place. Brian was the first to break the silence. "Bloody 'ell Kevin. Didyow see that?"

"Ar I did........ Cheeky sods! That's a new boat that is. I 'ain't even paid furit yet! They berra not bluddy bend it. That's all I can say!"

The custodian arrived to give solace and comfort. "I've phoned the Police." He informed the pair. "That's kidnapping that is, and they haven't moved their van either."

Police Constable Prichard's wife took the message at home. The washing machine had just burst a hose and was leaking all over her kitchen floor. She had switched it off and was busy mopping up. Being a policeman's wife she was used to taking odd messages and further more knew exactly how to get her priorities right. She completed her clean up operation, phoned Gibbons the plumber and then set about contacting her husband. She phoned him at Ashdale Field Centre with the news that a gang of armed men had stolen two speed boats from the Neyland Yacht Club and were heading in the direction of The Jolly Matelot. Oh, yes and something about abducting a pair of women too and by the way Gibbons the plumber had a hose in stock and for him to collect it on his way home.

PC Pritchard had only a bicycle and was also several miles away. Obviously this gang of armed men were one and the same. He did what any sensible Police officer would do under the circumstances. More so when instructed to pick up a spare washing machine hose. He too commandeered transport. And thus it came about that a policeman, wearing trainers and driving the Asdale Lada pickup, ended up on the neat and tidy lawns of The Jolly Matelot. Along with some early morning drinkers. Watching the antics of MI6 and the CIA, plus two terrified female water skiers, as they pursued each other up and down the reaches of the Cleddau River. He phoned headquarters in Carmarthen and then his cousin telling him to bring the Range Rover over as fast as possible and not to forget his boots either.

At Heddlu, which is Welsh for police, headquarters in Carmarthen, the story of armed men immediately rang a bell with the desk sergeant. Recently Mad Myreg as he was known locally had been making firebrand speeches. Well, it was assumed that they were firebrand speeches, and that's what the

English/Welsh translation leaflet had said. Firebrand speech on behalf oh the Welsh Nationalists. Though there was little chance of any fires starting anywhere with the amount of spit that Mad Myreg was throwing every which way.

The Welsh Nationalist Party having Spin Doctors of its own, in the image of, if lacking the sophistication of the New Deal Democratic Party. They basically operated along the lines of telling Myreg to get up and spout and spit for a set period of time, and wave his arms about a lot. Then gave the speech they had concocted to the translator, who just read it. A ploy that suited all persons concerned. Personally he thought that Myreg should stand for London Mayor, every other odd ball in the country seemed to want the job. He informed his superior, and so it got passed up the line until finally, the Chief Constable was informed. He knew that the SAS were holding abseiling exercises from helicopters up and down the cliffs. Their major belonged to the same Masonic Lodge as himself and they had been drinking together the previous evening. He decided that it was a job for them, and, accordingly, phoned his friend.

The resultant confusion with two boats, complete with female water skiers in garish wet suits, chasing one other boat and helicopters flying overhead, with soldiers in combat jackets and camouflage face paint, hanging from ropes. Trying in vain to deposit themselves into three separate speed boats was worthy of the very best of Hong Kong spy movies, and would provide subject matter for discussions at all levels for years to come. Home videos were made, and though themselves subject to the Official Secrets Act, many would be clandestinely copied and sold. It was after all, one of the biggest security cock-ups of all times, and certainly the best one for America since The Bay Of Pigs. Finally, boats, helicopters and skiers, having put on quite a show for the patrons of The Jolly Matelot, and brought all traffic to a stand still on the Cleddau Toll Bridge, shot off up stream to appreciative applause. Folks naturally thinking that it was all part of some new Bond movie. PC Pritchard sat half in and half out of his Lada, easing his aching feet, clad in red and blue trainers, and licked his pencil stub thoughtfully. He was rather a loss of what to write. He decided to have a pint of Hoghtons best badger bitter and give the matter some thought whilst he awaited the arrival of his cousin with official Police transport and his boots.

It was the weed that eventually brought all matters to a stop. Literally. All three boats sheared their props and came to a sudden halt. The hysterical and terrified skiers glided to a rather anticlimactic and gentle standstill, and the helicopters hovered. The furore that then subsequently ensued was of magnificent proportions. The CIA all claimed to be ecological attaches attached to the American Embassy and thus had diplomatic immunity. The two females, still having hysterics were incarcerated for their own good under section two of the mental health act. There they could be assessed, or more to the point, checked out to see how much they knew. Their husbands were cautioned under the Official Secrets Act, but not before they had began legal action for the theft of two powerboats. Action once started had to be allowed to stand as it had been lodged prior to their being cautioned. Their solicitor, seeing the chance of building himself a nice little pension fund, immediately referred the case The Court Of Human Rights in Strasbourg. Their wife's case being taken up by Amnesty International and both women featuring on the cover of Time Magazine.

Willie Clayton meanwhile, with his beloved Lulu in tow, had jumped aboard Airforce One to fly to Britain, retrieve his sea weed and sort those Limey Jerks out once and for all.

Meddlesome programmed Toni to cordon off the whole area with razor wire and armed troops. A message that Bradford found hilarious as he knew that his father's farm was now effectively in the centre of a military exclusion zone.

The SAS, having been denied the chance of shooting at least one person, became very miffed, and all packed up and went back to Hereford, refusing to have any more to do with the matter.

The Welsh Nationalists however, seeing their window of opportunity opening up before them, but still in the dark as to what exactly all the fuss was about. Claimed traditional Bardic rights over all blue stone areas under some archaic Eisteddfod ruling dating back to Owyn Glyndour. A claim that was taken up by the whole Welsh nation, both within and outside Wales. No one at that point may have known what exactly was involved, but they were bright enough to work out that if Whitehall was prepared to go to such lengths to obtain it, then it was of value. Pretty soon however, within hours, word was out that it concerned seaweed. Speculation as to what exactly were the properties of this seaweed at that point became rife. Beyond all doubt though, it grew in Wales, and only on Blue Stone. It followed then that it came under the control of Wales, who after all now had an elected Assembly. An elected Assembly that had been forced upon them by Whitehall. Game, set and match.

Willie Clayton was pissed off. He had organised the IRA to arrange for the break out of Solly and his gang from The Maze Prison. He had even supplied the explosives with which to effect the escape. Some new chemical that his military people had assured him was vastly superior to anything else on the market and since it was also brand new, having never been used before, untraceable. The IRA though, were having problems of their own. All of the old hands, having now either made sufficient money out of raiding banks in the name of freedom to retire, or having become politicians, and thus availing themselves of making considerably more. They were no longer interested in blowing up prisons, no matter how worthy the cause. It then fell upon the younger and less experienced members to undertake the work. Which they did with more will than actual hands on knowledge. Whilst the zeal of their younger contemporaries merited applause, it would have perhaps have been expedient for them to have tempered their youthful enthusiasm with caution. The end result being that the whole of the south walls of The Maze were vaporised along with the demolition team. The remainder of the prison suffering severe structural damage. Consequently, as everyone rushed to view the huge smoking crater in the South, a rather dazed and totally deaf Solly and his gang staggered out of the creaking front gate, at the North. From there they had made their way, albeit unsteadily, though no one takes much notice of a staggering Irishman, to the waiting submarine and the passage home to America. Willie wasn't bothered too much about that lot. What had concerned Willie was the subsequent plan that involved Solly breaking into the offices of Shock Weekly, bugging the place and taking any evidence that incriminated him with Lulu. That had been a foul up of Biblical proportions.

Not only had Solly ended up in the wrong building, he was even in the wrong district! All of his men and Solly himself still deaf and suffering from post traumatic stress. Instead of breaking into a nice quiet newspaper office with perhaps a couple of old janitors playing chequers amongst the pipes in the basement, at the best. Solly found himself breaking into The Convent Of The Little Sisters Of Mercy. Which in actual fact was a front for an anti government, para military survival group known as The Right Wing American White Brotherhood. An organisation that had been, unbeknown to them, under surveillance from the Black Panthers, who occupied the building opposite. Solly suddenly found himself in the middle of a shooting match between red beret wearing blacks on the one hand and bearded, white, abseiling nuns carrying Ruger machine pistols on the other. Not to mention the crack addicts and junkies down in the street who were letting loose with whatever handguns they carried, assuming it was police raid. The whole experience, coming on top of only just recently having been blown up, proving just too much for Solly to take. He had resigned his commission as head of the Jewish Mafia and retired to a trailer home for senior citizens in Florida.

Naturally the New York Tribune and The Boston Post were now investigating the minor war that had taken place, and the body count involved. An investigation that stood the very high chance of being carried out with greater expertise and vigour shown by the editor and employees of Shock Weekly.

What irked Willie even more was that Shock weekly had subsequently run their story on him. However, as shock Weekly was confined to being sold off super market shelves and normally confined itself to such journalistic gems as, "My dog was abducted by aliens", or even one feature that claimed that Prince Philip had once been a drummer with Meat Loaf, no one had batted an eye lid or had taken any notice what so ever. Now however, there had been mayhem in the streets of Washington DC. The CIA were up to no good on the other side of the Atlantic and The President was suddenly off over there again, along with that blond piece with the big tits. If two and two didn't quite at this point add up to four, then for sure if they could hint it added up to five and a quarter. That would sell papers, and that was their business. Willie was well pissed off! So much so that he sat in his big leather swivel chair on Air Force One, swinging from side to side for the whole trip. Even though Lulu was in the on board state bedroom wearing her leather, dyke on a bike gear.

Toni had been placed in Charm and smarm mode. Meddlesome could see that the sea weed's potential was enormous. If Britain controlled it, and it was Britain's turn to head the EEC. Then there was the potential for Britain to control Europe with Toni at its head. Therefore, if he could dump Gobbleton and Heigar, he would effectively be in control.

Heigar too could see the same possibilities, though she planned to dump Meddlesome and Gobbleton. The snag being that she was no longer sure just what programmes Meddlesome was running. Still, IT experts were ten a penny, so she saw no difficulties in getting a tame one later.

Gobbleton and Te'Upp naturally wanted the sea weed for themselves. He being under the impression that he would retire to a life of oriental luxury in Taiwan, with Te'Upp at his side, or better still, underneath. She, on the other hand, planned to pass the sea weed on to her Government in Hanoi and dump the munt with the hairy, groping hands as fast as possible.

Gerald now found his pig farm, to his consternation, not only the focus of attention, but in the centre of a military exclusion zone, and politically, being in a position of being unable to do other than to support his parties policy and grin and bear it.

Al Arrod was no further forward in obtaining his much-coveted British Passport and in an exposed position.

Myreg and the Nationalists had already decided that the seaweed belonged to Wales, and no one else. They were busy mobilising the Free Welsh Army.

Bradford and Peter monitored all messages and progress with glee, and Tiffany started to knit baby socks.

Toni met Willie Clayton in private in number ten. Toni was in smarm and charm mode. Lulu, who had never been inside number ten had insisted on coming along. She claimed that Willie owned her that much, as he had ignored her on the flight over. Willie by this time had other things on his mind, namely getting this stupid, plastic Brit to hand over his seaweed. Toni however was being difficult.

"Well you see Willie, one has to look at the global picture. Take more of an overview, so to speak. I mean, after all is said and done, it is actually growing in Britain."

"So am I Toni, but you don't own me!"

"Yes, I take your point. But we all know who you are, I mean how do you actually, I mean sort of positively identify this seaweed as being yours? The Welsh for instance, claim that it's theirs."

"Jesus Toni! Everyone and their dog will claim it, given the opportunity."

"Well. Er, yes. Quite. Exactly the point that I personally was making."

"Look, Goddamnit! Ask yourself a question Toni. Was the sea weed there before that damn ship went down?"

"Well, personally, frankly Willie, I mean, er, I can't say. I mean, er, it might have been. If one looks at the big picture, that is."

"Give me my Goddam seaweed Toni! Before I send the marines in and Damn well take it!"

"Now Willie. Er, that's no way to talk. Special relationship and all that."

"Stuff your special relationship, you Limey faggot!" Willie Clayton had to stop. He was purple with rage and beginning to choke. Lulu, who had witnessed the whole conversation from the settee was looking up at him with ever growing alarm.

"Willie sweetie pie, calm down, don't shout so. It's only a bit of old seaweed. It's not worth getting upset about." Willie Clayton sort of half suffocated in anger and turned the whole of his fury on her.

"A bit of old sea weed! You stupid Bitch!" He stormed out of the room, leaving Toni and a now sobbing Lulu.

Toni was still in charm and smarm mode. "There, there. Not to worry. Just a little tiff. How about a nice cup of tea?" He sat down beside the distraught Lulu.

"He's never spoken to me like that before." Lulu sobbed.

"Well, er, not to worry. Look at this way...." It was at this point that Bradford, having perfected his duplicate signal, activated it. Toni switched to earnest and sincere mode. "I actually find you a very attractive young lady and it really does touch me right here." He indicated his heart, "To see you so upset."

"Really Toni? Does it?"

"Oh yes. I feel that his behaviour was quite uncalled for. More so when one realises that he was addressing a charming and sweet person such as yourself." Toni gave her the benefit of his best earnest and you must believe me look.

"Oh Toni, you say the sweetest things. You have the cutest accent too." Bradford sent the second signal. Toni moved into Confident and aggressive mode. "Let me wipe your eyes with my handkerchief." He produced a large linen handkerchief from his pocket.

"Oh Toni, you have such strong hands, but so gentle too." Lulu looked at him and held his hand. Toni smiled down at her, exuding confidence. Bradford changed the signal again. Toni immediately placed his hand upon Lulu's more that adequate breasts.

"Why Toni, you mustn't. "But she made no attempt to move his hands. Toni was now exploring inside of her blouse with one hand, whilst investigating the contents of her skirt with his other. "Oh Toni." Gasped Lulu. But Toni was locked into sex mode and was removing her clothing with the speed of an eight-armed Indian God on viagara. "Oh Toni." Was all Lulu managed to gasp as her bra flew one way and her panties another. She lay there, her naked and more than voluptuous body ready for the taking. Toni threw off his clothes, displaying his massive throbbing phallus.

Lulu's eyes goggled at the enormity of his purple-headed weapon. "Oh Toni." Was all she managed to gasp as he was upon her.

With one deft move, Toni threw her legs open wide and plunged himself into her, as the door opened and Willie Clayton stood aghast at the scene unfolded in front of him. "This means WAR! You Limey Bastard" He slammed the door.

"Oh Toni." Murmured Lulu.

CHAPTER. 9

Two things had really upset Willie Clayton. It wasn't just that the Prime Minister of Great Britain was stuck up to the hilt in his woman. Alliances with foreign countries he knew, were peculiar animals, and sometimes one had to take a rather broader view of things. One should not be too judgmental in these matters, even if the other party did appear to have more faults than normal. He would for instance, have been perfectly happy had he have found Toni stuck up his wife. No, what really pissed him off was that Toni had not only ignored his standing in the doorway, it was the size of Toni's tackle! He always had the feeling that this Limey Jerk was a pepperoni short on the pizza but that donger of his really was abnormal! Obviously that was where he kept his brains. No wonder all that stupid cow of a woman could do was murmur, "Oh Toni!" It was a wonder the end of his dick wasn't poking out of her mouth at each thrust. America was the country that was supposed to build everything bigger and better. He was after all supposed to be the most powerful man in the World, and here was this little, plastic, Limey faggot, not only hung like a Godamn Donkey, but also giving it to his mistress like a steam engine, and ignoring him too. He was going to mobilise, grab his seaweed and to Hell with the consequences.

It was Heigar that eventually discovered Toni. A Toni still programmed for sex, still giving it to Lulu and still with an erection. The rest of Toni though was not holding up so well. He had a glazed look about his sweat-streaked face, and was on the verge of collapse. Lulu had long ago fainted off into cloud of ecstatic, sexually stimulated oblivion, and apart from lying totally supine, was not capable of anything, other than to still give the occasional moan of, "Oh Toni."

Heigar managed to pull Toni from off her, and on to the floor. There he lay on his back. On the Persian carpet. Still maintaining an erection, and weakly moved up and down rhythmically. She phoned Meddlesome with instructions to get around to Number Ten immediately. This was an emergency!

Meddlesome arrived, and took in the scene before him in one glance.

"Dear God Heigar! What the Hell have you been doing? Look at his colour! All the blood in his body has rushed to his dick. Get his head down and his legs up in the air, before he passes out and suffers brain stem death. Not that anyone would notice." He muttered under his breath, as Toni still continued to pump up and down weakly. "Hit the sleep mode Woman."

"I already have!" Heigar replied angrily. "Something has gone wrong with your programme." She pushed in futile exasperation at her hand held console. Coincidentally, at that point, Bradford exited from his programme and Toni, now once again under Hegira's control passed out. "Shit! He's died on us. Start mouth to mouth!"

"No, he hasn't Heigar. He's still breathing. Look, his dick is going down and the colour is coming back to his cheeks. Good God Heigar, what the Hell did you need a sex programme for. He's got prick the size of a babies forearm!" He looks like an advert for Viagara!"

"That's my business. What has gone wrong with your programme I want to know? Do you know who that is?" She indicated the naked, sweating mound of flesh that was Lulu. A Lulu that could not have been further beyond recall than if she had been smoking opium. A Lulu that continued to murmur, "Oh Toni." and lie there like a sack of wet potatoes.

"Of course I do. It's that ugly fat cow Clayton likes to poke. So what?"

"What happens if Clayton finds out?"

"Oh sure. The President of America is going to make a public fuss over the fact that his girl friend has been given one on the settee in Number Ten by The Prime Minister Of Great Britain. I don't think! No, though he may well get the CIA to lace your corn flakes with anthrax. Just get her up, dressed, back on this planet, and send her on her way rejoicing. It's the programme that we have to worry about, not the damage he's done to her. Anyway, nothing a good plastic surgeon and 30 or 40 internal stitches won't fix. Willie will never know the difference. Mind you, she probably will. No doubt Claton's willie will feel like a baby carrot compared to that bloody great marrow she has just eaten! I have to hand it to you Heigar; you can take a Damn sight more than I can. You make me feel quite envious!"

Willie Clayton flew back to Washington alone. He would mobilise. Irrespective of the wishes of the Congress, or the Senate. He was head of the American Armed Forces, and he was getting his seaweed back. He would teach that Prime Minister of Britain that he might be able to fuck with Lulu, but no way was he going to fuck with Willie Clayton. He picked up the phone and placed America on an War footing.

CNN broke the news to a stunned world. The special Alliance was off. Sea weed, or else!

Myreg Cwmyurr had been enjoying life. Not only was he head of the Welsh Nationalist Party and as such got to eat regularly, but that little dark haired minx of a secretary, Rhonan Phillips was sleeping with him too. The salary wasn't much good, but the allowances he received from being a member of the Welsh Assembly and the perks in the shape of Rhonan, were, on the whole, pretty good. Now, though, it seemed that this miracle, feed the world seaweed was growing on the Blue stone of the Cleddau River estuary. Furthermore, the Yanks were prepared to go to war to take it, claiming that it was theirs. How the Hell anything that grew in Wales, could be anything other than Welsh, was beyond the logic capabilities of both Myreg and his party. Obviously, this seaweed needed defending. Myreg mobilised The Free Welsh Army. A shadowy organisation that consisted of eleven members in total. Six of them being out of work sixteen year olds. Drafted in on a Government sponsored work experience scheme, by an over zealous clerk from the Punjab. Who worked in one of Cardiff's Job Centres and hadn't as yet quite got the hang of the job. The other five consisting of four academics from Aberystwyth University and one "Baron De Clacey" A homicidal maniac with delusions of grandeur, who had recently escaped from a secure mental institution near Oswestry.

There was an emergency meeting of the Cabinet called to be held in Number Ten. Both Heigar and Meddlesome were terrified that Toni would run amok again. So much so that they had hot-wired him to the mains. As the slightest hint of problems they would give Toni a quick boost of 240 volts and claim sudden illness. Toni, though obviously weak and needing assistance to stand, this being put down to the stress of office, ran perfectly. The only thing that Meddlesome could come up with was for Toni to insist that obviously Willie Clayton was suffering from an illness, jet lag, food poisoning brought on by the tinned salmon soufflé. They had to stall for time. They would appeal to the Secretary on the United Nations. The fact that the UN in the main consisted of America and Britain was studiously ignored. In short, as usual, The New Deal Democratic Party hadn't a clue.

Back in Wales, the sudden crisis was all too coincidental for Bradford and Peter. They sat together, whilst Tiffany plied them with pizza that she had recently mastered the art of cooking.

"It can't just be coincidence Brad." Said Peter, through a mouth full of pizza. "I mean, the signals are coming from Heigar's home in Austria. Her father, is some crazy professor. She being married to the PM and all. Then you blip the airwaves, and Bingo! Third world War."

"Another interesting thing that I discovered Peter is about our dear Heigar's old man. I did my homework and guess what? Seems like the nutty professor has had some bee in his bonnet about stimulating the brain with electrical currents to produce a known reaction. Daughter Heigar has a Doctorate in neuro psychology, what ever that is. And then there is the meteoric rise to power of our friend Toni. I mean, anyone with only half a brain can see that he is just some plastic front man for The Party."

"OK Brad, but where does that leave us?"

"Yes, who exactly is The Party?" It was Tiffany posing a question. She had joined them around the cosy AGA and was busy cutting up another pizza.

"Exactly Tiff." Exclaimed Peter. "Who is the party. Who is controlling whom and what are their ambitions?"

"Well, who ever they are, then they are pretty sinister, but I don't believe they intended to allow things to go this far." Bradford shook his head. "No. Spin-doctors run the machine. The snag is they are all spinning so fast and in so many directions at once, Toni must have lost his balance. Maybe it's coincidence and Toni is not connected to the strange signals. Though the odds seem pretty long. When I ran through that programme, I hadn't expected to open up this can of worms. I wonder what the five signals are? I mean what do they control. What is their purpose?"

"Hmm." Said Tiffany, sitting down with them, "Let's Just consider friend Toni for the moment. Think what all politicians need."

"Personality and the ability to lie with ease and conviction, I suppose." Replied Peter rather cynically through a mouthful of pizza.

"True Peter, true." Agreed Tiffany. "But wouldn't he, or she also need to come over as being sincere and at times be able to force a point and also shout down the opposition now and again? OK, by moving the goal posts and sloping the pitch, I agree. There again, you look at Toni, how he performs. Patently, he is plastic. Anyone can see that. He never answers a question. Or if he does, he does so in a way that removes himself from all accountability. If he is pushed into corner, then he promptly attacks the opposition parties record, alters the facts a little, moves the argument. Poses his own question, and then answers it and moves on. All of course to the cheers of his parties benches. Which are actually shouts of relief that he has wriggled out of the net again. Look how he dealt with the scandal over State old peoples homes. First of all he reduced their funding so that they could hardly provide a service. Then when families were loath to put poor old granny into such a cesspit, he closed the lot down on the pretext that they were under used and costing money. Then sold the lot off to some private medical company, that rumour has it is owned by some relation to the Minister for Health. I don't for one instance believe that he has the brainpower to work out these ploys by himself. Someone is running him. He is just the front man. He gets away with it due to his personality. Smarm, false sincerity and a bit of bullying. Oh yes and that God awful grin of his."

"Well, that takes care of three programmes Tiff." Laughed Brad. "What about the other two. Are you going to eat that other pieces of pizza Pete? This is jolly good Tiff. I never knew that you could cook."

"Oh, I'm getting better at all sorts of things Brad." Replied his sister smiling. "You two boys don't have to fight over the last piece, there is plenty more in the oven, along with something else."

"So." Said Peter. "We think that we may be able to account for three programmes. Programmes whose signals we believe are being transmitted from Castle Kutzanburnz in Austria. Signals that it would seem sensible to assume, are tied in with Heigar and her father. So, what do we have? A self-learning programme on a main frame computer set up in Herr Doktor's dungeons. A computer that is triggered to run one of five programmes. Those five programmes being triggered by a signal that originates from close to Toni. Toni then runs as if on rails. So who is running him? Obvious Heigar at this end. Her father knows nothing about computers, neither does Heigar. He is then just left alone in the castle to pop coins in the meter and make sure the electricity doesn't go off. Who is close to Toni at this end who knows his way around a Computer programme?"

"Meddlesome and Gobbleton!" Exclaimed Peter and Tiffany together.

"Exactly! Two Spin-Doctors! So all we have to do now, if to confirm which signal serves what function, and we control the PM." Bradford sat back with a smile. This situation appealed to the hacker inside of him.

"So how do we go about that Brad?" It was Tiffany asking the question.

"Elementary, my dear Watson. By observation. Now let's put ourselves in their position. My burst of signals must have snarled things up no end. More so since I forgot to shut down for a while. Since they are using the mobile phone microwave system, when I left my end open, I blocked them. All they were getting was the engaged tone. No this needs some more work. I need to build in a feed back system. I want to be able to transmit my signal. If they then notice and retransmit their signal, I need to know. I can then either, switch it back again, and shut down. Then they can transmit again and so on, we play ping pong. Or I transmit and leave the line open, thus blocking their signal. What we need to do is to be close enough to friend Toni to be able to observe the effect. That way, by a process of elimination, we establish which signal indicates which command. My guess right now is that they will stall for time, and either Gobbleton or Meddlesome will shoot off to Austria to check through the main frame for a glitch. Difficult without shutting down. More so in the present Global crisis."

"A serious note, brother in law of mine. But what happens if America does actually decide to invade? Had you considered that angle?"

"Come on Pete. The sea weed is all around Dad's farm. We pinch a bit, give it to the Green Brigade. They will start having the stuff grown somewhere in secret. But let everyone know that they have it and will give it out free to any country that requests it. Let them appear not only as saviours of the World food crisis, but preventors of a nuclear holocaust too. Easy."

Myreg Cwmyurr was bemused. He was bright enough to realise that things were running not only too fast but away from him too. Being head of the Welsh Nationalist party was one thing, but having to defend not only Welsh territory and Welsh property, but against the Worlds mightiest nation. A nuclear nation to boot, and with what? he asked himself, all eleven men of the Free Welsh Army. Meanwhile the USS Terminator was, apparently on its way. On the whole, Myreg realised that he much preferred, waving his arms about at rugby football matches and spitting. Having a few pints with the boys. Picking up his allowances from the Welsh Assembly and then going home and poking Rhonan Phillips each night. Now he found himself sitting behind a desk in Narbeth Village hall. A hall that he had to share with the Scouts on a Tuesday evening and The Women's Institute on a Thursday. A hall that proudly displayed for the entire world to see, was now in fact, the Headquarters of The Free Welsh Army. And now all of this lot had arrived on his doorstep and Myreg had no idea of what to do, and if he asked for advice, no one understood him!

The IRA had a vast quantity of ordinance on its hands. It didn't actually want, nor knew quite what to do with the huge amount of weapons and explosives that it had over the years managed to acquire and accumulate. Senn Fein had duly elected MPs in Westminster. The Government at Stormont, in Northern Ireland was still suspended. Senn Fein had politicians ready and waiting to take their rightful place there. Thus, at last would Senn Fein share power with the Unionist MPs for the first time and actually get to have a say on how things should be run in the North. Or would have been able to have done so if the terms of the Good Friday accord could be met. Namely, that the IRA decommission its arms. The IRA wanted to decommission its arms. Its leaders were all now in cushy jobs. Like the Mafia, the IRA had gone respectable and into legitimate business. No one wanted to be associated with the wild boys and their guns any longer. Times had moved on. Shots had been fired, martyrs made, positions taken, and stances posed. That was all over now, and no one wanted them back. People had grown tired of having their auntie's disembowelled by flying glass, from a bomb in Woollies or having masked men burst into their homes and shoot their uncle George through the knee caps because he happened to have a thing going with a protestant, or catholic or what ever. But the IRA were in a quandary as to whom to surrender their arms. Arms that were increasingly becoming a liability. The Brits, naturally were insisting that the IRA hand their weapons over the army. This did rather stick in the craws of several people, and was not really a good political move. It hinted too much of unconditional surrender. The British, naturally took a different view. Only the army was entitled to play with guns, therefore it fell upon the army to take responsibility for decommissioned weapons. Stalemate was the obvious result.

Now, with a stroke of genius, Senn Fein handed over all its weapons to The Free Welsh Army. Thus, not only could the terms of the Good Friday agreement said to have been met, and Senn Fein representatives take up their seats and government be restored to Northern Ireland. The Brits couldn't very well object to the Free Welsh Army getting them to protect the mainland from outside aggression. In the event of any conflict, Senn Fein was planning to align Ulster with the South and remain neutral. Thus it was that a rather bemused and somewhat agitated Myreg found himself signing for a consignment of mixed ordinance and explosives. A consignment that occupied eight 40 Ton lorries. All of which were now parked outside of Narbeth Village hall and blocking the road. The Vicar was also jumping up and down, pulling out what little hair remained on his head and insisting that no weapons enter the hall, for which, under Parish Council rules, he was custodian. Not that the hall in question had the capacity to accommodate the shipment anyway.

To add to his problems, the four academics, had pulled rank and said no way were they going to unload boxes and crates. Myreg didn't feel that he ought to let the six young lads loose with automatic machine pistols, no matter how keen they were. It was at this point that a ninth truck had appeared. A low loader that was carrying a small tank. This had promptly inspired the totally mad Baron De Lacey to claim it as his own personal transport. He had last been seen cutting a swathe through farm land and hedges alike as he headed over the horizon. His last words being that he had some old score to settle with a High Court Judge and this seemed to be just the thing!

Meddlesome was in a muddle. Heigar was giving him grief and pressing him to sort out the glitch in the programme. For that is what Meddlesome believed it to be. To effect this properly, Meddlesome knew that he would have to fly to Austria. Then shut down the programmes, clean the memory and start again. First of all there wasn't time with the USS Terminator looming ever closer every second. Toni could in no way be allowed to take control of the situation and the country without electronic supervision. God alone knows what might happen if Toni were in charge. Also, his rushing off during this time of crisis would look suspicious. His place was by the side of the PM and to be seen to be there. Gobbleton should be seen too. Where was Gobbleton? Shacked up with that piece of oriental pussy of his and conducting his own private search for sea weed. A search over which Meddlesome had no control. Meddlesome needed Gobbleton's help. But he did not trust him sufficiently to send him off to Austria alone. No, Gobbleton might just play with the existing programme to further his own ends. Meddlesome decided that only he would be involved in any memory cleaning operations. The only solution was to leave the main memory banks in Austria alone for the moment. Run Toni as per usual, but monitor his every action.

Meanwhile Gobbleton now had been located. For some obscure reason he was apparently, down in West Wales. On the scene so to speak. Getting a first hand look. The Hell he was! Meddlsome knew beyond all doubt, Gobbleton was hot on the trail of the sea weed. Meddlesome's paranoia grew, feeding upon the latest piece of information. Gobbleton was against him and could not be trusted. Heigar and her mad father certainly had their own agenda.

Gobbleton had phoned him. He had been very brief, it was an open line. He had said something about an arms shipment. Though the details were as yet unclear. Meanwhile, the whole area was under military control, along with Fatslobe's farm. Meddlesome felt powerless and he didn't like it one bit. He brooded and seethed.

The UN was powerless to act. Their two major players were on the brink of hostilities. Toni was now head of the EEC. Every now and again the EEC played a game of musical chairs and everyone got a turn to be king of the castle. Myreg appealed for help from the EEC.

Denmark demurred. On the grounds that they had made a point over the last hundred years or so, of not picking a fight with anybody. Hence, they were a little out of practice.

Holland and Belgium, both said that the last time that they had fired shots in anger was in Indonesia and The Congo respectively, and in both places, the locals, generally armed with spears, and pointed sticks, had seen them off.

Germany said that its track record of winning wars during the twentieth century was pretty poor, so best count them out.

Italy claimed to be a nation of lovers, not fighters, why not ask Spain?

Spain said, sorry, but they only specialised in fighting among themselves.

Switzerland said that it wasn't a member of the EEC and had no wish to join. They were, and wished to remind everyone concerned, a neutral country. However, on the basis of that and naturally wishing to further good relations, whilst at the same time wishing to appear open handed to all. They were quite prepared to sell, organise the sale of and act as a banking facility for all parties concerned. They were also willing to offer some gold bullion, albeit it still carried the Reichstag mark, against suitable collateral, if anyone was interested.

France offered to help. On a strictly commercial basis and only on the understanding that the official language of the EEC became French. Someone in the Houses of Parliament christened them, "The Jackals of Europe" Which did not go done too well in Paris. Then added insult to injury by pointing out that as a fighting nation, France's air force was untested. It no longer had a navy, Oran and Trafalgar respectively having put paid to it. And why France kept such a large army was beyond comprehension, as no one could remember when France had actually last won a war. Even their famed Foreign Legion having met with a decisive defeat the last time it went into action. In what was then French Indo China, but after that debacle, became Vietnam.

The French naturally went into a Gaulic huff and promptly blocked the Channel ports with their lorries. Which didn't actually bother Britain at all. Since the only interest that the British had with regard to ports of entry to France was the Channel Tunnel. And they only used that to skip over in their white Transit vans to fill up with cheap booze and fags from Tesco. Since Tesco was located within the precincts of the Tunnel approaches. It was thus not affected by the lorries on the other side of the motorway. The Brits just gave two fingers to their French cousins on the other side of the wire, and carried on as normal. It was the thousands of bogus asylum seekers, that were hidden away in the depths of the back of the parked trucks, under piles of soap and washing powder that suffered. Many just starving to death. It was at this point that France, realising that it was about to experience a major public health scandal, closed its boarders to the Eastern European hordes. Naturally the National Front in the UK claimed this as a victory. The fruit growers of Kent, still smarting under the EEC directive that had banned the sale of their Coxs Orange Pippins, suggested that the French feed the poor unfortunates on Golden Delicious apples and not dump any more of their surplices on the UK in future.

Generally then, there was complete turmoil, and the world watched and waited nervously. But none more nervously than Meddlesome, who was forced to monitor Toni's every move. He sat in front of his computer screen, poised to intervene electronically the moment that Toni showed any signs of not following the script. This he found nerve racking and very stressful. Heigar persistently nagged at him to get the programme sorted out. A situation that was not improved any by him knowing full well that Heigar didn't know the difference between a programme and a postman. Gobbleton meanwhile was still swanning around in Wales. Meddlesome knew that he had to take charge, though he was at a loss as to know exactly what to do. This just made it all even more frustrating and wearing. He began to wonder if it was all some huge plot, hatched up by Heigar and Gobbleton? The more he sat there in the gloom with only the glow from his visual display unit, full ash trays and dirty coffee cups for company, waiting nervously to intercept any faux paux made by Toni. The more it became clear to him that this was in fact the case. They were out to get him! Meddlesome was getting really paranoid and cracking up.

On the other side of the Atlantic, things were no better for Willie Clayton. He sat behind his desk in the Oval Office brooding. Half the population of the USA was behind him. Thinking it was time those uppity Europeans got a dusting, just to keep them in line. Others, less informed perhaps, were shouting, "No Intervention in European Wars." The fact that they were acting as the aggressor, having somehow slipped past them. The native American population, along with most of South America, was complaining that Spain had not been included on the cruise missile hit list. As they voiced the opinion that they saw Columbus as having been the root cause of all of their misfortunes. Whilst the remainder of America were loading up their Winnabaygo's with tins of beans, Winchester rifles and survival booklets. The Senate and Congress were in total disarray and at a loss to control The President. The Tribune and Post were screaming about having sufficient evidence for impeachment and Lulu was complaining about the size of his member and had taken to calling him Little Willie.

It was actually Te´Upp that provided the answer. She and Gobbleton had quietly driven down to Pembrokeshire. They found the whole county isolated, and under a military blockade, but Gobbleton had his Government Pass. Te´Upp could see quite clearly that the last thing that would do anyone any good was an open war. She planned to steal some sea weed and send it off to Hanoi when an idea struck her. What if Vietnam was to offer to undertake a police action? They were part of ASEAN. Britain under that nice Prime Minister who had smoked a pipe and behaved as if he advertised rain coats had kept Britain out of the Vietnam war. They had beaten America hands down once. No, the population of the USA would not want a second bite of that particular cherry. The memory of all of those green body bags was all too recent.

So it came about that with the USS Terminator in position, that Vietnam donned the Blue Betets of the UN and began their peace keeping mission in West Wales. Myreg breathed a sigh of relief and the Welsh Nationalist Party, not wanting to miss an opportunity to make a quick profit, sold the donated arms from the IRA to Hanoi. Minus one small tank, that seemed to have been mislaid. The terms of the Good Friday accord having now been fulfilled. Stormont reconvened and settled down to ignore the threat of nuclear destruction looming on their doorstep and go about their normal day to day running of Ulster. Namely, the organising of orange sashed and bowler hatted marchers on the one hand and their disruption on the other.

Gobbleton was ecstatic and all most beside himself. Any day now he and his beautiful Te´ Upp would have their sample of sea weed. Then, having finally cut himself loose from his scrawny wife and boring family, together he and Te´Upp would flee to Taiwan. Te´Upp, however had other plans. She would return to her beloved Vietnam, having dumped her hairy Gobbleton en route and as fast as possible.

Meddlesome was loosing weight. He was existing on a diet of black coffee and cigarettes. His eyes were dark from lack of sleep and his mind was darker still as the paranoia insidiously took over.

A summit meeting was proposed. Gerald Fatslobe offered his farm as the venu. It was after all in the middle of a military isolation zone, and at the heart of the matter, so to speak.

The Vietnamese peace keeping force would be arriving any day now.

By scheduled flight to Heathrow and Gatwick courtesy of Singapore Airlines and MAS. Vietnam itself lacking suitable transport facilities.

Willie Clayton was flying in on Airforce One. With his considerable entourage.

The PM was due to fly in to Cardiff Airport and complete the 100 odd miles by road. No suitable air field with long enough runways being available any closer. Gerald was of the opinion that if he could somehow get in on the sea weed deal, then he had no use for either pigs, rabbits or Al Arrod. Other than for the pleasure of slaughtering purposes. The thought of slaughtering Al Arrod crossed his mind and he found it wholly pleasurable.

Meddlesom sent Gobbleton an E mail telling him of the planned summit. Naturally Bradford intercepted it too. Tiffany had been cooking lunch for them all.

"What is this Tiff? It tastes good."

"Spicy chicken breasts in soy sauce Brad. Do you like it?"

"Yes, it's jolly good. What do you think Pete?"

"I like all of Tiff's cooking Brad. I'm putting on weight. She is too." He pointed his fork in the direction of his wife, but Tiffany just smiled.

"Anyway Pete, I have an idea."

"What's that then Brad?"

"Well, we want to prove one way or another that the PM, Toni Cacophony is just as plastic as he seems. And in fact is no more that some automated puppet, programmed to perform as someone else pulls the strings."

"That someone being either Meddlesome, Gobbleton or Heigar, or any combination of all three. That is what we are thinking isn't it Brad?"

"Yes. That's about the size of it. Now what I have planned is this. I'll nip back home. They have to let me in. I will bug the bedroom that Toni and Heigar will use. Oh, I'll bug the others too, whilst I'm about it. There is plenty of gear in the cellar."

"Don't they brush or sweep for bugs Brad?" It was Tiffany looking up from her matinee jacket knitting pattern.

"Yes sis, but I can get around that. I will run some thin piano wire across the loft, between the floor boards and the ceiling below. I will have the bugs, all deactivated in a little box at the end. Each bug will have a little hook, so that it can run along the piano wire. Then I will run nylon fishing line down between the cavity walls and run the lines down into the basement. They can sweep all they like. Once they are happy, they will stop checking. Then, when we are ready, I pull the bugs into place by pulling gently on the nylon lines, and switch on. Then we transmit our signals and watch what happens.

Bradford arrived at the check point just as the first continent of Vietnamese troops rolled up. In the general confusion, he slipped by and drove the familiar road to his home. Once home, he again entered quietly. He saw no point in advertising his arrival. He settled down to rig his bugs.

First of all, he checked out his electronic equipment in the cellar. All of the computer equipment was now with Peter and Tiffany, so Bradford took out anything that might be construed as suspicious, and with some tools went up into the loft. He met his mother on the way. She smelt of alcohol and gave him a cheery, if somewhat bleary hello, then she weaved off towards the lounge, clutching a depleted one litre bottle of gin.

Up in the loft, Bradford lifted some floor boards. Some to store his cache and others to enable him to run the piano wire. He hitched each bug to its wire and deactivated it, clustering all of the bugs around one junction box, the wire of which could be seen running up from the flooring in the loft and along the wall. By doing that, and putting his main activating switch there, he hoped that any weak signal given out by the small battery pack in his bug, would be shielded and confused with the electromagnetic force radiated normally from a live 240 Volt household cable. He then ran his nylon lines down through the cavity walls and into the cellar. Bradford replaced the floor boards, tidied up. Then made things look a bit untidy, as lofts are supposed to look like, and he went in search of something to eat. On his way to the kitchen, he met his father.

Gerald was not in a good mood. Al Arrod was being difficult. He was pushing for his passport. Gerald wasn't ready. Not yet. There was this sea weed thing to consider. Certainly that crazy Yank wouldn't attack. Yes. OK, he might very well sit in the Irish or was it the Celtic Sea now? And make noises, but surely to God, he couldn't be crazy enough to actually attempt an invasion? Could he? There again, what good did a massive aircraft carrier do him? I mean, he wanted some sea weed. No point in blasting everything to kingdom come, when all you wanted a bit of marine growth. The obvious thing was to stall and talk to him. OK, maybe it was originally his sea weed, then there was the question of how it ended up here, in piles, on his, Gerald's foreshore? That was another thing. Under British law, his title deeds extended down to the low water mark. Anything cast ashore was his. It began to dawn on Gerald that he actually had a case for claiming the sea weed was his property. If indeed it did have the capabilities to feed the World, then obviously America wanted it back. America fed most of the World at the moment and the threat of starvation was a powerful political weapon. No, what was needed here was an agreement between Britain and America, though no doubt that would have to include the EEC in some way. Gerald began to feel better. He was Agricultural Minister after all. He would suggest to Toni that things be put on hold for the moment. A proper scientific study would have to be made. He rubbed his hands, there would be an opportunity to make a few quid there, since all of the boffins would be working on his farm. Maybe he could get a few asylum seekers to run a little sandwich and coffee van?

Once the results of the study were clear, then Britain and America could come to some agreement. An agreement that could be proclaimed throughout the World as being the answer to the World's food shortage. Oh, yes, Clayton would see the sense of that. Better to go down in history as one of the joint saviours of malnutrition, than the guy that nuked England! The New Deal Democratic party would be the EEC driving force and he, Gerald Fatslobe, Agricultural Commissioner to the EEC, would sit at its head. At last, here was the way to rule his empire from Poland to Dublin. Never mind pigs, or rabbits or Al Arrod for that matter. He would obtain British Citizenship for Al Arrod, but later, and on his terms. Actually it was he Gerald that held all of the aces. Gerald smiled in happy contentment to himself. Good Lord was that Bradford? He hadn't seen him around the place for a while, didn't think he still lived here. Oh, well, leave the lad alone. Never did understand him. Had his head full of Ohms and power factor or something. Gerald smiled benignly at his son and murmured a polite good morning. Bradford knew immediately that his father was preoccupied with yet another dodgy deal.

Bradford made himself a cheese and pickled onion sandwich. Then he went down into the cellar and carefully removed a brick, so as to expose his nylon lines. He marked them up and one by one pulled and labelled each, so that he knew which line pulled which bug into position. He then went back up into the loft and carefully positioned each bug to where it should sit for maximum effect. Then he ran return lines, numbering each. Finally and for the last time he replaced everything, and messed it up again. In the cellar, he fixed an old cupboard to the wall over the removed brick. Making sure that he could remove one board from the back of the cupboard. Finally placing some paint tins and old brushes in the cupboard. Now he was ready. All he had to do was pull out the board from the back of the cupboard. Activate the bugs by a radio signal, and pull each one into place. He would then monitor each bug in turn and be able to hear what was being said in the room below. Using his mobile phone, he could then phone Peter. Peter could then transmit each signal in turn. Bradford sitting in the cellar could then observe its effect. He would test his systems using a small radio to represent his targets. That way he could get the sound levels right, and fine tune his surveillance systems. Then all would be ready and in place. Bradford decided that he had better have a word with the cook. He wanted to eat by himself. After he had eaten a quiet evening meal, he would take up position and wait.

Gerald's farm was swamped with people. Trailers had to be set up in the yards and generators hooked up to supply the power. Port a Loos had to be brought in. The International press were to be catered for. Also all the diplomatic trappings of White Hall, not to mention America, plus all of their hangers on too. The Americans demanded ice cream machines and air conditioned trailer homes. The press vied with each other, fighting and squabbling with each other like angry sparrows, for the better spots and a lot of folding money changed hands between various greasers and tradesman. No one seemed to consider the Vietnamese, who were directed towards a barn. They appeared to be quite happy with their lot, and bedded down amongst the straw, having set themselves up a field kitchen. Long before even the haggling and jostling was over among the other parties, the Vietnamese had liberated a few chickens and a couple of rabbits from Western, Capitalist Imperialism, eaten, held a political lecture, sang some jolly songs about peasants and rice harvests, and all gone off to sleep. No one had taken any interest in a non descript Bradford.

A very worn and haggard looking Meddlesome had arrived with the Prime Minister and his wife Heigar. Gobbleton having slipped in much earlier, as he was already in the area. Actually he had been down on the foreshore and had already placed his samples of sea weed in their plastic bags and given them to Te´Upp to forward via DHL to Taiwan. Te´Upp had of course had already given them to the representative of the Vietnamese Embassy that had arrived to greet his countrymen. At that very minute it was on its way to Hanoi via The Diplomatic Bag. Te´Upp had also included a letter in which she requested that she now be allowed to tidy up any loose ends at the UK end, ditch Gobbleton and fly home to her hero's welcome.

The President of the United States of America arrived. Along with his full complement of bodyguards, secretaries, drivers, cooks, shoe blacks and of course Lulu. The resultant confusion and turmoil that this produced was of almost apocalyptic proportions. The secret service not wanting the Vietnamese to get anywhere near Willie Clayton. The Vietnamese obliged, and went back to sleep. They were all jet lagged anyway.

Finally, when it had all settled down, Heigar and Toni were alone in bed. Bradford activated his surveillance systems

CHAPTER. 10

Willie Clayton was fed up. Congress and the Senate had cut off his funding. OK, he still had the CIA secret funds but the head of the CIA had pointed out to Willie just how much it cost to run an aircraft carrier. The gross national budget of several small countries was considerably less. So now he was haggling with the CIA to get back the illegal funds that he had given them in the first place. The CIA were naturally loath to hand over any money and The President couldn't very well make too much fuss over funds that were in fact both illegal and clandestine.

The out come had been a face saving exercise for all concerned. Congress being well aware such funds existed. Yes, the USS Terminator could take up position. But under no circumstances was it even to point its weapons anywhere, let alone arm or fire them. Probably end up shooting down Concord, or worse still. One of those cheap package tour jets owned by that gentleman whose name sounded like a chutney company. That really would stir things up. The gentleman concerned, having sufficient money to finance his own private war in retaliation! No, navy planes could fly around, carefully, and certainly not in a manner that could be in any way construed as being provocative.

Since both Senate and Congress had rather been pipped to the post by Willie's premature mobilisation action, it would now seem foolish to stand down without gaining a few points. But the sooner that America was taken off this present war footing, the better. As it was the National Parks were full of survival groups all shooting at each other. Which, in the general view of things wasn't viewed as being such a bad thing, as it took their minds off shooting members of the Senate and Congress. But they were also shooting deer and other animals out of season and pretty soon, once all of this present turmoil was over, some one would have face the wrath of the conservation lobby.

Then there were the marches on the White House to contend with. Every freak in the country was bearing arms and shouting from his corner. Frankly the Government was amazed at the weaponry that some of these freaks were toting. No one would have been too much surprised if some group or another produced a small thermo nuclear device that they had purchased from a mail order company. Legally too. Naturally with all this firepower now out on the streets, shootings, bank raids and general mayhem were the order of the day. Britain, whilst under the threat of immanent attack, was peaceful by comparison. Some Boston newspaper statistician had already produced figures that detailed the over all cost to the American taxpayer in damage and lost revenues. And not a shot had been fired. Willie had wanted to charge him with treason, but had been advised against it on the grounds of right or wrong, the legal costs would have been enormous. That and the case would have dragged on for years. He fumed over the fact that he was President and he couldn't even sue some jerk. This job wasn't quite so good as he had imagined, he mused.

Now, Willie had been instructed in no uncertain terms. By both upper and lower houses. Go over there, get the best deal possible. Which would mean sharing things some with the Brits and leave the advisors to sort out the details and proclaim a victory. Meanwhile the Terminator could be down played and eventually slipped into the role of protecting the blasted sea weed from outside interference from an unnamed foreign power. North Korea or Libya springing to mind as being likely candidates at whom to point fingers. Generally one could point a finger at either of them and blame them for anything. No one ever questioned it. Then, depending on how well he pulled it off would depend if he got impeached. Both the Tribune and The Post were down in Florida chasing up some leads with regard to some break in some place. There was also the matter of Lulu.

Willie had worked out that if he was going to survive this little lot then maybe, just maybe Lulu could be of assistance. If that donkey dick of a British PM fancied her, well maybe he could use her as a bargaining chip.

For sure all the stupid cow had done since she returned was talk about Bloody Toni and the size of his prick! He was also pissed off about the way she now called him, "Little Willie." So Congress had cut off his funding and it felt like Toni had been instrumental in cutting off his balls. Further more, if he didn't pull this deal off, he would get impeached. No doubt that would suit his hatchet-faced wife who had threatened to run against him in the next campaign. All in all, The President of the United States of America was not a happy camper.

Naturally, upon arrival there were the jolly handshakes, and the plastic smiles, for the benefit of the press and TV. Once that was over, Willie said he was tired, it would be a big day tomorrow etc. and he took himself off to bed, only to find that some dick head had placed Lulu's bedroom, way down the corridor.

Bradford was sitting in the cellar. He carefully checked each of his bugs in order, listening quietly. Toni and Heigar, the rhythmic sounds of sleep. Meddlesome too. Someone had placed Lulu in the bedroom he had assumed would have been used by Gobbleton, but Gobbleton had made other sleeping arrangements. Lulu seemed restless. It was time to test the signals. He dialled Peter on his mobile phone. "OK Pete, fire one."

Back in the farmhouse Peter transmitted the first signal. Toni woke up and instantly went into smarm and charm mode.

Toni was a little confused. He knew that he had to be nice to someone, but no one was talking to him. He had no input. Toni had been programmed to react. He had never been programmed to produce any original thoughts of his own; thus he reacted to the only stimulus that was around. The gentle snoring of his wife Heigar, as she lay on her back in a huge, floucey nightdress. "Had I ever told you that I find the sound of your nocturnal, nasal breathing mellifluous?" Heigar slumbered on. Toni continued, having prompted no reaction. "To lay here next to you and listen to happy buzz saw noises, reminds of a spring day, walking in the woods in my youth. The chirp of crickets, the happy hum of be....."

Heigar awoke. "Shuddup!" She scrabbled around in the dark for her hand held console and groggily punched the sleep button. Toni collapsed.

Peter relayed the information about Heigar's signal to Bradford. "Pay dirt! What's next Brad?"

"Hang on Pete. We have isolated two signals. Smarm was the first and sleep must have been the last. That leaves us with three to decode. Press number two." Peter activated Toni's earnest and sincere programme. Toni woke up again.

"Heigar. It is my firmly held belief that the cornerstone of our British way of life, fundamentally is that of a secure family relationship. It is upon such foundations that the new social order, as offered by The New Deal Democratic Party, can and will move forward. All pulling together, not ignoring our duties, but as of one, keeping our eyes firmly on the future. The heartland's behind us, pushing us forward, ever striving......."

"Shaddap!" Heigar again hit the sleep button and Toni, obligingly, went back to sleep. Heigar was annoyed and she muttered to herself, "I swear I'll kill that raving queer Meddlesome if he doesn't get his programmes sorted out and the glitch removed from the system. I'll send him off to Austria tomorrow on some pretext. That idiot Gobbleton can stand in and monitor Toni. Anyway it's about time he earned his corn instead of spending all of his time shagging that skinny oriental bitch. Can't see what he sees in her. More meat on a butcher's pencil." All of which Bradford took a careful note.

"OK Pete. That was the Earnest and you can trust me role. I guess that Heigar must have pushed the sleep button again. Try him on the third signal." At the other end, Peter placed Toni into confident and aggressive in mode.

Again Toni awoke. "Heigar. It is the right of every husband to expect a certain standard of behaviour from his wife. Therefore, I feel that it is only fair to give you advance notification of my intention to have sex with you....."

"Swein Hunt! Slaffen fur Christ's sake!!" Again she hit the sleep button, and again Toni slept.

"That one is, "Pushing my point" Mode." Said Brad confidently. "Now I wonder what the last one is? Go for it Pete."

Heigar registered the fact that the bedclothes were rising in response to Toni's erection.

She reached for her console, but was too late. Toni was upon her, and her floucy nighty was up around her face somewhere. She tried flailing her arms but it was of no use. They got caught up in all the ribbons and roses. OK, she thought, maybe it's just sex that is overriding the programmes. After all Freud had pretty well proved that it was a dominant driving force. Since Freud had originated in her neck of the woods, Heigar was inclined towards believing in his theories. Maybe let him wear himself out some. Release some testosterone. Then switch him off. Heigar decided to lay back and enjoy the experience. Once Toni slowed down some, and she felt it was time, she would suggest another position. Then make a grab for the console and switch him off.

"What's happening Brad?" It was Peter.

"Would you believe that the PM is going like pile driver? That is sex mode, from the way he is grunting and the bed is bouncing."

"What's Heigar doing?"

"Laying back, dreaming of the Tyrol, edelweiss, and enjoying it by the sound of it."

"Shall I switch him off Brad?"

"Naw! Not yet. Let me get signal strength on old Heigar's moans. If we time it just right, we can switch him off just as her bubble is about to burst. That really should frustrate her!"

With perfect timing, Peter hit the sleep mode and Toni collapsed on top of a very upset Heigar!

"Mein Gott in Himmel! Wass ist wrong mit you?" Heigar struggled to uncouple herself. "Enough!" She cried. "You sleep on your own." And she dragged a recumbent Toni into the passageway, leaving him lying on the floor, and stomped back to bed, rearranging her night dress as she did so.

"What's happening Brad?"

"Dunno Pete. I think the old cow has dragged the poor sod off some place. We really must have pissed her off. Maybe next time I had better rig the place for sound and vision. Hang on, that's the bedroom door closing. Old plastic smile Toni must be out on the landing. Let's wake him up again."

"Which button Brad?"

"Sex was pretty interesting. Fire up his hormones again." Peter obliged.

Lulu was upset. Toni had been fantastic. The last time she had enjoyed sex like that had been with two East German discus throwers in Minsk. Even they though, and both together, could not match up to Toni's standards. She wondered idly if all Englishmen were built along the same lines and if her choice of adopted country required rethinking. Still, Willie's willie was better than no willie at all and he was sort of sweet. She decided to try and pay him a visit. He had been pretty grumpy with her of late. She had tried to explain that it had not been her fault. She had even claimed it as having been rape. Willie however had rejected this out of hand on the basis that she had been enjoying it too much! Lulu slipped quietly out of her bedroom and ran slap-bang into Toni. Toni responded as he had been programmed to do, and pushed her back inside her bedroom. Lulu couldn't believe her luck.

"Oh Toni!" She murmured as she willingly led him back to her bed, closing the door behind them.

"Bloody Hell Pete! The old ram is screwing Lulu."

"Shit! What shall I do Brad?"

"Nothing Pete. She's telling him that he is all man and she has never stopped thinking about the last time! What last time is that I wonder? He puts it about a bit does our Toni. No wonder Heigar sticks him out at night. He's like a old tom cat!"

Willie Clayton couldn't sleep. The Brits never had air conditioning and their beds were too soft and the pillows too hard. Furthermore he was jet lagged. He decided to check out Lulu's bed, Maybe if he rolled around with her for ten minutes or so, then he could sleep. He got up and padded off in his silk dressing gown. He didn't bother knocking on Lulu's door, and went straight in. He pulled up short at the sight that met him. "Jesus Toni! Don't you ever stop?"

"Quick Pete. Smarm and charm mode!" Peter switched programme.

"Willie! How nice to see you. Just let me put this away." Toni stood up, "Lulu, close your legs. It's regarded as impolite in front of a visitor. Come Willie. Let's sit over her. Now how can I help you?"

Willie Clayton was caught flat-footed. This guy could not be for real. He found himself replying as if in a daze, "Well for beginners, you could start by ceasing to shag my woman every time my back is turned!"

"Willie, don't be foolish." Toni declared expansively. "Believe me. That's only my way of furthering East West relationships. It's nothing. Anyway, she enjoys it. Why don't you take advantage of our old English hospitality whilst you are here? Go and shag Heigar.

Fatslobe's wife too, if you like. Get her sober and she would probably enjoy it."

Willie was completely bemused. "What is this? Some kind of Limey tradition? Pass the host's pussy?" Willie was tired, annoyed and he didn't understand the Brits. Furthermore he didn't want to.

"Exactly Willie. It's an Old English Country House Weekend. Very traditional. Sometimes we play sardines first. Get a willing little housemaid in a dark cupboard with three of you, and boy can you have fun.

Willie considered Toni's words. This guy is for real, he thought. Maybe it is some crazy old Limey tradition. I mean they dressed up in funny clothes and chased foxes and everyone knows that they are inedible. Who knew what these weidos got up to inside the confines of their own homes? And his brief was not to upset them. He decided to play along and see where it led. "Can't say I fancy Fatslobe's wife. Too skinny for my liking."

"Well there you are then. One can not say that about Heigar."

Willie mulled on that statement. Was this guy offering swapsies? That big wife of his was a fair piece of ass. Willie went on a fishing trip. "You're right there buddy. Fair piece of meat that woman of yours. And you say this is an old English tradition then?"

"Give us sincere and earnest Peter." Bradford had been monitoring the conversation.

"Absolutely Willie. Trust me. I can say with all sincerity that you are welcome to work your way into her affections at any time you wish. Host's hospitality and all that. Nothing would please me more than to see your aspirations fulfilled in that direction."

"Third programme now Peter. Let's push the point."

Toni clapped his hand on Willie's shoulder. "You go for it old friend. Come on, up you get, and up you get, if you get my meaning." Toni gave his grin for which he was famous. "Get in there and give old Heigar a good poking. She'll love it. So will you old boy. Goes like a train does my misses." He ushered The President out of the door. "Stick him back on sex Pete, I'm switching bugs to see how Willie gets on."

Willie had meanwhile slipped into bed with Heigar. Heigar was sleepy. "Toni, sleep yah?" She reached for the console and realised that it was not Toni. Heigar stopped in mid move. Her Logical Teutonic brain examined the possibilities. It was a mistake. Dismissed. She was about to be raped. Dismissed. Too quiet. Any way, she never got that lucky.

Someone fancied her. Who?

"Heigar, it's me."

Good God! It's The President. Well, that's OK then. He would never have to tell because of the fifth amendment. Heigar settled back to have completed that which Peter had so recently and rudely interrupted.

After 30 minutes Peter placed Toni into sleep mode, and everyone in both households went to bed to sleep. With the exception of Willie and Heigar. Good old Toni had been quite correct. She did go like a train. Willie Clayton, when he did finally go to sleep, slept soundly. Both He and Heigar had silly smiles on their faces.

Next morning the old relationship between America and Britain was back on line. Meddlesome was controlling Toni and Toni was behaving perfectly. Heigar decided to delay sending him to Austria for two reasons. There was no way that from a political point of view that he could have disappeared at a time like this, and any way Toni was behaving normally. They decided that perhaps it was his biological needs overriding the programme. Well, that could be sorted out quite easily. Anyway she didn't want the boat to be rocked. She wanted Willie to hang around as long as possible.

Gobbleton had been down inspecting the seaweed and declared that there was mounds of the stuff, all washed up along the foreshore in front of the farm. Toni was steered away from the question of ownership and they decided to all stroll down after breakfast and look at the stuff for themselves.

"Looks like it's hardly worth a small rowing boat Willie, let alone The Terminator." Toni was in charm mood. He playfully kicked at the piles of seaweed with his foot. He was on walk a bout and for the press and TV was wearing jeans and an open neck shirt with the sleeves rolled up and his famous silly grin. He did a lot of waving.

"You know Toni, you could be right. We don't actually know if this stuff is all that it is cracked up to be. It looks pretty nasty, and smells odd too. Can't say I'd fancy sitting down to a plate of it myself." Willie Clayton poked at a pile with a stick. "How about if we get the scientific boys to have a look at this stuff?"

"Yes Willie. Exactly what I was thinking too. Oh Lord! Here comes Gerald and his performing ferrets." All TV cameras had now focused on the arrival of Gerald Fatslobe. He stood a little above them all on the riverbank, wearing his country gentleman's outfit. Tweeds and gum boots. A ferret peeked out of each lower side pocket in his jacket. He waved his walking stick in greeting in their direction. "God! I hate it when he up-stages me Willie. He's so fat he fills a wide screen TV all on his own." Come on; best get over there before he says something stupid. Gerald however had more important things on his mind than just getting his face on TV. Gerald had found that his pigs quite liked eating the strange seaweed. Maybe all of his financial problems with regard to pig feed costs could be solved overnight. Thus his negotiating position with Al Arrod would be strengthened.

So the Summit continued, and eventually drew to a successful outcome. Having decided that the Vietnamese would remain as a token force to protect the seaweed. Assisted by the Free Welsh Army. The four academics having been promoted to Brigadiers, the six work experience lads becoming Sergeants and mad Baron De Lacey not being mentioned. He having seemed to have disappeared off the face of the earth, along with his little tank.

Willie was happy sleeping with Heigar. Lulu was happy sleeping with Toni. Who now seemed to be operating on his own at night quite well without external stimulus. Meddlesome could get some sleep and Gobbleton continued to make his own arrangements.

Myreg breathed a sigh of relief and went back to spitting, waving his arms, poking Rhonan Phillips and collecting his allowances from the Welsh Assemble.

The USS Terminator steamed into Portsmouth on a Good will visit and school children were given rides in munition lifts and allowed to play virtual reality war games called Hunt Saddam.

The World breathed a sigh of relief. The Swiss all appeared, if a little sheepishly, from out of their nuclear shelters and the French lifted their ban on the Channel ports. Bogus asylum seekers again began to flow. Africa carried on starving. The Chilli Chicks released a controversial record called, "The sea weed in my face." Which was banned by the BBC. Thus guaranteeing it a place as number one in the charts, and generally things returned to normal. Te'Upp was not so happy. She had planned on dumping Gobbleton as fast as possible and returning to her beloved Vietnam. Hanoi however had other plans for her. For Vietnam to be acting as a peacekeeper now became a liability. Not only was there the cost involved, the troops were also being exposed to unnecessary, decadent Western trappings. Such as a 24-hour supply of electricity and indoor plumbing. Plumbing of any nature being a novelty. Not only that, they were developing a taste for chips, Worcestershire sauce and pizza and ignoring their sacks of rice and salt fish. Since they were actually employed to guard the seaweed, it made it a little difficult for Vietnam to cultivate the samples already sent and then to proclaim to the world that it had been their discovery all along. No, something more subtle was needed. Gobbleton provided the answer. Hanoi knew full well that Gobbleton was under the impression that Te'Upp was Taiwanese. Also, that Gobbleton thought that he would soon be retiring to some oriental love nest with Te'Upp. Hanoi saw how to exploit this loophole. What if Gobbleton could be brought to Vietnam, whilst under the impression that he was in fact going to Taiwan? As long as Te'Upp was with him, he would not be suspicious. Once in Vietnam, then some statement could be cobbled together to the effect that he had defected to the worker's paradise and given them the secrets of the seaweed. That only there could the seaweed be grown under true socialist conditions. To be given freely to a starving World. All blame would then be focused upon him. No mention then would have to be made of any deals and political trade offs that resulted in Vietnam feeding the starving third world in the process. Much better that way. Vietnam didn't have to provide an excuse for possessing the weed. All blame would fall squarely upon his shoulders. Te'Upp was instructed to remain faithfully by the side of her lover. Later would she receive instructions as how the journey was to be effected. Te'Upp voiced her objections. As a freedom-loving daughter of the glorious revolution, she could not in all honesty remain at the side of the capitalist exploiter for the rest of her life. She was going to add, fat, hairy pawed, groping, and suffering from halitosis, but thought better of it.

Hanoi was understanding. They fully realised the sacrifices that their comrade sister had made and sure, she could dump the slimeball, once he was on Vietnamese soil and had made his confession and had appeared to the world on a suitably doctored piece of video footage.

Meddlesome, though sleeping better was not of a forgiving nature. He began to plot the demise of both Heigar and her father in earnest. A skiing accident would be best. If he were to secrete some small waterproof explosive charges above the Schloss Kutzanburnz, along with a radio controlled firing device. Then later, when the snow was around, he would detonate them. The resultant avalanche should remove all traces of both Heigar, father and evidence. The idea appealed to him. He gave it closer and more detailed thought. Once they were out of the way, he would install his own computer system elsewhere and then have sole control of Toni. Then he would deal with Gobbleton too.

Gerald meanwhile began to feed his pigs on the seaweed in earnest, allowing them to wander along the foreshore and forage for themselves. Te'Upp had persuaded her Gobbie to come to Taiwan. She depicted their idyllic life together. A house by the sea. Overlooking the azure waters. The sound of wind chimes. Sunshine and servants to wait upon them and her Gobbie in a silk dressing gown, with a dragon on it. She also dressed in silk, awaiting upon the every whim of her Lord and Master. Anyway, now that Taiwan had the seaweed, time was running out for them both. Either come with her, and rest in her arms. Or stay and face the inevitable scandal. Gobbleton said that on the whole, a life of ease and nuptial bliss with her in Taiwan was preferable to a long spell of porridge in Wormwood Scrubs, and promptly enquired as to when would they be leaving?

Secretly they slipped aboard a ferry for Ireland and from there, equally secretly boarded a Vietnamese tanker in Wexford. Gobbleton was on his way. Te'Upp was not looking forward to being cooped up with him for the voyage, but consoled herself that it would not be long before she was rid of him. Then she could claim her hero's accolade of The Ho Chi Minn Medal for service to her country and settle down and marry some decent political cadre from within the party.

Back in Pembrokeshire Gobbleton's disappearance was noticed. Meddlesome was suspicious, but kept his own council, awaiting events to unfold. Nothing happened. It was as if Gobbleton had been swept from the face of the earth. Meddlesome immediately suspected Heigar. Yes, it was obvious! She had done away with Gobbleton and he would be next. Meddlesome decided to eliminate Heigar and her father, before he too suffered a fate similar to that of Gobbleton.

The general feeling in Britain however, was that perhaps Gobbleton had drowned. The Cleddau was dragged. More seaweed was disturbed and washed up on Gerald's foreshore. The pigs flourished.

The scientific team produced their conclusions. The seaweed was indeed some new species. It did indeed only grow on Blue Stone. It was absolutely useless as a food base. Apart from a very unpleasant taste and slimy texture, it had no nutritional value what so ever. It did have some very odd strings of hydrocarbon molecules that as with any hydrocarbons contained energy. There was no way though, that a human gut could break them down. You might just as well try feeding people on sawdust. In fact, sawdust on the whole tasted better. They got ready to go home. The seaweed bubble had burst.

The world groaned. A couple of African leaders, wanting to take the heat off themselves, and their Mercedes cars and personal Swiss bank accounts, promptly accused the West of deliberately suppressing the truth in a racist bid to keep their populations oppressed and in debt. Since most of their population's could neither read nor write and were too busy trying to scrape a living, and knew full well that the boss man was crook. It tended to get ignored.

The Vietnamese UN force got ready to go home, but at the last minute decided to defect en mass and seek political asylum. Back in Hanoi, Gobbleton, not speaking Chinese and still being under the impression that he was in Taiwan was wondering why there were water buffalo carts in the main road and no BMW saloons. Te´Upp was called before the Central Committee and asked to explain how it was that not only was the sea weed useless, they had just worked out how much the policing exercise had cost, and there were insufficient funds within Vietnam to foot the cost. Not only that, all of the troops employed had opted to remain in the UK. Far from receiving her accolade, she was banished to a worker's collective for re education through labour and worse still, instructed to take Gobbleton with her.

The only one who breathed a sigh of relief was Kenu. He went and lit a few candles and incense sticks in the small Shinto shrine he had built in his garden and he banged a gong quietly, so as not to disturb his sleeping and ever attentive Brenda.

Life in Britain returned to much as it had been before the Summit. The Vietnamese had joined forces with the Free Welsh Army and were swapping recipes for salt fish and lava bread on S4C TV. All of the arms, with still the exception of Mad Baron De Lacey's little tank, had been quietly handed over to the British authorities. Since there was no where to house this latest batch of asylum seekers, all other Government designated hostels etc. bursting at the seams. It was decided to leave them at Gerald's farm. Gerald saw the advantage of this. The Vietnamese understood pigs had time on their hands and the British Government had to feed them. Gerald effectively had a free work force. Not only that, but he could be seen as being philanthropic too. Willingly allowing his farm to be used to house poor, unfortunate asylum seekers. He quietly made all his other staff from cook down to farm labourer redundant.

The scientific team was still hanging around. No one was quite sure what he or she was doing, and if asked, no one understood the answers. Obviously they had not used up all of their funding and would remain until such times as they did. So they were ignored and allowed to carry on with what ever they were up to.

The Vietnamese slipped into the farm and the community with grace and ease. They set themselves up a whole cottage industry in manufacturing coloured kites, candles, polished stones and carved driftwood. All of which they sold at a Sunday market in Haverfordwest. Being small, neat and polite they were also a hit with the local girls. Something that didn't go down too well with some of the local lads. But after a couple of skirmishes in which the Vietnamese bounced the much larger and heavier local boys around like ping pong balls, and then apologised for doing so, it was though better to accept them. So they formed their own football team and applied to play in the local league.

It was the Vietnamese who first reported the change that had come over the pigs. They had been harvesting the seaweed from across the river each day. The pigs preferred it fresh. The pigs had quietened down, so much so as to have become almost docile. They were jolly and fat. They were no longer displaying any signs of nervousness. They approached you to have their snouts patted, or their backs scratched and grunted appreciatively if you obliged. That could have been put down to all of the extra attention that they were getting from the attentive Vietnamese. But it seemed to be more than that. The pigs quite obviously were happy and contented. So much so that none of them had exhibited any signs of BDS. The pigs were no longer prancing around, farting and defecating in all directions. Furthermore, they no long stank. In fact, they no longer smelled bad even. Obviously something had happened. The scientists, with both time on their hands and funds available, decided to satisfy their enquiring natures and began to investigate.

It was discovered, to the amazement of the scientific group, that the pigs were all free of BDS. Had the disease died off of its own accord? The mysterious prion having vanished? Or was the seaweed something to do with it? That having been the only variable in the equation. The scientists were intrigued. Both they and Gerald decided that it would be best for the moment to maintain silent and keep the information quietly to themselves. No point in setting any premature hares running.

A paranoid and agitated Meddlesome had visited the Schloss Kutzanburnz. He had done what checking of the programme that he could without a total shutdown. He had found nothing. No further aberrant behaviour had been observed in Toni. Heigar and her father were both of the opinion that an excess of testosterone had caused the sudden glitches and the programme going haywire. It fell upon Heigar's lot to then reduce his hormone balance and maintain them within controllable levels. Meddlesome had not given up on his plan to rid himself of both Heigar and her father though. He took to taking long walks around the castle. Something that arose the suspicions of the Herr Professor, who unbeknown to Meddlesome, spied upon him through a pair of ex SS Panzer Division binoculars. Tracking his every move. The good Herr Doctor having no love for Meddlesome. Since Meddlesome obviously only regarded him, the famous and about to be World recognised Herr Professor, Doctor Frantz Kutzanburnz, as just some custodian of that electrical monster in the cellar. The Herr Professor puffed himself up in rage and frustration. He knew that limp wristed Englishman was up to no good, but what exactly was he planning? He followed Meddlesome's wanderings with renewed and intense interest. Reminding himself how much he hated perverts, and gypsies, and people with long hair, in fact the list was almost endless. Still, soon he would be famous and together; he and his daughter would control Europe. Via, Toni, of course. Then the World would sit up. Oh yes. There would be no room for limp wristed Meddlesomes in his New Order!

Meddlesome during his walks mulled over the problem with Toni and his hormones. There were obviously only three answers. Change the programme for one that over rode his urges. Supply a substitute for Heigar once she and her father had been safely disposed of. A substitute that would really have to be introduced soon. Or castration! The latter certainly held appeal.

On the other side of the Atlantic, Willie was not so happy. The seaweed had proved to be a fiasco and an expensive one at that. Lulu wasn't the same. Hardly surprising when one considered the amount of punishment that her body had been absorbing. The effects of which were all too apparent to Willie. Those Damn journalists were still sniffing around in Florida and

Impeachment was on the cards. Willie really had upset both houses when he had mobilised without their consent. Now the bean counters were busy producing costing's. Willie began to cast around for something to take the mind of the people away from him and onto something else. He almost wished that Iceland would plant a flag on his shores.

Gobbleton was equally unhappy. Taiwan had somehow become Vietnam and his delightful little submissive Te´ Upp had transformed into a bullying midget. Also the promised house by the sea and life of luxury had not materialised. Now she had informed him that they were move from Hanoi and live in the Mekong Delta. The reason she gave was that his seaweed, it had now become his seaweed, he noted, was useless. Gobbleton was confused. It wouldn't have been so bad if Te´ Upp was nice to him. As it was she was worse than living with that bitch of a wife of his. He wondered what the other six families with which Te´Upp had informed him they would be sharing a home, would be like? He thought perhaps a nervous breakdown was in order. But dismissed the idea as he thought that it was unlikely that either Te´Upp, or her masters would understand, or be sympathetic.

Meanwhile, back on the farm, the scientists continued to make more discoveries. The prion had gone and it was the seaweed that effected this miraculous cure. They tested the theory on infected pigs. Fed them sea weed and low and behold they were cured and declared free from infection. They tried it out on other infected animals too. Sheep, goats and cattle all underwent the same recovery. The seaweed was the panacea for BDS. Would it work on humans? Gerald spoke to Toni. Toni spoke to Meddlesome. The problem was one of getting the seaweed tested on humans and then if it was a success, getting the drug onto the market. Stringent laws were in force with the regard to new drugs. Toni and the New Deal Democratic Party needed to bypass this gate somehow. If the drug could be tested and was proven to effect a cure, the NDDP would be seen as saviours. They needed to involve Willie. A secret message was sent. A message that naturally Bradford picked up too.

Willie could see the problem. It was two fold. First of all the drug needed testing. Then if successful, he needed to bypass the food and drug people. Then there were the Brits. Whilst they could be allowed credit for the discovery of the cure, commercial exploitation and profits were definitely the domain of America. If he pulled this one off, then the pressure would be off him. Also he could shuttle back and fore across the Atlantic and reacquaint himself with Heigar's sexual preferences at the same time. So, first things first, test the drug.

This proved to be surprisingly easy. The prison system of America was bursting at the seams with prisoners on death row. Each time one got shot, hung, fried or injected, there was an outcry. What could be simpler that to cut a deal with these guys? Guinea pig in exchange for life? If they died, so what? If they survived, well both sides came out smelling sweet. 500 prisoners were quietly and deliberately infected with the BDS disease. Then the tests and trials began. All of the prisoners that received treatment were pronounced cured. The drug was a success. The next trick would be to get it past the food and drug boys. The obvious method of achieving this would be to claim that it was a natural product.

Del Minki, who had remained remarkably quiet and patient throughout all of the events since their chief scientist had disappeared, along with their genetically modified sea weed, now saw their opportunity to press their case and claim their share of the cake. They had not been idle in the intervening time but had preferred to maintain a very low profile. If things had gone wrong, then they didn't want any fingers pointed in their direction. There again, if events turned out well, then they wanted their share of any profits to be made. So though keeping in the background, and seeming to take no interest, they had in fact been bringing their not inconsiderable resources to bear in the form of both a through investigation and observation of the facts and subsequent events. It was Del Minki that eventually supplied the solution

Though they too had failed to locate their missing scientist and also assumed that he was dead. This was no longer regarded as being important. His original task, that of growing genetically modified seaweed as food, had been a failure. This was however now superseded by a whole new objective. That of obtaining the sole licence to market the drug that could cure BSD. As for having the sole rights to market the seaweed as animal feed? Well that would prove to be difficult, as the stuff only appeared to want to grow on the Blue Stone. They would do some quiet research on that later. Either way they didn't need Kenu Itayaku and since he had absconded with the product in the first place, and subsequently disappeared, presumed drowned. They were not liable for death benefits, or had any responsibilities towards him at all. Del Minki washed its hands of Kenu. Del Minki, via its Washington contacts began to put pressure on Willie Clayton at this stage.

The Brits had the seaweed. Seaweed that had originally belonged to Del Minki. Seaweed that hadn't existed in the Universe until Del Mini produced it. They hinted that it was all a bit like God and Genesis, but on a smaller scale. They could see that now the seaweed was growing in Wales and there was no way that America was going to be able to claim it. Del Minki at this point subtly substituted America for Del Minki, in the conversation. As a source of food for human beings, it was not the best. That they agreed. But as source of food for animals, it was great. So, in the long term, it should not be too difficult to get the stuff to grow elsewhere. But, there again, that was open to exploitation by anybody. All anyone needed was a few cuttings. That would be impossible to stop from happening. No, the real money-spinner was the cure for BSD. Del Minki had the where with all to make this drug. After all, it was only basically ground up seaweed. As such it could be claimed to be a natural product and there fore not subject to federal food and drug regulations. There were no rulings with regard to products obtained from genetically modified seaweed. The stuff had never existed before, so there were no regulations that covered it. Any way, it could be argued that the seaweed was no longer the same plant as the one that had left Japan. In fact the Brits had already used this argument against America when they discovered it growing in their waters. This growth was something that might or might not be connected to their original product. Who could prove what? The lawyers could argue for years and make millions.

No, market the BSD cure now. Market the product as a herbal remedy, called, oh, Kelp Help, or Marine-Aid or something, and pip the Brits to the post. That they could do now. Regulations already existed with regard to not only the validity of herbal products, but with regard to patent laws too. Regulations that were recognised and adhered to by the UK. The market window would only be open for a set length of time. For as long as it took for all sufferers of BSD to be cured. America must strike now, whilst the iron was hot. Get in and get in fast and clean up. Once it became public knowledge that America had a sure-fire cure, it didn't matter if the UK dragged its feet with regard to legislation. As with viagara, public pressure would force the issue.

Willie Clayton could see both the political and economic sense in taking this course of action. Del Minki would make a profit, thus ensuring work for Americans and revenue via tax for the country. There was also the kudos to be gained and no doubt a suitable contribution towards his party's re-election funds from a grateful Del Minki. America would have the sole rights to produce and market Kelp Help, and some licence could be granted to the Brits to produce the drug, sorry, herbal remedy themselves. The Brits could be left alone to harvest and market their own seaweed. This they could sell as both animal feed and a cure for the animal strain of BDS. They could also sell, at a suitable cost sufficient amounts for the herbal cure to be manufactured. This price would have to be sufficiently low for the herbal capsules to be made economically, bearing in mind that America controlled the patent. Since Britain had a state controlled National Health system, then they would not want to be placing themselves in the position of effectively having to buy in the product for which they supplied the raw materials at a cost that was prohibitive. Hence, they would have to keep down the cost of raw seaweed. Meanwhile, since Del Minki would be receiving the raw seaweed for the production of the Kelp Help, they would be in a position to attempt to grow it themselves and then in turn enter the animal feed market. The Kelp help market would diminish whilst the animal feed market would grow. Game, set and match.

Willie Clayton agreed. Del Minki received the green light to start producing "Kelp Help Kapsules" as it was decided that the product would be named. Their marketing team would begin to fire up the sales campaign. Maybe at first a few deliberately leaked rumours. Hints that cure had been discovered. In America. Then perhaps a muddled denial. Just to muddy the waters. Then proof positive, in the form of leaked memos. Then perhaps a Del Minki representative could go on prime time TV. He could make a point of saying that the so-called miracle cure was as yet untested. No need at this point to mention prisons and death row inmates, it hinted of exploitation. Also that it was a natural product an actually really a herbal remedy. Down play the drug side. No need at this to mention seaweed. That could come later, and at no point in the early stages would the fact that the seaweed in question was in fact growing in the UK. Certainly under no circumstances ever, would the words genetically modified be used at all. That should stir things up in Europe. Then a learned paper. Stating that this was a 100% natural product and did in fact indicate that it would indeed provide a cure for BDS. Public pressure should then be sufficient to over ride any UK Governmental doubts. So once again Willie Clayton found himself looking forward to yet another spell with Heigar, and he would bring along Lulu to keep Toni sweet too.

It was the Vietnamese down on Gerald's farm that made the next discovery, but were so confused that at first they kept it to them selves.

CHAPTER. 11

It was the fact that Gerald's pigs stopped smelling like pigs that first alerted the Vietnamese workers that something was not as perhaps it should be. Pigs are supposed to smell, everyone knew that, but Gerald's pigs didn't. Since the root cause of the smell that pigs produce is due to the stuff that comes out of the back end, and that in turn is dependant upon what goes in the front. It didn't take a genius to work out that Gerald's pigs no longer stank because they were eating seaweed. The Vietnamese thought it as being odd, but there again, they were British pigs and white. They were more used to the black pot bellied pigs of their homeland.

Meanwhile, Willie Clayton and Toni were busy cooking deals. Willie had tested the drug for basically his own interests but had been happy to let Toni think that he was doing it for him. After all, it was only Britain and the EEC that suffered from BDS. Now Willie gave Toni the good news. The cure for BDS had been found. So Willie outlined his suggestion. Britain could continue to collect, dry and market the sea weed as animal food and America would produce the wonder cure. America would purchase the raw materials from Britain, in the form of dried seaweed. In turn Britain could also manufacture the drug, but under licence from America. By the way, best to stress that it wasn't a drug. Just a herbal remedy, produced from a naturally occurring substance. In fact, best not to mention it's source at all at this stage. It was from America and made from seaweed. The actual seaweed, being kept a trade secret. Any seaweed being sent to America would be shipped under the heading of animal feed and kept totally separate. Toni, under Meddlesome's direction agreed.

Bradford and Peter sat and observed but did not interfere. Bradford had much bigger plans in mind. Having infiltrated the main computer database of Meddlesome's in Austria. The computer that controlled Toni. Since Britain was now heading the EEC, it therefore had the potential for now controlling Europe. Bradford was now working on a scheme to steal all of that database electronically. His plan was to down load it in secret into his computer's own memory banks. Then he hoped to be able to modify the programme, so that at any time he wished, he could transmit his own signal. This signal would effectively change Toni's instruction signals onto five other frequencies and at the same time place a malignant virus into Meddlesome's database. Full control of Toni then switched from Meddlesome to himself. It was a bold plan, but demanded all of his attention and considerable intellect. Peter was fully involved in renovating the farmhouse. His sister Tiffany was putting on weight, he noticed. Rural life was obviously suiting her.

The British scientific team had used up their funding. Since no more was going to be forth coming from the Government, sensibly they all packed up and left. Joining other projects or going back to doing what ever it was they had been doing before having been seconded. Del Minki saw the window of opportunity open. They promptly stepped in. Under the guise of being part of the USA team that would be assisting Britain to manufacture Kelp Help under licence. They moved in to the trailers and port a-cabins so recently vacated by the British crew. They too were surprised that Gerald's pigs no longer stank. They immediately set about finding out why. The answer to the question amazed them. They notified their headquarters in America in a coded e-mail. An e-mail that was sent from the trailers parked in Gerald's farm. An e-mail that Bradford now also received as a matter of course. He called in Peter to run the decode programme. What they eventually read was very interesting.

Attention. Dr. Kleinhausen.

We have noticed a peculiar phenomena. Pigs that eat fresh, wet GM Sea weed, as their sole diet no longer smell. My team have carried out a series of experimental investigations and have come to the following conclusions. 1 In the pig's stomach and gastric tract is a new and unknown enzyme. 2 We have designated it as ZT/115 3 As far as we are able to establish, this enzyme is peculiar to those pigs fed only on the wet seaweed. 4 We are undertaking further investigations to isolate the reasons for the occurrence of the enzyme. 5 Effect of ZT/115 within the pig brings about a specific chemical reaction to the sea weed in the gut. 6 The pig's faeces become odourless. 7 The protein content increases dramatically. 8 It resembles tofu in both texture and colour. 9 With suitable purification this product would provide a valuable high protein food source for humans. Observations: The pig has effected naturally by a process of digestion and fermentation within its gut a change to the GM sea weed turning it into a high protein food source. Also in the process, the animal has also managed to adequately and effectively feed itself. Conclusion. Pigs fed on fresh, wet GM seaweed thrive. Later to become a valuable food source them selves. In the process they produce naturally a secondary source of protein.

From Dr. Alan Gollygee.

"Well, what do you know? Dad's pigs have turned the sea weed into a food source!"

"Bloody Hell! Brad. It will take one of a Hell of an advertising campaign to convince people to eat pig shit! I notice that the scientists described its texture and colour, They made no mention of its taste!"

"True. So you either don't tell people what they are eating, or make it terribly up market. Snails are eaten, but and I wouldn't pop out into the garden and gobble down a couple. And how about Bloops?"

"What the heck is a bloop Brad?"

"Exactly. It's a chicken egg that is fertile and has a part formed chick inside. You know, beak, eyes and feathers."

"Yuck! Brad. That's really disgusting!" Tiffany had joined the conversation.

"Even so Brad. None of that has actually already passed through an animal's digestive system, Has it?"

"Again true Pete. Which brings me to my final question, and then the defence will rest its case. So, M'Lud, I put it to you. In East Africa, which coffee is the best in Kenya?"

"Brad. I haven't the faintest idea. The one in the handy jars with the free washing up sponge. Which coffee is the best?"

"The one that the elephant has already eaten!"

"What do you mean Brad?" Tiffany stopped knitting the little matinee jacket. "Do the elephants in Kenya pop along to their local Mombassa coffee bar and order a capacino then?" She took on her deepest voice. "Fifteen bucket sized capacinos pal and heavy on the cream and sugar."

"No. Of course not Tiff. There again who knows with the advance of tourism? No, I was referring to coffee beans. Which coffee beans command the highest market price?" Brad looked at his two bemused companions over the top of his huge spectacles. They shook their heads. "So I will tell you. What I meant was that the Elephants eat the coffee beans. The beans don't get fully digested. Just attacked by the enzymes in the elephant's gut. So eventually, in the fullness of time, they pass through. Those are the beans that are regarded as making the best coffee and command the highest price."

"Jeepers! You mean to tell me some poor old Kenyan is following some heard of elephants around a safari park all day and poking through their steaming turds with the end of a stick for coffee beans?" Tiffany joked.

"Correct little sister of mine. The conclusion being, that all protein is edible. Just that some is a doubtful delicacy! Furthermore, human beings will eat just about anything, once they get used to it. It's one of the reasons that as a species we have been so successful."

"So what are we going to do about it, wise brother of mine?"

"I don't know Tiff. Should we do anything at this stage? Is there anything that we can do? We seem to have been down this road before."

Brad looked at both Peter and Tiffany. They in turn looked back at him expectantly.

"We have finite resources. Though I'm working on that problem too. Our strengths are that we are a small cell. No one out side of this room knows, or cares about us. No one suspects us. What we are good at is in fact hacking into systems and decoding secret information. We then make conclusions, based upon that information. We assume that in doing so we actually have all of the information. That of course in not necessarily true. What we have is the piece of information that the sender wishes the receiver to know. It may not be the truth, or the whole picture, as we have discovered."

"Let's examine what we know to date." Brad settled back more comfortably in his chair. "First of all someone some where had the bright idea of feeding bits of dead animals to ruminants. The animals became sick. The sickness was passed to humans."

"Totally separate to that, over in Japan, Del Minki are genetically modifying sea weed. Their stated intention being to feed the World. This may not be true. Food is one of the oldest weapons in the book. The whole idea of siege was based upon that principle. Also, you can feed your friends and starve your enemies. Not forgetting of course, that if you control all the food, then no one with any sense wants to become your enemy."

"Due to political games, and our input too. That seaweed ends up here, washed ashore on dad's farm. Then it gets very interesting. It proves to be worthless as a food source crop for humans." Brad stopped, as if in thought.

Peter raised a point. "Why then would they have thought that it was in the first place and have gone to all the trouble to hi jack the boat?"

"Exactly what I was thinking Pete.

"So either it's not the same sea weed, or it's some new strain that has mutated, or cross pollinated. Or whatever sea weed does." Tiffany had been following the conversation.

"I think that you must be correct Tiffany. We will never know, and for the purpose of this discussion, it doesn't matter." Both Tiffany and Peter nodded. Brad continued. "Then we learn that animals that eat the sea weed are cured of BDS. So immediately there is a market in dried seaweed. Not in itself any small item. Meat reappears on the tables of Europe."

"Then that a cure for BDS in humans has been discovered using the same sea weed. That really is a breakthrough."

"Now the latest discovery is that pig crap is going to be the new food source of the twenty first century. Pigs that have been fed on wet sea weed. It's all gone around in a circle."

Peter looked at Brad and then said quietly. "And how did we find all of this out? Because our worthy PM is wired up to some computer and Meddlesome and Heigar are pulling his strings. That is much more sinister. A Prime Minister who is at this moment head of the EEC. Nor should we forget that his partner in crime, Gobbleton has mysteriously disappeared. We believe that in fact he has toddled off to Taiwan with his mistress and seaweed samples. BUT, WE DON'T KNOW. Maybe our thieves fell out. If so, then we really are playing for serious stakes and we had better watch our backs. They are sad, mad, bad and dangerous to know. How much of the story do you think that your father knows Brad?"

"Hmm. Good point Peter. Tiffany, what do you reckon Dad knows? I've never had much to do with him."

"Not too much would be my guess. Otherwise he would be more active and trying to work out some edge whereby he made a profit." Tiffany stated cynically.

"OK, I agree with that sister. So Brad, what should we do?"

"Nothing for the moment. Let's wait and see. In the mean time I won't be eating any meat, nor any new wonder food either."

Del Mini's chief executives met. The meeting was held in secret. Del Minki were still smarting over the way they had lost the GM seaweed in the first place. They decided not to make the same mistake again. The first thing to be done would be to carry out secret and stringent tests with regard to the strange properties of the new product. The question was raised that was this effect peculiar to just Gerald's pigs, or was it wide spread. Del Minki decided to investigate, and in doing so, naturally began to investigate Gerald Fatslobe. What they uncovered not only was of interest, it was, they considered a possible point of leverage.

The first thing that Del Mini did was to increase the staff numbers at the farm and begin to check if any other animals were being fed on the seaweed. They discovered that truckloads of seaweed were being moved by Gerald. These they secretly followed. So the extent of Gerald's pig farming activities within the UK became known to them. It was a simple step to follow these leads and uncover the vast extent of his illegal empire. An empire perilously close to ruin. An empire that when their forensic accountants did their sums, was one that could not have survived without having had access to out side funding. The next question was from whence had that funding originated. The trail led straight back to Al Arrod.

Meanwhile, the scientists had checked on the actual seaweed. It still only grew on Blue stone outcrops that it had attached itself to, and was growing upon, every available outcrop below the high water mark. Though its growth rate was prolific, due to the limiting factor of the availability of Blue Stone, it had now reached its boundaries. The scientists knocked off a few lumps of Blue Stone from above the high water mark and threw them in the river. Immediately they were colonised. Thus they came to the conclusion that it would be possible to lay out organised weed beds, and grow the weed commercially. They also sent samples of both weed and stone back to their labs in America. In an effort to copy the conditions in the Cleddau River. The results however were disappointing. The weed seemed to be happy only in its present location. Del Minki redoubled their efforts.

A further discovery was made. It was only the pigs that were allowed to free range over the fore shore that produced the tofu, or torpooh, as some wag had christened it. Pigs that were fed on the seaweed at Gerald's other farms, did not produce any thing more interesting than a high aroma fertiliser.

The next breakthrough for Del Minki came in America. The samples of faeces sent from Gerald's pigs were indeed high in protein, but they also held yet another secret. A highly marketable secret. One that could make a fortune for who ever patented and marketed it. The secret was yet another strange and new enzyme. An enzyme that was code-named, Skin/E/1. Del Minki had struck gold.

What Del Minki found was that if an obese person was fed a diet of Torpooh, as they had decided to name the product, their metabolism changed and they burned off the excess fat as if by magic. At last, the slimmer's dream! Del Minki decided to keep this valuable piece of commercial intelligence very much to themselves. They secretly planned as exactly how they would go about cornering the World health food, diet and fitness resort markets.

CNN broke the news that both the Chinese and the North Koreans had suddenly started throwing off their clothes, dancing and farting. It didn't take the Del Minki team long to connect the "Empty" banana containers with Gerald's farming activities. Banana containers that suddenly seem to have found some other system of being dispatched. Yet no other port in the UK was handling such a cargo. Nor were the full banana containers that they followed through the system behaving in the manner of the one's that had previously exited through Milford Haven. A further check quickly revealed that had in fact all of the containers that left Milford Haven originally contained bananas, once added to the normal import quota. It transpired that every man; woman and child in the UK would have had to eat the equivalent of eight kilograms of bananas every day for a year! Del Minki dug deeper.

They estimated the maximum number of pigs that Gerald could have owned, spread all over his UK holdings. These they compared to the present live stock numbers. A huge discrepancy was discovered. Where had all of the missing pigs gone? Now China and North Korea had the human form of BDS. Obviously; Gerald had not only been involved in massive fraud with regard to his farms. He had been moving and exporting his infected live stock too. Furthermore Gerald was The British Minister For Agriculture! If Gerald were to be convicted, then on that charge alone, they would throw away the key. Let alone beginning to consider the National and Global political implications! The small investigation team returned to America, along with their top-secret report.

Del Minki chief executives rubbed their hands in glee.

The scientists back on the farm. Who had not been privy to their colleagues findings were instructed to investigate why it was only the free-range pigs exhibited the interesting systems. The answer was yet again to do with the Blue Stone.

As is common in estuaries, shellfish abound. One of these is the lowly periwinkle. A small sea snail. It goes about it's business of eating alga and plants quietly and steadily, not bothering anyone, and no doubt hoping no one will bother it. It was these small molluscs, caught up in the still wet seaweed that ended up by accident in the pig's stomach along with the weed. Molluscs that were still alive and which had been grazing the under water alga that also grew on the Blue Stone. The combination of these factors, were what made all the difference. Once the weed was transported by road however, the molluscs died. The pigs could still eat the weed, but the internal reactions were no longer the same. They notified Del Minki headquarters in America. An e-mail that Brad as usual intercepted. Now Del Minki headquarters had all of the pieces of the seaweed jig saw. Except two. They did not know about Toni's implants and they were sublimely unaware of Brad and his team. The Del Minki management met again and again in secret.

They decided to adopt the following strategy. Certain facts they would release. Others they would keep to themselves. Obviously, there was a huge market to be exploited in selling "Torpooh" However, it would not be very wise to disclose exactly how the product was manufactured.

Another problem would be one of securing a reliable supply of raw material. It was decided to approach the matter on two fronts. The first the open and visible front and the second, the hidden agenda, that depended upon the success of the first ploy.

Kelp Help Kapsules would require seaweed. The seaweed depended upon Blue Stone. Blue Stone was only available in West Wales. West Wales was an economically depressed area with little or no industry. Therefore any thing that brought jobs into the area would not only be welcomed by both the British Government and the Welsh Assembly, (What ever that was!)

Del Minki would propose that Blue Stone beds be laid out in the river in question and the weed cultivated on a commercial basis. This weed being harvested and Kelp Help Kapsules produced from it, in both the USA and Britain. The latter under licence. Naturally the market for these Kapsules would eventually dry up. Though now there were reports of BDS breaking out in both China and North Korea. So much the better for sales.

The second industry would be the harvesting of the weed for feeding livestock. A smaller, but ongoing operation. Finally there was the real money-spinner. The hidden agenda of Torpooh.

Gerald Fatslobe was vulnerable. He had exploited his political position for personal gain. Tax free gain too. Now, financially he was on all but on his knees. Up to his eyebrows in debt to Al Arrod. Del Minki would wipe out all of his debts in one fell swoop, providing he co-operated with Del Minki. Gerald would be put back in the pig farming business. His empire would be expanded. But his land would be used to grow the seaweed that Del Minki intended to feed to his pigs. Sea weed that would be transported in such a way as to ensure that the periwinkle snail remained alive and well. Seaweed that would be fed to special battery pigs. Forced fed like Strasbourg Geese, if necessary. The odourless waste being collected by a Del Minki subsidiary specially set up to perform this task. Waste that would be dried and pressed and then vacuum wrapped and shipped to another Del Minki subsidiary in America. Shipped under the heading, "Dehydrated hydro carbon briquettes" Home barbecue use. Or even, "Animal feed stock base." Which ever was the most viable and least suspicious.

Once in the USA, the raw material for Torpooh would be purified, and have various other down stream, by products added. Such as rejected soybeans. In fact anything to add bulk and that normally would constitute a waste disposal problem in its own right. This would then be sprung upon an unsuspecting world as either an expensive diet, or health food. There would be a whole new market to exploit by setting up their own health centres. With most of the population's in Europe and America over weight, the prospects for huge profits were enormous. Just so long as no one ever got wind of the fact that their healthy diet and almost magical slimming that then came about, was in fact a result of in the main, of eating processed pig shit!

Thus Del Minki moved into phase two of their plan. The ensnaring of Two Ferrets Gerald Fatslobe.

Gerald was in a pickle. Gerald knew that he was in a pickle. Al Arrod
had refused point blank to start up operations again. Gerald, apart from his
Ministerial salary, had no income. He still had huge outgoings though. He
was feeding his pigs on the seaweed, but there were still all the other costs
to be taken into account. Gerald could see that he was going down hill. Al
Arrod wanted his passport. He wouldn't pay another red cent out to Gerald
and Gerald knew that once Al Arrod had his passport, he would no longer
have any reason for financing Gerald any longer. Then out of the blue came
this gift from heaven! Del Minki threatening to expose him. They had just
come straight out. No beating around the bush. If you don't agree to our
terms, you are exposed Fatslobe! And what terms! What marvellous and
wonderful terms!

Del Minki would extend and expand his farm. Put in weed beds. Set
up a pill industry and sea weed exportation industry. Pay off all of Gerald's
debts. Help him to restock and expand and all he had to do was smooth
everything through Parliament. Feed all of his pigs on the seaweed. And
allow them to collect the waste from the pigs for some crazy scheme they
had for making barbecue briquettes or some thing. Gerald could not believe
his good fortune. Gerald said yes. Having first of all made all the suitable
whining and pleading noises. At last, he would become King Pig of Europe
and legally too. He could forget Al Arrod and his passport.

The developments at Gerald's farm proceeded rapidly and without
hitch. That a natural cure had been found for human BDS was received
with joy amongst those sufferers and super market managers alike. There
was a perception of optimism within Europe that a light was shining at the
end of the tunnel and soon, not only would elderly vicars and overweight
females cease to strip off their clothes and dance gleefully along the aisles,
but that soon meat too would be back on the those shelves.

Myreg Cwmyurr, naturally was allowed to take all the credit for bringing
the new sea weed industry into a depressed West Walian economy and both
Westminster and The Welsh Assembly in Cardiff breathed a sigh of relief.

Willie Clayton was equally happy. He had managed to slip away from
impeachment. Kelp Help Kapsules would soon be sold off super market
shelves and he was skipping back and for over the Atlantic to reinforce

"The Special Relationship" that a confident Britain was now sharing with America. And Willie was sharing, on a more personal basis with Heigar.

Heigar was happy. Willie was sharing her bed. He was far less demanding than Toni. Anyway, a change was pleasant.

Meddlesome however, was now fully in the grip of his paranoia. A Meddlesome that now looked dark and haggard. A Meddlesome that had large black rings under his eyes. A Meddlesome that stayed out of sight and slunk from shadow to shadow. A Meddlesome that regarded everyone else as persons that only provided a difficulty to every solution. He had however now finalised his plans for the tragic deaths of both Heigar and her father. During his visits to the Schloss Kutzanburnz, He had secretly placed the small explosive charges in the rocks above the Her Doktor's home. He would now wait for more snow.

Tiffany was happy, her pregnancy was proceeding well, and both lads seemed not as yet to have noticed. Being a small slim girl by nature, it wasn't showing too much she thought.

Brad and Peter continued to monitor the activities down on the farm but since they had no knowledge of Del Minki's real purpose, put it all down to the natural greed of Gerald Fatslobe.

The only persons unhappy were Al Arrod, and Gobbleton. The latter had suddenly found himself transported to a farming commune in the rice growing area of the Mekong Delta and sharing the place with six other families and a very annoyed Te'Upp. Gobbleton was bemused and in shock.

Xmas was fast approaching, and as is usual in both America and Britain, all thought of World events was drowned and forgotten beneath the sounds of Jonnie Mathis and "A little drummer boy" and information with regard to the number of shopping days remaining.

Quietly the first of the seaweed growing pens was commissioned. The launch of Kelp Help was to be effected on both sides of the Atlantic simultaneously in January of the New Year. It was to be claimed as a triumph of Anglo-American co operation.

Willie secretly gave Heigar a fetching little number in black silk that consisted of a mask, fish net black panties, stockings and matching suspender belt.

Lulu gave Toni a shapeless cardigan that she had valiantly hand knitted and Tiffany began to look at Mother Care magazines.

Brad began to move money. Del Minki's money.

Systematically the seaweed beds were installed on Gerald's farm, and the weed propagated. Some of the subsequent crop being shipped out to America and going to Del Minki to make Kelp Help Kapsules. Some to their Welsh subsidiary. Red Dragon Capsules as they were marketed in the UK had people beating a path to the door of the manufacturers. The rush for a cure for the human form of BDS was on.

In the general hubris with regard to the seaweed, no one took any notice of Gerald's activities. Gerald of course had wet sea weed carefully collected, along with its all important periwinkle lodgers, and shipped out to all of his various pig farming enterprises all over Europe. Pigs were going to be back in fashion. Bacon would be back on the breakfast menu. Gerald was stocking up. Once meat was cleared throughout the EEC, he would be back in business in a big way. In fact Gerald would just about have the monopoly on pigs in Europe. Gerald's dreams were about to come true. Mr. Slice would again rule supreme! Gerald began to drool in happiness. There was only one small cloud on the horizon. There was a limit as to how far he could transport the seaweed by road and keep the periwinkle alive. There was no chance of getting it to Poland or Eastern Germany, where Gerald had big pig interests. Still, he could feed all of his farms in the UK. Then, given time, restock the rest of his empire from the BDS free animals bred in the UK.

This was a problem that Del Minki had not as yet solved either. Therefore they were dependent upon the raw material for Torpooh from Gerald's UK based farms only. Del Mini had quietly set up a waste collection company called Green Waste. They had instructed Gerald to award Green Waste the contract for the cleaning and removal of all pig waste from Gerald's farms. Gerald went along happily with the arrangements. If Del Minki wanted to take all of his pig crap away for nothing and set Gerald up in business in the process, lovely! Waste that was then secretly freeze dried, pressed into 50Kg plastic wrapped bails and shipped to America under the heading of animal feed base. Del Minki was about to launch Torpooh on the world's markets.

Del Minki however had not bargained on the their supply of raw materials being confined to the UK. Still, it was only a question of solving the transportation problem of the periwinkle. They would solve that given time. Then, once the problems of cultivating the seaweed in places other than the Cleddau Estuary were also resolved, Del Minki would really be in business on a money-spinner. Feeding people on the one hand to make them fat. And supplying the cure to make them slim again on the other.

Del Minki however had decided not to market Torpooh under their own name. No, they would put in place a whole new health fad industry first. They would market trainers and sports wear. Fitness equipment and have health centres and spars. All under the name of "Keepsuslim."

Keepsuslim was not just a supplement, but a complete diet. Suitable adverts would be placed in certain Sunday newspapers. An intensive campaign would be run on TV. Package tours for the whole family. Fat mum and dad getting slim, whilst the kids were catered for and fed ice cream so that later, they too would be returning. Or if Del Minki were lucky enough to hit upon a whole family of fatties, take them all on board. Torpooh was not going to be cheap, but affordable, just! And hopefully would soon be viewed by everyone, both in America and Europe, not to mention Australia as being a necessity. Del Minki quietly put their infrastructure in place and then launched their new and exciting product upon an eager and overweight Western World. It didn't take Brad, Peter and Tiffany long to work out what was happening. Meanwhile Keepsuslim was acquiring literally a huge following of grateful and very obese disciples. Over night, the share value of Keepsuslim tripled and continued to rise. Their world wide web site was one of the busiest. The fatties of the World united behind Keepsuslim and shed pounds. Meanwhile the starving in the third world looked on bemused and had they have been aware, would have perhaps reflected upon the immortal words of millionaire John F Kennedy. "Live is not fair."

"It's too circumstantial Brad." Declared Tiffany, "Where did Keepsuslim suddenly appear from? Complete with gyms, clothing, dumb bells and package health tours too!"

"It's got to be Del Minki Tiff. What do you think Brad?"

"I'm sure that you are correct. I have been doing a bit of quiet checking on that wheeling and dealing father of ours. He has pig-breeding stations all over the UK. The ban on moving and selling meat is about to be lifted. Naturally dad, being Min. Of Ag. Is well behind that and pushing hard. Toni is head of the EEC. He is pushing Europe. The seaweed is being shipped out all over the place as a cure. BUT, and this is the interesting bit. Special loads of wet weed are sent out to dad's farms. Why I wonder? It has to be the effect that feeding wet weed has upon the pigs. Pigs that produce a very special kind of waste. Waste that is collected by a company called Green Waste. A company whose sole contract is to collect from dad's farms. Now that really is suspicious. More so when we discover that the farms in question are all held under false names and the waste is then processed and shipped off to America!" Brad looked pleased with himself. "Haven't I been busy? Not only that but the good news is that I have finally downloaded all of the mad professor's programme. Any time we like, we can take over control of Toni!"

"So we are in charge." Tiffany clapped her hands. "Let's shut down all of Dad's pig farms and tripple the tax on gin. That would really upset both of our worthy parents." Tiffany laughed and clapped her hands at the thought.

"Steady on Tiff. They are your parents when all said and done."

"Oh I know that Pete, but dad is a crook and mum is an alcoholic. Not exactly a pair of shining examples of the sort of person that I would choose as a grand parents." She smiled and patted her stomach.

"So that's why you are putting on weight!" Peter looked surprised. "And there was I thinking that I would have to sign you up for a Keepsuslim clinic!"

"That would not be a very good idea, considering their track record Pete." Declared Brad firmly.

"So;I am about to become an uncle. When's it due Tiff?"

"Oh not for a little while yet. You still have time to sort out Toni, and Del Minki too, and see what you can do about dad while you are at it!"

"Oh I already have little sister. I already have. And now that you are budding I have even more reason for forward planning."

"What do you mean Brad? What have you been up to?"

"Well, I discovered that our father, the Honourable Gerald Fatslobe MP and Minister For Agriculture has a whole load of farms in the UK, all under false names. All containing pigs. And all making a profit. A profit that is slid sideways. So I just put the systems in place to slide it a bit further. When ever I want to, that is. I'm not ready yet. There are a few other little financial transactions that need completing. Still an empire like that would make a nice little gift to that lump that you are carrying around Tiff." He polished his glasses in a self-satisfied manner.

"What else have you been up to, wise old brother of mine?"

"Oh nothing very difficult Sis. I have breached a few security systems that's all. I can siphon off dad's profits electronically any time I like!"

"How very clever of you Brad." Peter looked impressed. "Almost the perfect crime. I mean, he can't very well make too much noise, as he won't want to draw attention to himself will he? What else have you been up to?"

"Well, I have got into Del Minki too. All sorts of charities have suddenly been the beneficiaries of anonymous and large donations. Oh, we are a company by the way. Registered in the Cayman Islands naturally."

"What sort of company Brad?"

"A very wealthy one Tiffany."

"Oh, that's nice. Have I got a credit card? Can I order things from Mother Care?"

"Give that brother of yours another ten minutes Tiff and he'll have you a platinum account with them, by the sound of it. Brad, have you any idea of what you are worth? There are still wicker baskets full of money down in the cellar."

"I, or rather we, are worth whatever we want to be worth Peter. I don't care about the money, you know that. You know I am going to have a lot of fun teaching my nephew or niece the art of international hacking. What will you name he or she Tiff?"

"I hadn't really thought about it. What do you think Pete?"

"No use asking me Tiff. This has come as a surprise to me. Anything that makes you happy I guess. Though I would advise caution in choices such as Beau Regard Butterfly. Or Camellia Parkyourballs."

"But you don't mind?"

"Mind what? Names, well I just said that I would adv....."

"No Silly! Me, being pregnant."

"No. Of course not. I thought that you were taking the pill. I thought you didn't want a baby. I'm very happy; to be a daddy, but I never pushed you as I didn't want to try to make you do things that you didn't want....... A bit like the green hair and safety pins I suppose."

Brad swivelled around towards them. He was seated in his favourite place. A large swivel, leather arm chair. Placed in front of his computer console. "OK. Good. We have all played Happy Families but I am serious. We have several problems. Our dear old dad is so crooked that he couldn't lay straight in bed. Toni is being controlled by a raving queer and some megalomaniac wife and her insane father. Del Minki is about to subtly try to take over the World. Furthermore Del Minki we all know relies upon genetic engineering. We all know what happens when we little old humans start a-messing with genetics. We have no idea what will be the end result of this Keepsuslim nonsense."

"Consider this. There is Del Minki, an American company remember, remaining very, very quiet when their seaweed was hijacked from Japan. Why would that be I wonder? Because quite simply they want to control the Worlds food supplies and use it as a political weapon. For Del Minki from now on read USA. Because believe me, Willie Clayton, or anyone else that sits in the White House is going to be controlled just as effectively by the Del Minki Corporation, as our dear sweet and totally brainless Prime Minister is by the string pullers here."

"Then consider us. No one knows about us. We have limitless financial resources. I'm pretty sure that I can move money from anywhere to anywhere. Just so long as I only do it once. We are a bona fida off shore company. How about if we decided to take charge?" He waited for their reactions.

"To what end Brad?" It was Peter who spoke. "I mean, we don't need the cash and personally I have no desire to be in charge. I quite like Tiff to be happy and for me to potter."

"That's fine Peter. It does however presuppose that the World will go on turning the way it does. What about if Del Minki has other ideas? Not to mention Meddlesome and that crowd. How safe is your pottering and Tiffany's happiness then?"

"I take your point Brad. So you feel that we should exert our influence on Global events?"

"Exactly. Step in here to help out a famine. Step in there to level the playing field. Nothing too drastic. Just the odd spanner in the works now and again on the side of the good guys."

"Can we do that Brad?" Tiffany asked her brother, "I mean like now? Really?"

"No. Not at the moment. We will take charge, but not before all of our systems are in place and we are good and ready. Then we will strike. But it won't be for personal power. It will be for the betterment of mankind." Brad took off his glasses and polished them vigorously.

"I like that idea Brad." Said Tiffany. A better World for our child. Mmmm, if you are to teach our child all the secrets of your black arts we had better call him, or her Geek! But come on tell us more. What exactly is your plan?"

"Simple really. We take control of Toni and in doing so we use him to gain access to the EEC computers. From there we take over the reigns of the EEC farming surpluses. We don't attempt to control the EEC that would be too difficult. Anyway, with all of them pulling in different directions and all at the same time, it would be impossible. No, all we need to do is exercise control over what happens to the crop excesses. Agriculture is the single largest industry within the EEC. Furthermore the EEC produces far more food than it can consume. At the moment they are ploughed back into the soil."

"Once this BDS thing is finally eradicated, then the EEC will be back to producing too much milk. We turn it into powdered milk, instead of butter and cheese mountains. All the excess fruit can be dried along with excess grapes. Don't produce the wine. Dry the grapes instead. Mix the currants with the excess grain. It could form a basic high-energy food stock. It may not be to palatable, but if it's that or starve........ Actually, with a little thought it could be made into a highly palatable and nutritious basic diet."

"Potatoes are another example. Easy to freeze dry and powder. No, if only a small percentage of the energy that is expended by corporations such as Del Minki were to be utilised in actually feeding the World and not in chasing profits. There would be far less famine. But it's Governments that have to lead the way. This we can do, and in doing so gain the respect and friendship of people Worldwide at a grass root level. If you grow up knowing that it was the EEC that saved your life, then you will be far less liable to show aggressive tendencies later in life, towards those that fed you as a child. For the moment though, we wait, and we watch, and we keep well away from Keepsuslim. We also keep a very close eye on Del Minki because remember, they also, have intentions to control the world through food. Though their method of control is directly opposite the direction that we will choose. So are you game?"

Peter looked at Tiffany. They both looked at Brad and nodded their agreement.

CHAPTER. 12

Keepsuslim was launched to a fanfare of publicity. This was the answer to one of the major problems in the Western World. Overeating! Two thirds of the planet didn't get enough to eat and the other third was having triple bypass heart operations brought on by a diet of cigarettes and stuffing themselves like Strasbourg geese. Del Minki couldn't loose. On the one hand they supplied the high fat, high calorie food that made people fat. Then on the other, the expensive diet that would once again make them thin. Presumably then to start the cycle all over again! The whole of the Western World was on the Keepsuslim fad and they loved it. Eat as much as you like. Drink as much as you like. Sign up for a two-week intensive course of Keepsuslim at one of the expensive health centres. Or take the package tour, if your pocket only ran to the lower end of the market. Miraculously, you would shed the extra pounds. Someone compared Keepsuslim with the Catholic Church. Fall by the wayside, confess, do penance, and low and behold you are restored. Certainly Keepsuslim was adopted with all the fervour of a new religion.

Apart from shedding kilograms, and one of the Keepsuslim TV adverts showed the gross Global figure for human fat lost in tonnes! There was a very healthy business in designer sports and leisurewear. Naturally, Del Minki was laughing all the way to the bank and had given a handsome contribution towards Willie Clayton's re election campaign. Equally naturally, the source of Keepsuslim was shrouded in secrecy. Several false trails were set including copies of, "genuine documents" that alluded to Amazon rain forests and rare plants.

Relations between the USA and Britain could not have been better, and Toni was running smoothly and heading up the EEC. Kelp Help and Red Dragon capsules were effectively curing the human form of BDS and dried seaweed for its manufacture was being harvested.

Gerald Fatslobe was restocking in the UK and in his shadowy EEC farms with BDS free pigs. Dried seaweed was also being used as animal feed, and Myreg Cwmyurr being seen as the person who brought work back to the valleys etc. Such was his popularity in Wales that he was offered the job as Lord Mayor of Cardiff. This post being one of the most highly paid but least advertised facts in The Principality. It was there that he made his famous speech that some how slipped by the censor's net. There had been a suggestion that a Gondola be put on Roath Park Lake in Cardiff. Myreg thought this to be an excellent idea, and suggested that two be acquired then perhaps they would breed.

Tiffany was about to give birth. She had told her parents, but her mother had killed off so many of her brain cells with gin, it didn't register, and her father was far more interested in his pigs. Soon he would have sufficient to start slaughtering again.

Al Arrod was fuming. His plans had been thwarted. He had spent a lot of time and money and still was no closer to obtaining his coveted British Passport. He demanded to meet in secret with Fatslobe.

Meddlesome's moods had grown darker. The paranoia was eating away at his soul. He was positively looking forward to executing the demise of the family Kutzanburnz.

Gobbleton's brain somehow could not wholly cope with his situation. He was drifting away from reality, and firmly believed that he was dreaming and would soon wake up. Consequently he was quite happy mastering the art of ploughing wet paddy in bare feet. With a pair of water buffalo.

On a dark wet winter's night in West Wales, Al Arrod went to meet Gerald Fatslobe in secret at his farm. Al Arrod was annoyed. Al Arrod was far more than just annoyed. Al Arrod was enraged, and he felt a strong sense of injustice. Gerald, he felt had cheated him and deprived him of his birthright. Al Arrod felt British. He spoke English. He was rich and successful. It wasn't so much the money that he had invested in Fatslobe that he cared about. It was the fact that Gerald had some how evaded him and come out on top. Al Arrod felt used. Again the English had treated him like a foreigner. Why was it that he could not obtain a British Passport? Then he too could look down upon foreigners. Al Arrod did not like people besting him. Nor did he like feeling that he was a second class citizen in what he regarded as his own country. He bore a grudge. Al Arrod wanted his passport and he wanted it now!

The problem was that now there was only Fatslobe upon whom to try to exert pressure. That idiot Gobbleton had gone and got himself drowned. Al Arrod had thought about Gobbleton's disappearance for a long time. Al Arrod had no doubt that Gobbleton was in fact dead. Te'Upp had disappeared too. Al Arrod believed that Te'Upp had double crossed him and done away with Gobbleton herself. Then disappeared, taking all the money with her. Money that Al Arrod saw as being rightly his. He waited quietly in the cold darkness of one of the pigarries, for Fatslobe to arrive. The rain began to fall more heavily and lightening from an advancing storm cloud front occasionally lit up the dark and hostile Western sky. The pigs moved nervously at the noise and flashes of the approaching storm.

Al Arrod thought that he heard a noise. He listened intently but was only rewarded with the sound of the West wind and the hard rain beating down on the corrugated metal roof of the piggary. He shivered and drew his expensive coat closer around himself. Al Arrod did not want to be seen. He had taken explicit precautions not to be seen and to keep this meeting a secret. He had even driven himself to the farm in small hired car. A car that he had been careful to hire under a false name and then conceal. He wasn't quite sure what he intended to do to Gerald, but Al Arrod certainly wanted to frighten him. He was going to show that fat Englishman that it didn't pay to cross a son of the desert. He would make Gerald understand that if he knew what was good for him he would produce the passport and quickly. He fingered the curved blade, the twin of Mr. Slice that he had secreted in his belt. Al Arrod wondered if the noise that he thought that he had heard was that of one of Gerald's Vietnamese workers? He quietly climbed over the low wall that separated him from the pigs and slipped into the shadows.

The pigs snuffled and moved uneasily in the darkness. They pressed back, grunting amongst themselves. Finally turning in a semi circle to face him, their wet snouts cocked up at an angle and their little beady eyes squinting at him from the darkness. Al Arrod ignored them. He had no love for pigs.

A dark shadow filled the doorway and Gerald's voice hissed out from the darkness. Al Arrod stood up from his crouched position, "Over here Fatslobe."

Gerald joined him; the pigs retreated a little, but maintained their almost defensive, semi circle.

"Where's my passport Fatslobe?" Al Arrod began without his usual polite preamble.

"These things take time Al Arrod."

"You have had time Fatslobe, and money too. My money."

"Yes, yes, well I can repay the loan. Very soon in fact." Gerald spoke almost flippantly. He knew that he had no use for Al Arrod and Al Arrod had nothing with which to threaten him. No, he would pay back what he owed. Less expenses, of course, and in his own good time. Meanwhile this obnoxious little Middle Eastern gentleman should be dissuaded from making foolish and threatening noises.

"You know what will happen if you don't get me my passport Fatslobe?" Al Arrod's voice held a menacing tone.

"Nothing at all actually." Replied Gerald cheerfully. "I have new backers. Backers that are vastly superior to anything that you can produce Al Arrod. So don't try to frighten me little man, or maybe it's you who will be receiving a knock on the door at midnight. Or better still, I could arrange for the fraud squad to be given certain evidence that involved you in some nice juicy conspiracy. Oh yes Al Arrod, better you go and play your little games somewhere else. In fact, I might even have a word with the Home Secretary, perhaps we could get your work permit or whatever revoked." Gerald laughed. Gerald was feeling quite bold, he held Mr. Slice behind his back. He thought that perhaps he would flash it little, Just enough to have Al Arrod running for the door and rain. "Yes, better you toddle off back to London before something very nasty happens to you."

Al Arrod was incensed. He too decided to flash his curved blade. Both of them, unbeknown to each other and in the darkness, raised their weapons. It may have been the sudden flash of lightening, or perhaps the almost instant crash of thunder that caused the pigs to bolt. The effect upon both Gerald and Al Arrod though was the same. They were knocked upon each other. Each perhaps thinking the other had attacked. Both automatically defended themselves. Their two arms struck downwards and the wicked curved blade performed the task for which they had been designed. Each inflicted a mortal wound upon the other and together they sank to the concrete floor bleeding profusely.

The pigs now boldly approached the two twitching bodies. They sniffed. They became excited, grunting and snuffling. Pigs eat anything. Pigs fed upon genetically modified seaweed tasted blood for the first time, and they liked it. Eagerly they tore at the still warm bodies and their newfound food source. And so it was that as Tiffany's baby daughter took her first lung full of air, so Gerald's pigs finished off the last juicy morsels of Al Arrod and the British Minister for Agriculture. Leaving behind only a few torn and bloody clothes, a pair of gumboots and two identical curved daggers.

Gerald was presumed identified from the gumboots. The other person eaten by the pigs remained a mystery. Al Arrod's disappearance was not noticed for a few weeks and no one showed particular interest. Bradford naturally put two and two together, and as Al Arrod was no longer alive and hence presumably would have no use for money where ever he had gone. Brad helped himself to one or two million. By hacking into Al Arrod's secret bank accounts. Naturally Bradford and Tiffany inherited Gerald's empire. Having first taken the trouble to have their mother detained in a home for hopeless alcoholics under section two of the mental health act. They then set about reorganising things and decided to go organic, placing Peter at the head of the company. Meanwhile the pigs that had eaten Gerald and Al Arrod digested them and passed them out as normal waste. Waste that was carefully collected by the Green Waste Company and processed as raw material for Keepsuslim. Gerald and Al Arrod had been recycled.

Within the ranks of Parliament, whilst making suitable noises, Gerald's loss was not mourned. His ferrets had been a nuisance, disturbing the ritual postprandial slumbers of MPs. His passing though was of interest. He was after all, the first Minister For agriculture that had been eaten by pigs. There was hard core cadre of disillusioned farmers who were cruel enough to voice the opinion that it was a pity that the threat didn't hang over the head of every Min. Of Ag!

Whilst it had been raining in Wales. It had been snowing in Austria and Meddlesome had been summoned to the Schloss Kutzanburnz by Heigar. Heigar and her father were planning to poison Meddlesome and put him through the animal incinerator. A bit at a time. They were of the opinion that once any glitches in Toni's programmes had been removed, they would run him single-handed. Toni would become the front man in Europe. A united Europe. A united Europe that Heigar and her father secretly controlled. They would use this position to build an empire that would last a thousand years. The Teutonic peoples would at last grasp their destiny and step forward into a new dawn. The National Democratic Peoples Party would rule Europe and then the World. She could control that weak American President as she had controlled Toni. He would be the next in line for the electrode treatment. So she summoned Meddlesome. She informed him that she thought it was time that Meddlesome sorted out the programme.

Meddlesome went in secret to the Schloss Kutzanburnz and fumed. "She thought, she thought." What would she know about programmes? And to summon him too. Who did she and her father think they were? "The programme." It wasn't "The programme". It was HIS programme. Further more he had found nothing wrong. There was nothing wrong and he had told them both so. What were they doing? The pair of them. He knew that they were plotting. Well, he had his little secrets too. In the fading light of the evening, Meddlesome went to inspect his charges.

The good Herr Doktor espied upon him with his SS Panzer Division binoculars. Heigar stood by his side. They stood in the shadow of the wall of the Schloss, looking up the snow-covered slopes to where a mere 1000 meters away and above Meddlesome held something in his hand. Inspecting it.

"What is he doing Father?"

"I don't know Heigar. He is holding something." Her father passed the binoculars to his daughter and used the telescopic site on his heavy Mauser hunting rifle. "Shall I shoot him now Heigar? No one knows that he is here. No one has ever known that he has been here. The programme is good. That idiot of a husband of yours is head of the EEC and the time is perfect for us to take control. Then we can plan to operate upon that stupid American President too. The snow will cover Meddlesome's body and he won't be found until spring. An unfortunate victim of a hunting accident." Or we can dig him up later and incinerate him. Better if he is frozen solid when we saw him up. It is less messy that way. He gently squeezed the trigger.

The heavy bullet passed straight through Meddlesome's back as it was intended that it should, exploding his heart, and then travelling on, exiting out through his chest. There it didn't stop but flew on its deadly path. Amputating his right thumb and striking the fulminate of mercury detonator that he had been holding in his hand as it did so. A detonator that was connected to five others and their respective charges. The resultant avalanche swept down the mountain taking Meddlesome's body with it, and smashing it beyond recognition. A perfect crime, there would be no trace of any bullet wound now. Well, it would have been the perfect crime if the avalanche had not then have buried both Heigar and her Father under several tons of snow as it swept up and over the wall of the Schloss Kutzanburnz.

In Britain the country mourned the loss the Minister for Agriculture and the wife of the PM. The Nation's sympathy went out to Toni and with it his standing grew.

Bradford by default inherited, along with his sister, Gerald's empire. An empire that he had promptly set about rearranging, so that Peter could run it along organic lines. An empire that no longer was at the beck and call of Del Minki. Del Minki were infuriated but were powerless to do anything. A Del Minki that was suddenly plagued by computer crash downs and funds that unaccountably disappeared. They could see the source of their raw materials for Keepsuslim drying up and they didn't know quite how to resolve the problem. They decided to do nothing for the moment other than to call a secret meeting. A meeting at which they would decide how best to force the new owners of Gerald's farms to play ball according to their rules. Suddenly though Del Minki began to get rumours that all was not well with other aspects of Keepsuslim. They were beginning to get disturbing whispers and there was nervousness on Wall Street. Partakers of the capsules and World wide now there had been millions, began to develop very alarming symptoms.

Women who had shed their surplus fat with the ease that a snake sheds it's skin, now began to regain that weight. Naturally they took more Keepsuslim. For men it was a similar story. Then more and far more sinister side effects began to develop in both sexes.

Men stopped being interested in football and beer and instead preferred to watch soap on TV. Some took up knitting. They shaved off their beards and began to display an interest in cosmetics and hairstyles. They preferred to go shopping, in groups, and hold hands rather than sit in the pub.

Women however became more aggressive. Not only that, their skins took on a very positive pinkish hue. What was even more alarming was that their eyes started to become squinty. The horrible truth dawned; Keepsuslim affected the hormones in the body. Men were becoming effeminate and the women were turning into pigs. Boars to be more exact!

It would have been impossible to have kept the facts hidden. Too many people were affected, even the President of the United States of America.

Both Willie Clayton and Lulu had been amongst the first to use Keepsuslim. A public advertising triumph for a delighted Del Minki. Now however the secret was out and the opposition party had the video. No longer did Willie play a dominant role in the bedroom. In fact, his secret service had found him tied with silk handkerchiefs to the bed whilst a fat and prancing, squinty eyed and very large pink Lulu dressed in a Gestapo uniform wielded a whip and snorted. The President was not alone in a World that had suddenly undergone a fundamental change.

Kenu Itayaku sat cross-legged on the plastic simulated rush mat in his completed teahouse. Brenda, resplendent in her new kimono and with black pins in her hair kneeled before him, pouring tea. Kenu was at peace with the world. At last he had found happiness. Brenda too was happy. The do it your self-pregnancy kit she had purchased in Boots in Haverfordwest had showed positive. She would tell Kenu later. He would be pleased, she knew.

Gobbleton turned the two water buffalo again. He looked over the small bund into the next paddy fields where a line of bare footed and black pyjama clad females all were bent down planting paddi. He wondered which one of the identical black bottoms pointing his way belonged to Te'Upp. He also wondered when the strange dream would end.

The lights from the large bay windows of Justice Charles Wiggery's large and expansive home, spilled out onto the immaculate swathe of grass outside. The Judge was holding a dinner party for the Chief Constable, The Sheriff of the County and a few other distinguished friends. Baron De Lacey had parked his little tank hull down, just peeping over the top of a small rise, about half a mile away. He thought that perhaps a white phosphorous shell would liven up proceedings in the household below. He smiled to himself and hummed a happy tune as he loaded and sighted carefully.

Bradford sat in his favourite swivel chair, in front of his huge computer console. He held his baby niece carefully and lovingly on his lap. He spoke to her gently. "Let's see what that funny uncle Toni is up to today baby. He has an important meeting to attend. We won't want him saying the wrong things now will we? Your Uncle Bradford is going to teach baby all about computers and the Internet and how to control who does what, where and how. It's easy and one day Little Geek," He tweaked her cheek and the baby gurgled in delight, "One day, all this will be yours. It was a prophecy you know. Yes it was." He rocked her and she smiled back. "Someone, somewhere once wrote that it would be the Geek that inherited the Earth." He tuned in to Toni and Little Geek watched with interest.